Robert Coover's first novel, *THE ORIGIN OF THE BRUNISTS*, was the winner of the 1966 William Faulkner Award as the best first novel of that year. In honoring Mr. Coover, one of the judges wrote of the book: "*This is solid, masculine, bountiful art, a novel tough-minded in its vision and robust in its manner, a triumph of intelligence and a courageous heart, of a youthful spirit and a seasoned insight.*"

Mr. Coover has published short stories in *New American Review, Evergreen Review, Playboy,* and other magazines. His other published titles include *THE PUBLIC BURNING, A THEOLOGICAL POSITION,* and *THE WATER POURER.*

His book of *fictions*, *PRICKSONGS & DESCANTS*, is available in a Plume edition.

"One of the most talented American novelists" —*Philadelphia Bulletin*

Also by Robert Coover

THE ORIGIN OF THE BRUNISTS

PRICKSONGS & DESCANTS

the universal baseball association, inc.

J. Henry Waugh, PROP.

ROBERT COOVER

A PLUME BOOK
NEW AMERICAN LIBRARY
NEW YORK AND SCARBOROUGH, ONTARIO

This is an authorized reprint of a hardcover edition published by Random House, Inc., and simultaneously in Canada by Random House of Canada Limited, Toronto.

PLUME TRADEMARK REG. U.S. PAT. OFF. AND FOREIGN COUNTRIES
REGISTERED TRADEMARK—MARCA REGISTRADA
HECHO EN WESTFORD, MASS., U.S.A.

SIGNET, SIGNET CLASSIC, MENTOR, ONYX, PLUME, MERIDIAN AND NAL BOOKS are published *in the United States* by
NAL PENGUIN INC.,
1633 Broadway, New York, New York 10019,
in Canada by The New American Library of Canada Limited.
81 Mack Avenue, Scarborough, Ontario M1L 1M8

First Plume Printing, April, 1971

10 11 12 13 14 15 16

PRINTED IN THE UNITED STATES OF AMERICA

for Pili: co-proprietor

It is here not at all requisite to prove that such an *intellectus archetypus* is possible, but only that we are led to the Idea of it . . .

—Kant, *Critique of Judgment*

THE UNIVERSAL BASEBALL ASSOCIATION, INC.

J. Henry Waugh, PROP.

1

BOTTOM half of the seventh, Brock's boy had made it through another inning unscratched, one! two! three! Twenty-one down and just six outs to go! and Henry's heart was racing, he was sweating with relief and tension all at once, unable to sit, unable to think, *in* there, *with* them! Oh yes, boys, it was on! He was sure of it! More than just another ball game now: *history!* And Damon Rutherford was making it. Ho ho! too good to be true! And yes, the stands were charged with it, turned on, it was the old days all over again, and with one voice they rent the air as the Haymaker Star Hamilton Craft spun himself right off his feet in a futile cut at Damon's third strike—zing! whoosh! *zap! OUT!* Henry laughed, watched the hometown Pioneer fans cheer the boy, cry out his name, then stretch—not just stretch—*leap up* for luck. He saw beers bought and drunk, hot dogs eaten, timeless gestures passed. Yes, yes, they nodded, and crossed their fingers and knocked on wood and rubbed their palms and kissed their fingertips and clapped their hands, and laughed how they were all caught up in it, witnessing it, how he was all caught up in it, this great ball game, event of the first order, tremendous moment: *Rookie pitcher Damon Rutherford, son of the incomparable Brock Rutherford, was two innings—six outs—from a perfect game!* Henry, licking his lips, dry from excitement, squinted at the sun high over the Pioneer Park, then at his watch: nearly eleven, Diskin's closing hours. So he took the occasion of this seventh-inning hometown stretch to hurry downstairs to the delicatessen to get a couple sandwiches. Might be a long night: the Pioneers hadn't scored off old Swanee Law yet either.

A small warm bulb, unfrosted, its little sallow arc so remote from its fathering force as to seem more akin to the glowworm than lightning, gleamed outside his door and showed where the landing ended; the steps themselves were dark, but Henry, through long usage, knew them all by heart. Cold bluish streetlight lit the bottom, intruding damply, seeming to hover unrelated to the floor, but Henry hardly noticed: his eye was on the game, on the great new Rookie pitcher Damon Rutherford, seeking this afternoon his sixth straight win . . . and maybe more. Maybe: immortality. And now, as Henry skipped out onto the sidewalk, then turned into the front door of Diskin's Delicatessen, he saw the opposing pitcher, Ace Swanee Law of the hard-bitten Haymakers, taking the mound, tossing warm-up pitches, and he knew he had to hurry.

"Two pastrami, Benny," he said to the boy sweeping up, Mr. Diskin's son—third or fourth, though, not the second. "And a cold six-pack."

"Aw, I just put everything away, Mr. Waugh," the boy whined, but he went to get the pastrami anyway.

Now Swanee Law was tough, an ace, seven-year veteran, top rookie himself in his own day, one of the main reasons Rag Rooney's Rubes had finished no worse than third from Year L through Year LIV. Ninety-nine wins, sixty-one losses, fast ball that got faster every year, most consistent, most imperturbable, and most vociferous of the Haymaker moundsmen. Big man who just reared back and hummed her in. Phenomenal staying power, the kind old Brock used to have. But he didn't have Brock Rutherford's class, that sweet smooth delivery, that virile calm. Mean man to beat, just the same, and to be sure he still had a shutout going for him this afternoon, and after all, it was a big day for him, too, going for that milestone hundredth win. Of course, he had a Rookie catcher in there to throw to, young Bingham Hill, and who knows? maybe they weren't getting along too well; could be. Law was never an easy man to get along with, too pushy, too much steam, and Hill was said to be excitable. Maybe Rooney had better send in reliable old Maggie Everts, Law's favorite battery mate. What about it? Haymaker manager Rag (Pappy) Rooney stroked his lean grizzly jaw, gave the nod to Everts.

"How's that, Mr. Waugh?"

"Did you put the pickle?"

"We're all out, sold the last one about thirty minutes ago."

A lie. Henry sighed. He'd considered using the name Ben Diskin, solid name for an outfielder, there was a certain power in it, but Benny spoiled it. A good boy, but nothing there. "That's okay, Benny. I'll take two next time."

"Working hard tonight, Mr. Waugh?" Benny rang up the sale, gave change.

"As always."

"Better take it easy. You been looking a little run-down lately."

Henry winced impatiently, forced a smile. "Never felt better," he said, and exited.

It was true: the work, or what he called his work, though it was more than that, much more, was good for him. Thing was, nobody realized he was just four years shy of sixty. They were always shocked when he told them. It was his Association that kept him young.

Mounting the stairs, Henry heard the roar of the crowd, saw them take their seats. Bowlegged old Maggie Everts trundled out of the Haymaker dugout to replace Hill. That gave cause for a few more warm-up pitches, so Henry slowed, took the top steps one at a time. Law grinned, nodded at old Maggie, stuffed a chaw of gum into his cheek. In the kitchen, he tore open the six-pack of beer, punched a can, slid the others into the refrigerator, took a long greedy drink of what the boys used to call German tea. Then, while Law tossed to Everts, Henry chewed his pastrami and studied the line-ups. Grammercy Locke up for the Pioneers, followed by three Star batters. Locke had been rapping the ball well lately, but Pioneer manager Barney Bancroft pulled him out, playing percentages, called in pinch-hitter Tuck Wilson, a great Star in his prime, now nearing the end of his career. Wilson selected a couple bats, exercised them, chose one, tugged his hat, and stepped in.

Henry sat down, picked up the dice, approved Everts' signal. "Wilson batting for Locke!" he announced over the loudspeaker, and they gave the old hero a big hometown hand. Henry rolled, bit into pastrami. Wilson swung at the first pitch, in across the knuckles, pulling it down the line. Haymaker third-sacker Hamilton Craft hopped to his right, fielded the ball, spun, threw to first—*wide!* Wilson: safe on first! Henry marked the error, flashed it on the scoreboard. Craft, one of the best, kicked the bag at third sullenly, scrubbed his nose, stared hard at Hatrack Hines, stepping now into the box. Bancroft sent speedster Hillyer Bryan in to run for Wilson.

"Awright! now come on, you guys! a little action!" Henry shouted, Bancroft shouted, clapping his hands, and the Pioneers kept the pepper up, they hollered in the stands.

"Got them Rubes rattled, boys! Let's bat around!"

"Lean into it, Hatrack, baby! Swanee's done for the day!"

"Send him down the river!"

"Dee-ee-eep water, Swanee boy!"

"Hey, Hatrack! Just slap it down to Craft there, he's all butter!"

The dice rattled in Henry's fist, tumbled out on the kitchen table: *crack!* hard grounder. Craft jumped on it this time, whipped the ball to second, one out—but young Bryan broke up the double play by flying in heels high! Still in there! Bancroft took a calculated risk: sent Hatrack scampering for second on Law's second pitch to Witness York—*safe!* Finishing his sandwich, Henry wondered: Would the Rookie Bingham Hill, pulled for inexperience, have nailed Hines at second? Maybe he would have. Pappy Rooney, the graybeard Haymaker boss, spat disdainfully. He knew what he was doing. Who knows? Hill might have thrown wild.

Anyway, it didn't matter. Pioneer Star center-fielder Witness York stepped back in, squeezed his bat for luck, swung, and whaled out his eleventh home run of the season, scoring Hines in front of him, and before Law had got his wind back, big Stan Patterson, Star right fielder, had followed with his ninth. Wham! bam! thank you, ma'am! And finally that was how the seventh inning ended: Pioneers 3, Haymakers 0. And now it was up to Damon Rutherford.

Henry stood, drank beer, joined in spirit with the Pioneer fans in their heated cries. Could the boy do it? All knew what, but none named it. The bullish roar of the crowd sounded like a single hoarse monosyllable, yet within it, Henry could pick out the ripple of Damon's famous surname, not so glorified in this stadium in over twenty years. Then it was for the boy's father, the all-time great Brock Rutherford, one of the game's most illustrious Aces back in what seemed now like the foundling days of the Universal Baseball Association, even-tempered fireballing no-pitches-wasted right-handed bellwether of the Pioneers who led them to nine pennants in a span of fourteen years. The Glorious XX's! Celebrated Era of the Pioneers! Barney Bancroft himself was there; he knew, he remembered! One of the fastest men the UBA had ever seen, out there guarding center. Barney the Old Philosopher, flanked by Willie O'Leary and Surrey Moss, and around the infield: Mose Stanford, Frosty Young, Jonathan Noon, and Gabe Burdette, timid Holly Tibbett behind the plate. Toothbrush Terrigan pitched, and Birdie Deaton and Chadbourne Collins . . . and Brock. Brock had come up as a Rookie in Year XX—no, XIX, that's right, it would have to be (Henry paused to look it up; yes, correct: XIX), just a kid off the farm, seemed happy-go-lucky and even lackadaisacal, but he had powered his way to an Ace position that first year, winning six straight ball games at the end of the season, three of them shutouts, lifting the long-suffering Pioneers out of second division into second place. A great year! great teams! and next year the pennant! Brock the Great! maybe the greatest of them all! He had stayed up in the Association for seventeen years before giving way to age and a troublesome shoulder. Still held the record to this day for total lifetime wins: 311. 311! Brock Rutherford . . . well, well, time gets on. Henry felt a tightness in his chest, shook it off. Foolish. He sighed, picked up the dice. Brock the Great. Hall of Fame, of course.

And now: now it was his boy who stood there on the mound. Tall, lithe, wirier build than his dad's, but just as fast, just as smooth. Smoother. More serious somehow. Yes, there was something more pensive about Damon, a meditative calm, a gentle brooding concern. The calm they shared, Rutherford gene, but where in Brock it had taken on the color of a kind of cocky, almost rustic power, in Damon it was self-assurance ennobled with a sense of . . . what? Responsibility maybe. Accountability. Brock was a public phenomenon, Damon a self-enclosed yet participating mystery. His own man, yet at home in the world, part of it, involved, every inch of him a participant, maybe that was all it was: his total involvement, his oneness with the UBA. Henry mused, fingering the dice. The Pioneer infielders tossed the ball around. Catcher Royce Ingram talked quietly with Damon out on the mound.

Of course, Pappy Rooney cared little for the peculiar aesthetics of the moment. It was his job not only to break up the no-hitter, but to beat the kid. Anyway, old Pappy had no love for the Rutherfords. Already a Haymaker Star and veteran of two world championships, four times the all-star first baseman of the Association, when Dad Rutherford first laced on a pair of cleats for the Pioneers, Rag Rooney had suffered through season after season of Haymaker failure to break the Pioneer grip on the UBA leadership, had gone down swinging futilely at Brock's fireball as often as the next man. So maybe that was why it was that, when the Haymaker right fielder, due to lead off in the top of the eighth, remarked that the Rutherford kid sure was tough today, Rooney snapped back: "Ya don't say. Well, mister, take your goddamn seat." And called in a pinch hitter.

Not that it did any good. Henry was convinced it was Damon's day, and nothing the uncanny Rooney came up with today could break the young Pioneer's spell. He laughed, and almost carelessly, with that easy abandon of old man Brock, pitched the dice, watched Damon Rutherford mow them down. One! Two! Three! And then nonchalantly, but not arrogantly, just casually, part of any working day, walk to the dugout. As though nothing were happening. *Nothing!* Henry found himself hopping up and down. One more inning! He drank beer, reared back, fired the empty can at the plastic garbage bucket near the sink. In there! *Zap!* "Go get 'em!" he cried.

First, of course, the Pioneers had their own eighth round at the plate, and there was no reason not to use it to stretch their lead, fatten averages a little, rub old Swanee's nose in it. Even if the Haymakers got lucky in the ninth and spoiled Damon's no-hitter, there was no reason to lose the ball game. After all, Damon was short some 300-and-some wins if he wanted to top his old man, which meant he needed every one he could get. Henry laughed irreverently.

Goodman James, young Pioneer first baseman making his second try for a permanent place in the line-up after a couple years back in the minors, picked out a bat, stepped lean-legged into the batter's box. Swanee fed him the old Law Special, a sizzling sinker in at the knees, and James bounced it down the line to first base: easy out. Damon Rutherford received a tremendous ovation when he came out—his dad would have acknowledged it with an open grin up at the stands; Damon knocked dirt from his cleats, seemed not to hear it. Wasn't pride. It was just that he understood it, accepted it, but was too modest, too *knowing*, to insist on any uniqueness of his own apart from it. He took a couple casual swings with his bat, moved up to the plate, waited Law out, but finally popped up: not much of a hitter. But to hear the crowd cheer as he trotted back to the dugout (one of the coaches met him halfway with a jacket), one would have thought he'd at least homered. Henry smiled. Lead-off man Toby Ramsey grounded out, short to first. Three up, three down. Those back-to-back homers had only made Law tougher than ever. "It's when Ah got baseballs flyin' round mah ears, that's when Ah'm really at mah meanest!"

Top of the ninth.

This was it.

Odds against him, of course. Had to remember that; be prepared for the lucky hit that really wouldn't be lucky at all, but merely in the course of things. Exceedingly rare, no-hitters; much more so, perfect games. How many in history? two, three. And a Rookie: no, it had never been done. In seventeen matchless years, his dad had pitched only two no-hitters, never had a perfect game. Henry paced the kitchen, drinking beer, trying to calm himself, to prepare himself, but he couldn't get it out of his head: *it was on!*

The afternoon sun waned, cast a golden glint off the mowed grass that haloed the infield. No sound in the stands now: breathless. Of course, no matter what happened, even if he lost the game, they'd cheer him, fabulous game regardless; yes, they'd love him, they'd let him know it . . . but still they wanted it. Oh yes, how they wanted it! Damon warmed up, throwing loosely to catcher Ingram. Henry watched him, felt the boy's inner excitement, shook his head in amazement at his outer serenity. "Nothing like this before." Yes, there was a soft murmur pulsing through the stands: nothing like it, electrifying, new, a new thing, happening here and now! Henry paused to urinate.

Manager Barney Bancroft watched from the Pioneer dugout, leaning on a pillar, thinking about Damon's father, about the years they played together, the games fought, the races won, the celebrations and the sufferings, roommates when on the road several of those years. Brock was great and this kid was great, but he was no carbon copy. Brock had raised his two sons to be more than ballplayers, or maybe it wasn't Brock's work, maybe it was just the name that had ennobled them, for in a way, they were—Bancroft smiled at the idea, but it was largely true—they were, in a way, the Association's first real aristocrats. There were already some fourth-generation boys playing ball in the league—the Keystones' Kester Flint, for example, and Jock Casey and Paddy Sullivan—but there'd been none before like the Rutherford boys. Even Brock Jr., though failing as a ballplayer, had had this quality, this poise, a gently ironic grace on him that his dad had never had, for all his raw jubilant power. Ingram threw the ball to second-baseman Ramsey, who flipped it to shortstop Wilder, who underhanded it to third-baseman Hines, now halfway to the mound, who in turn tossed it to Damon. Here we go.

Bancroft watched Haymaker backstop Maggie Everts move toward the plate, wielding a thick stubby bat. Rookie Rodney Holt crouched in the on-deck circle, working a pair of bats menacingly between his legs. Everts tipped his hat out toward the mound, then stepped into the box: dangerous. Yes, he was. The old man could bring the kid down. Still able to come through with the clutch hit. Lovable guy, old Maggie, great heart, Bancroft was fond of him, but that counted for nothing in the ninth inning of a history-making ball game. Rooney, of course, would send a pinch hitter in for Law. Bancroft knew he should order a couple relief pitchers to the bull pen just in case, but something held him back. Bancroft thought it was on, too.

Rooney noticed the empty bull pen. Bancroft was overconfident, was ripe for a surprise, but what could he do about it? He had no goddamn hitters. Even Ham Craft was in a bad slump. Should pull him out, cool his ass on the bench awhile, but, hell, he had nobody else. Pappy was in his fifteenth year as Haymaker manager, the old man of the Association's coaching staffs, and he just wasn't too sure, way things were going, that he and his ulcer were going to see a sixteenth. Two pennants, six times the league runner-up, never out of first division until last year when they dropped to fifth . . . and that was where his Rubes were now, with things looking like they were apt to get worse before they got better. He watched Everts, with a count of two and two on him, stand flatfooted as a third strike shot by so fast he hardly even saw it. That young bastard out there on the rubber was good, all right, fast as lightning—but what was it? Rooney couldn't quite put his finger on it . . . a little too narrow in the shoulders maybe, slight in the chest, too much a thoroughbred, not enough of the old man's big-boned stamina. And then he thought: shit, I can still beat this kid! And turning his scowl on the Haymaker bench, he hollered at Abernathy to pinch-hit for Holt.

Henry realized he had another beer in his hand and didn't remember having opened it. Now he was saying it out loud: "It's on! Come on, boy!" For the first time in this long game, the odds were with Damon: roughly 4–to–3 that he'd get both Abernathy and—who? Horvath, Rooney was sending in Hard John Horvath to bat for Law. Get them both and rack it up: the perfect game!

Henry hadn't been so excited in weeks. Months. That was the way it was, some days seemed to pass almost without being seen, games lived through, decisions made, averages rising or dipping, and all of it happening in a kind of fog, until one day that astonishing event would occur that brought sudden life and immediacy to the Association, and everybody would suddenly wake up and wonder at the time that had got by them, go back to the box scores, try to find out what had happened.

During those dull-minded stretches, even a home run was nothing more than an HR penned into the box score; sure, there was a fence and a ball sailing over it, but Henry didn't see them—oh, he heard the shouting of the faithful, yes, they stayed with it, they had to, but to him it was just a distant echo, static that let you know it was still going on. But then, contrarily, when someone like Damon Rutherford came along to flip the switch, turn things on, why, even a pop-up to the pitcher took on excitement, a certain dimension, color. *The magic of excellence.* Under its charm, he threw the dice: Abernathy struck out. Two down, *one to go!* It could happen, *it could happen!* Henry reeled around his chair a couple times, laughing out loud, went to urinate again.

Royce Ingram walked out to the mound. Ten-year veteran, generally acknowledged the best catcher in the UBA. He didn't go out to calm the kid down, but just because it was what everybody expected him to do at such a moment. Besides, Damon was the only sonuvabitch on the whole field not about to crap his pants from excitement. Even the Haymakers, screaming for the spoiler, were out of their seats, and to the man, hanging on his every pitch. The kid really had it, okay. Not just control either, but stuff, too. Ingram had never caught anybody so good, and he'd caught some pretty good ones. Just twenty years old, what's more: plenty of time to get even better. If it's possible. Royce tipped up his mask, grinned. "Ever hear the one about the farmer who stuck corks in his pigs' assholes to make them grow?" he asked.

"Yes, I heard that one, Royce," Damon said and grinned back. "What made you think of that one—you having cramps?"

Ingram laughed. "How'd you guess?"

"Me too," the kid confessed, and toed a pebble off the rubber. Ingram felt an inexplicable relief flood through him, and he took a deep breath. We're gonna make it, he thought. They listened to the loudspeaker announcing Horvath batting for Law. "Where does he like it?"

"Keep it in tight and tit-high, and the old man won't even see it," Ingram said. He found he couldn't even grin, so he pulled his mask down. "Plenty of stuff," he added meaninglessly. Damon nodded. Ingram expected him to reach for the rosin bag or wipe his hands on his shirt or tug at his cap or something, but he didn't: he just stood there waiting. Ingram wheeled around, hustled back behind the plate, asked Horvath what he was sweating about, underwear too tight on him or something? which made Hard John give an uneasy tug at his balls, and when, in his squat behind the plate, he looked back out at Rutherford, he saw that the kid still hadn't moved, still poised there on the rise, coolly waiting, ball resting solidly in one hand, both hands at his sides, head tilted slightly to the right, face expressionless but eyes alert. Ingram laughed. "You're dead, man," he told Horvath. Henry zipped up.

Of course, it was just the occasion for the storybook spoiler. Yes, too obvious. Perfect game, two down in the ninth, and a pinch hitter scratches out a history-shriveling single. How many times it had already happened! The epochal event reduced to a commonplace by something or someone even less than commonplace, a mediocrity, a blooper worth forgetting, a utility ballplayer never worth much and out of the league a year later. All the No-Hit Nealys that Sandy sang about . . .

No-Hit Nealy, somethin' in his eye,
When they pitched low, he swung high,

Hadn't had a hit in ninety-nine years,
And then they sent him out agin
the Pi-yo-neers!

Henry turned water on to wash, then hesitated. Not that he felt superstitious about it exactly, but he saw Damon Rutherford standing there on the mound, hands not on the rosin bag, not in the armpits, not squeezing the ball, just at his side—dry, strong, patient—and he felt as though washing his hands might somehow spoil Damon's pitch. From the bathroom door, he could see the kitchen table. His Association lay there in ordered stacks of paper. The dice sat there, three ivory cubes, heedless of history yet makers of it, still proclaiming Abernathy's strike-out. Damon Rutherford waited there. Henry held his breath, walked straight to the table, picked up the dice, and tossed them down.

Hard John Horvath took a cut at Rutherford's second pitch, a letter-high inside curve, pulled it down the third-base line: Hatrack Hines took it backhanded, paused one mighty spellbinding moment—then fired across the diamond to Goodman James, and Horvath was out.

The game was over.

Giddily, Henry returned to the bathroom and washed his hands. He stared down at his wet hands, thinking: he did it! And then, at the top of his voice, "WA-*HOO!*" he bellowed, and went leaping back into the kitchen, feeling like he could damn well take off and soar if he had anyplace to go. "*HOO-HAH!*"

And the fans blew the roof off. They leaped the wall, slid down the dugout roofs, overran the cops, flooded in from the outfield bleachers, threw hats and scorecards into the air. Rooney hustled his Haymakers to the showers, but couldn't stop the Pioneer fans from lifting poor Horvath to their shoulders. There was a fight and Hard John bloodied a couple noses, but nobody even bothered to swing back at him. An old lady blew him kisses. Partly to keep Rutherford from getting mobbed and partly just because they couldn't stop themselves, his Pioneer teammates got to him first, had him on their own shoulders before the frenzied hometown rooters could close in and tear him apart out of sheer love. From above, it looked like a great roiling whirlpool with Damon afloat in the vortex—but then York popped up like a cork, and then Patterson and Hines, and finally the manager Barney Bancroft, lifted up by fans too delirious even to know for sure anymore what it was they were celebrating, and the whirlpool uncoiled and surged toward the Pioneer locker rooms.

"Ah!" said Henry, and: "*Ah!*"

And even bobbingly afloat there on those rocky shoulders, there in that knock-and-tumble flood of fans, in a wild world that had literally, for the moment, blown its top, Damon Rutherford preserved his incredible equanimity, hands at his knees except for an occasional wave, face lit with pleasure at what he'd done, but in no way distorted with the excitement of it all: tall, right, and true. People screamed for the ball. Royce Ingram, whose shoulder was one of those he rode on, handed it up to him. Women shrieked, arms supplicating. He smiled at them, but tossed the ball out to a small boy standing at the crowd's edge.

Henry opened the refrigerator, reached for the last can of beer, then glanced at his watch: almost midnight—changed his mind. He peered out at the space between his kitchen window and the street lamp: lot of moisture in the air still, but hard to tell if it was falling or rising. He'd brooded over it, coming home from work: that piled-up mid-autumn feeling, pregnant with the vague threat of confusion and emptiness—but this boy had cut clean through it, let light and health in, and you don't go to bed on an event like this! Henry reknotted his tie, put on hat and raincoat, hooked his umbrella over one arm, and went out to get a drink. He glanced back at the kitchen table once more before pulling the door to, saw the dice there, grinned at them, for once adjuncts to grandeur, then hustled down the stairs like a happy Pioneer headed for the showers. He stepped quickly through the disembodied street lamp glow at the bottom, and whirling his umbrella like a drum major's baton, marched springily up the street to Pete's, the neighborhood bar.

N-o-O-O-o Hit Nealy!
Won his fame
Spoilin' Birdie Deaton's
Per-her-fect game!

The night above was dark yet the streets were luminous; wet, they shimmered with what occasional light there was from street lamps, passing cars, phone booths, all-night neon signs. There was fog and his own breath was visible, yet nearby objects glittered with a heightened clarity. He smiled at the shiny newness of things springing up beside him on his night walk. At a distance, car head lamps were haloed and tail-lights burned fuzzily, yet the lit sign in the darkened window he was passing, "DIVINEFORM FOUNDATIONS: TWO-WAY STRETCH," shone fiercely, hard-edged and vivid as a vision.

The corner drugstore was still open. A scrawny curlyheaded kid, cigarette butt dangling under his fuzzy upper lip, played the pinball machine that stood by the window. Henry paused to watch. The machine was rigged like a baseball game, though the scores were unrealistic. Henry had played the machine himself often and once, during a blue season, had even played off an entire all-UBA pinball tourney on it. Ballplayers, lit from inside, scampered around the basepaths, as the kid put english on the balls with his hips and elbows. A painted pitcher, in eternal windup, kicked high, while below, a painted batter in a half-crouch moved motionlessly toward the plate. Two girls in the upper corners, legs apart and skirts hiked up their thighs, cheered the runners on with silent wide-open mouths. The kid was really racking them up: seven free games showing already. Lights flashed, runners ran. Eight. Nine. "THE GREAT AMERICAN GAME," it said across the top, between the gleaming girls. Well, it was. American baseball, by luck, trial, and error, and since the famous playing rules council of 1889, had struck on an almost perfect balance between offense and defense, and it was that balance, in fact, that and the accountability—the beauty of the records system which found a place to keep forever each least action—that had led Henry to baseball as his final great project.

The kid twisted, tensed, relaxed, hunched over, reared, slapped the machine with a pelvic thrust; up to seventeen free games and the score on the lighted panel looked more like that of a cricket match than a baseball game. Henry moved on. To be sure, he'd only got through one UBA pinball tourney and had never been tempted to set up another. Simple-minded, finally, and not surprisingly a simple-minded ballplayer, Jaybird Wall, had won it. In spite of all the flashing lights, it was —like those two frozen open-mouthed girls and the batter forever approaching the plate, the imperturbable pitcher forever reared back—a static game, utterly lacking the movement, grace, and complexity of real baseball. When he'd finally decided to settle on his own baseball game, Henry had spent the better part of two months just working with the problem of odds and equilibrium points in an effort to approximate that complexity. Two dice had not done it. He'd tried three, each a different color, and the 216 different combinations had provided the complexity, all right, but he'd nearly gone blind trying to sort the colors on each throw. Finally, he'd compromised, keeping the three dice, but all white, reducing the total number of combinations to 56, though of course the odds were still based on 216. To restore—and, in fact, to intensify—the complexity of the multicolored method, he'd allowed triple ones and sixes—1–1–1 and 6–6–6—to trigger the more spectacular events, by referring the following dice throw to what he called his Stress Chart, also a three-dice chart, but far more dramatic in nature than the basic ones. Two successive throws of triple ones and sixes were exceedingly rare—only about three times in every two entire seasons of play on the average—but when it happened, the next throw was referred, finally, to the Chart of Extraodinary Occurrences, where just about anything from fistfights to fixed ball games could happen. These two charts were what gave the game its special quality, making it much more than just a series of hits and walks and outs. Besides these, he also had special strategy charts for hit-and-run plays, attempted stolen bases, sacrifice bunts, and squeeze plays, still others for deciding the ages of rookies when they came up, for providing details of injuries and errors, and for determining who, each year, must die.

A neon beer advertisement and windows lit dimly through red curtains were all that marked Pete's place. Steady clientele, no doubt profitable in a small way, generally quiet, mostly country-and-western or else old hit-parade tunes on the jukebox, a girl or two drifting by from time to time, fair prices.

Henry brought his gyrating umbrella under control, left the wet world behind, and pushed in.

"Evening, Mr. Waugh," said the bartender.

"Evening, Jake."

Not Jake, of course, it was Pete himself, but it was a longstanding gag, born of a slip of the tongue. Pete was medium-sized, slope-shouldered, had bartenders' bags beneath his eyes and a splendid bald dome, spoke with a kind of hushed irony that seemed to give a dry double meaning to everything he said—in short, was the spitting image of Jake Bradley, one of Henry's ballplayers, a Pastimer second baseman whom Henry always supposed now to be running a bar somewhere near the Pastime Club's ball park, and one night, years ago, in the middle of a free-swinging pennant scramble, Henry had called Pete "Jake" by mistake. He'd kept it up ever since; it was a kind of signal to Pete that he was in a good mood and wanted something better than beer or bar whiskey. He sometimes wondered if anybody ever walked into Jake's bar and called him Pete by mistake. Henry took the middle one of three empty barstools. Jake—Pete—lifted a bottle of VSOP, raised his eyebrows, and Henry nodded. Right on the button.

The bar was nearly empty, not surprising; Tuesday, a working night, only six or seven customers, faces all familiar, mostly old-timers on relief. Pete's cats scrubbed and stalked, sulked and slept. A neighborhood B-girl named Hettie, old friend of Henry's, put money in the jukebox—old-time country love songs. Nostalgia was the main vice here. Pete toweled dust from a snifter, poured a finger of cognac into it. "How's the work going, Mr. Waugh?" he asked.

"Couldn't go better," Henry said and smiled. Jake always asked the right questions.

Jake smiled broadly, creasing his full cheeks, nodded as though to say he understood, pate flashing in the amber light. And it was the right night to call him Jake, after all: Jake Bradley was also from the Brock Rutherford era, must have come up about the same time. Was he calling it that now? The Brock Rutherford Era? He never had before. Funny. Damon was not only creating the future, he was doing something to the past, too. Jake dusted the shelf before putting the cognac bottle back. He was once the middle man in five double plays executed in one game, still the Association record.

Hettie, catching Henry's mood apparently, came over to kid with him and he bought her a drink. A couple molars missing and flesh folds ruining the once-fine shape of her jaw, but there was still something compelling about that electronic bleat her stockings emitted when she hopped up on a barstool and crossed her legs, and that punctuation-wink she used to let a man know he was in with her, getting the true and untarnished word. Henry hadn't gone with her in years, not since before he set up his Association, but she often figured obliquely in the Book and conversations with her often got reproduced there under one guise or another. "Been gettin' any hits lately?" she asked, and winked over her tumbler of whiskey. They often used baseball idiom, she no doubt supposing he was one of those ball-park zealots who went crazy every season during the World Series and got written up as a character—the perennial krank—in the newspapers, and Henry never told her otherwise. Since she herself knew nothing at all about the sport, though, he often talked about his Association as though it were the major leagues. It gave him a kind of pleasure to talk about it with someone, even if she did think he was talking about something else.

"Been getting a lot," he said, "but probably not enough." She laughed loudly, exhibiting the gaps in her teeth. "And how about you, Hettie, been scoring a lot of runs?"

"I been scorin', boy, but I ain't got the runs!" she said, and whooped again. Old gag. The other customers turned their way and smiled.

Henry waited for her to settle down, commune with her drink once more, then he said, "Listen, Hettie, think what a wonderful rare thing it is to do something, no matter how small a thing, with absolute unqualified utterly unsurpassable *perfection!*"

"What makes you think it's so rare?" she asked with a wink, and switching top knee, issued the old signal. "You ain't pitched to me in a long time, you know."

He grinned. "No, but think of it, Hettie, to do a thing so perfectly that, even if the damn world lasted forever, nobody could ever do it better, because you had done it as well as it could possibly be done." He paused, let the cognac fumes bite his nostrils to excuse the foolish tears threatening to film his eyes over. "In a way, you know, it's even sad somehow, because, well, it's done, and all you can hope for after is to do it a second time." Of course, there were other things to do, the record book was, above all, a catalogue of possibilities . . .

"A second time! Did you say *per*fection or *e*rection?" Hettie asked.

Henry laughed. It was no use. And anyway it didn't matter. He felt just stupendous, not so exultant as before, but still full of joy, and now a kind of heady aromatic peace seemed to be sweeping over him: ecstasy—yes, he laughed to himself, that was the only goddamn word for it. It was good. He bought another round, asked Pete: "How is it you stay in such good shape, Jake?"

"I don't know, Mr. Waugh. Must be the good Christian hours I keep."

And then, when the barkeep had left them, it was Hettie who suddenly turned serious. "I don't know what it is about you tonight, Henry," she said, "but you've got me kinda hot." And she switched top knee again: call from the deep.

Henry smiled, slowly whirling the snifter through minute cycles, warming the tawny dram in the palm of his hand. It was a temptation, to be sure, but he was afraid Hettie would spoil it for him, dissipate the joy and dull this glow, take the glory out of it. It was something he could share with no one without losing it altogether. Too bad. "It's just that nobody's bought you two straight drinks in a long time, Hettie," he said.

"Aw," she grumbled and frowned at her glass, hurt by that and so cooled off a little. To make up for it, he ordered her a third drink. He'd had enough, time to get back, had to make it to work in the morning, old Zifferblatt had been giving him a hard time for weeks now and was just looking for a chance to raise hell about something, but Pete poured him one on the house. Not every day you pitched perfect games and got VSOP on the house. "Thanks, Jake," he said.

"Henry, hon', gimme some money to put in the jukebox."

Coins on the bar: he slid them her way. Stared into his snifter, saw himself there in the brown puddle, or anyway his eye.

It was down in Jake's old barroom
Behind the Patsies' park;
Jake was settin' 'em up as usual
And the night was agittin' dark.

At the bar stood ole Verne Mackenzie,
And his eyes was bloodshot red . . .

"The Day They Fired Verne Mackenzie": Sandy Shaw's great ballad. Dead now, Verne. First of the game's superstars, starting shortstop on Abe Flint's Excelsiors back in Year I, first of the Hall of Famers. But he got older and stopped hitting, and Flint, nice a guy as he was, had to let him go. And they all knew how Verne felt, even the young guys playing now who never knew him, because sooner or later it would be the same for them. Hettie leaned against him, head on his shoulder, humming the jukebox melodies to herself. He felt good, having her there like that. He sipped his brandy and grew slowly melancholy, *pleasantly* melancholy. He saw Brock the Great reeling boisterously down the street, arm in arm with Willie O'Leary and Frosty Young, those wonderful guys—and who should they meet up with but sleepy-eyed Mose Stanford and Gabe Burdette and crazy rubber-legged Jaybird Wall. Yes, and they were singing, singing the *old* songs, "Pitchin', Catchin', Swingin' " and "The Happy Days of Youth," and oh! it was happiness! and goddamn it! it was fellowship! and boys oh boys! it was significance! "Let's go to Jake's!" they cried, they laughed, and off they went!

"Where?" Hettie mumbled. She was pretty far along. So was he. Didn't realize he had been talking out loud. Glanced self-consciously at Pete, but Pete hadn't moved: he was a patient pillar in the middle of the bar, ankles and arms crossed, face in shadows, only the dome lit up. Maybe he was asleep. There was only one other customer, an old-timer, still in the bar. The neon light outside was probably off.

"To my place," he said, not sure it was himself talking.

Could he take her up there? She leaned away from his shoulder, tried to wink, couldn't quite pull it off, instead studied him quizzically as though wondering if he really meant it. "Hettie," he whispered, staring hard at her, so she'd know he wasn't kidding and that she'd better not spoil it, "how would you like to sleep with . . . Damon Rutherford?"

She blinked, squinted skeptically, but he could see she was still pretty excited and she'd moved her hand up his pantleg to the seam. "Who's he?"

"Me." He didn't smile, just looked straight at her, and he saw her eyes widen, maybe even a little fear came into them, but certainly awe was there, and fascination, and hope, and her hand, discovering he could do it, yes, he could do it, gave a squeeze like Witness York always gave his bat for luck before he swung, and she switched knees: *wheep!* So he paid Jake, and together—he standing tall and self-assured, Hettie shiveringly clasped in his embrace—they walked out. As he'd foreseen, the neon light was out; it was dark. He felt exceedingly wise.

"What are you, Henry?" Hettie asked softly as they walked under the glowing nimbus of a mist-wrapped street lamp. His raincoat had a slit in the lining behind the pocket, and this she reached through to slip her hand into his coin pocket.

"Now, or when we get to my place?"

"Now."

"An accountant."

"But the baseball . . . ?" And again she took hold and squeezed like Witness York, but now her hand was full of coins as well, and they wrapped the bat like a suit of mail.

"I'm an auditor for a baseball association."

"I didn't know they had auditors, too," she said. Was she

really listening for once? They were in the dark now, next street lamp was nearly a block away, in front of Diskin's. She was trying to get her other hand on the bat, gal can't take a healthy swing without a decent grip, after all, but she couldn't get both hands through the slit.

"Oh, yes. I keep financial ledgers for each club, showing cash receipts and disbursements, which depend mainly on such things as team success, the buying and selling of ballplayers, improvement of the stadiums, player contracts, things like that." Hettie Irden stood at the plate, first woman ballplayer in league history, tightening and relaxing her grip on the bat, smiling around the spaces of her missing molars in that unforgettable way of hers, kidding with the catcher, laughing that gay timeless laugh that sounded like the clash of small coins, tugging maybe at her crotch in a parody of all male ballplayers the world over, and maybe she wasn't the best hitter in the Association, but the Association was glad to have her. She made them all laugh and forget for a moment that they were dying men. "And a running journalization of the activity, posting of it all into permanent record books, and I help them with basic problems of burden distribution, remarshaling of assets, graphing fluctuations. Politics, too. Elections. Team captains. Club presidents. And every four years, the Association elects a Chancellor, and I have to keep an eye on that."

"Gee, Henry, I didn't realize . . . !" She was looking up at him, and as they approached the street lamp, he could see something in her eyes he hadn't seen there before. He was glad to see it had come to pass, that she recognized—but it wouldn't do when they got to bed, she'd have to forget then.

"There are box scores to be audited, trial balances of averages along the way, seasonal inventories, rewards and punishments to be meted out, life histories to be overseen." He took a grip on her behind. "People die, you know."

"Yes," she said, and that seemed to excite her, for she squeezed a little harder.

"Usually, they die old, already long since retired, but they can die young, even as ballplayers. Or in accidents during the winter season. Last year a young fellow, just thirty, had a bad season and got sent back to the minors. They say his manager rode him too hard." Pappy Rooney. Wouldn't let go of the kid. "Sensitive boy who took it too much to heart. On the way, he drove his car off a cliff."

"Oh!" she gasped and squeezed. As though afraid now to let go. "On purpose?"

"I don't know. I think so. And if a pitcher throws two straight triple ones or sixes and brings on an Extraordinary Occurrence, a third set of ones is a bean ball that kills the batter, while triple sixes again is a line drive that kills the pitcher."

"Oh, how awful!" He didn't tell her neither had ever happened. "But what are triple sixes, Henry?"

"A kind of pitch. Here we are."

Even climbing the stairs to his place, she didn't want to release her grip, but the stairway was too narrow and they kept jamming up. So she took her hand out and went first. From his squat behind the box, the catcher watched her loosening up, kidded her that she'd never get a walk because they could never get two balls on her. Over her shoulder, she grinned down upon him, a gap-tooth grin that was still somehow beautiful. Anyhow, she said, I *am* an Extraordinary Occurrence, and on that chart there's no place for mere passes! The catcher laughed, reached up and patted her rear. "You said it!" he admitted, letting his hand glide down her thigh, then whistle up her stocking underneath the skirt. "An Extraordinary Occurrence!"

She hopped two steps giddily, thighs slapping together. "Henry! I'm ticklish!"

He unlocked the door to his apartment, switched on a night light in the hall, leaving the kitchen and Association in protective darkness, and led her toward the bedroom.

"We're at your place," she said huskily when they'd got in there, and squeezed up against him. "Who are you now?" That she remembered! She was wonderful!

"The greatest pitcher in the history of baseball," he whispered. "Call me . . . Damon."

"Damon," she whispered, unbuckling his pants, pulling his shirt out. And "Damon," she sighed, stroking his back, unzipping his fly, sending his pants earthward with a rattle of buckles and coins. And "Damon!" she greeted, grabbing—and that girl, with one swing, he knew then, could bang a pitch clean out of the park. "*Play ball!*" cried the umpire. And the catcher, stripped of mask and guard, revealed as the pitcher Damon Rutherford, whipped the uniform off the first lady ballplayer in Association history, and then, helping and hindering all at once, pushing and pulling, they ran the bases, pounded into first, slid into second heels high, somersaulted over third, shot home standing up, then into the box once more, swing away, and run them all again, and "Damon!" she cried, and "Damon!"

2

8 **A.M.** Oh that boy. He did it. Yes, he did. Saw his own hand open, the dice fall, Hard John swing. Out! Unbelievable. The boy with the magic arm. Couldn't happen. But it did. And will happen again. And again. A new day. A new age. Glorious, goddamn it, *glorious!*

9 A.M. Awake again. More or less. Daylight filtering opaquely through the sheet over his head. Thoughts of phoning Zifferblatt at the office. Won't be in, dad. Yes, a little under the weather. Flu maybe. Chapped lips. Double entry fatigue. Cancer of the old intangibles, Ziff baby. Wasting assets. All washed up. But, no, feeling great. Just great. Still under the spell. Zifferblatt would hear the health, smell the secret laughter. Don't kid me, Waugh. You're finished. Thumb up, out of the game, off the team, out of the majors. You can't do that, Ziff. No vested authority. Waugh, we are amortizing you, wiping out your book value, man, closing the ledger: OUT! But then the boys trot out on the field. Ingram. York. Tuck Wilson. McCamish. Patterson. Hard John. They don't say

anything. They just give old Zifferblatt the eye and—*PFFFT!* —he disappears.

10 A.M. Up from the depths. Hoo boy, best night's sleep in several epochs, though maybe a little hung over. Dreams forgotten but a vague remembrance of massive and exhausting heroics. Reluctantly, he cracked the shell, broke out, slippered his feet, smiled at Hettie's mumbling protest, staggered to the bathroom to cancel accumulated liquid assets, wash up, gargle, assess resources and liabilities in the glass, and stir the cosmos with a creative wind or two. Then back in the egg to dream awake awhile, replay that whole impossible beatifical game, feeling goosey with the grace of it. Damon Rutherford. Yes, it was on, the great new thing. You could feel it with that first pitch. He laughed at old Pappy Rooney kneading his tortured stomach; sooner or later, Rooney, there's some things you gotta accept. Ahhh, shee-*it*. It'd cure that stomach trouble. I can live with it. Incorrigible bastard. What're ya gigglin' about, Hettie muttered. All those *per*fections and *con*nections, he said. She grunted and grinned, then slipped away again with a soft snore. A new Rutherford era. On the brink of a new Rutherford Era in the UBA. What about it, Barney? I don't know. Maybe. Wait and see. Right now, we've got the flag to think about. Bancroft was always cautious. But perceptive, too, and open, even if he was a born pessimist. He thought about things. A new Rutherford Era. It could be, it could happen. Maybe it was the extra drive that second sons seemed to have. The first son, Brock II, had come up in Year XLIX looking great, but after a fair start, he petered out. Brock's boys had to be pitchers, of course. Nevertheless, Bancroft had sent young Brock back to the minors, had trained him to play first base. There was glory in being a first baseman, too. But when he returned in Year LII, after hitting three home runs in his first two

games, he faded away to a .147, made seven errors in a half season of play. What's the main difference between them, Barney? I don't know. I had the same initial feeling about both of them: you know, chips off the old block. You mean chips off the old Brock, don't you, Barney? Yeah, heh heh, chuckles around. And they both had something extra the old man didn't have, a kind of elegance, you might almost call it. No offense to Brock, but he was always more open, more one of the boys. Sure of himself, but as though he'd had to prove it somewhere along the way. A kind of self-made man, you mean? Mmm, something like that. The boys were different. But, Barney, what has Damon got that young Brock lacked? Well, you know how second sons are. When they're still kids, they always have to try a little harder. And something else: you can't say Damon's brighter, but there's something up there that's, well, different; he's more responsive somehow. Yeah, I think I know what you mean, Barney—it's like some guy said up in the press box, all he said was: *He knows,* and everybody seemed to know just what he was talking about. Barney Bancroft nodded in understanding, gazed thoughtfully off.

11 A.M. Hettie came around at last, lit up a smoke: mingling of aromas generally pleasing to his nostrils. Old Mom looking a bit haggard in the honest morning light, but a freshening was taking place, or so she said and said she was grateful. And it was probably true, he knew how she felt. Didn't seem to come from live coals, that smoke curling up, more like from old ashes, but there was still a lot of life there, a lot of possibility. They laughed about the night's games. Doubleheader. Doubleheader, hell, that was a world series! Chortling, she padded off for a moment, leaving a chill in the sheets. In the interim, he tried considering Hard John Horvath striding to

the plate once more, two down, Damon one out from grandeur, but Zifferblatt's fat frown again intruded, making Henry restless. What was it doing out? Terrible storm maybe. No public transportation. Millions dying. Image of himself trapped on flooding streets. Hettie turned on faucets, making suitable water noises. Cities crumbling, whole populations getting washed out to sea. Zifferblatt apologetic: Didn't mean for you to get out in that, Henry; sorry. Too late to be sorry, Ziff, you can't apologize to a drowning man, we're through, I've had it. Hettie returned, slipping in with fresh odors and comforting warmth, though her feet were cold. He suggested going out for breakfast. But she was afraid, didn't want the separation, not yet, pulled him over on top of her. No pitches left, he protested, arsenal all cleaned out. Didn't matter, she said, just stay like that. They talked about time and people and history and how everything seemed to flow confusedly together. Here they were warm, two bugs in a rug, two fish in a blanket, and it was peaceful. Her body made subtle liquid shifts under him, seeking total attachment. Baseball was a lot better game than she'd ever guessed, she admitted. All those wild pitches. What'd he call that surprise one? Oh yeah, a sinker. Hee hee! a real beauty! Well, that's right, the kid had a bag of tricks, all right. Secret, though, was control. Power and control, that was Pappy Rooney's theory. Drive one on the fists, then throw one outside, mix 'em up, but always right where you want 'em. Control. A batter don't go up and swing from his butt on a pitcher like that. You take a short stroke, you don't swing a yard on him. In and out, speed, now and then a curve, change-up, in and out. Oh yeah, said Hettie. In and out. Pitch and catch. Great game. Of course, that wasn't really the truth about baseball. She made it sound easier than it really was. Mom in a protected crouch, holding up her big padded womb, Dad delivering the pitch, winging it in there, time after time. Looked easy. But she forgot about the batter, not to mention all his brothers. Standing there in the box. Frustrating old Dad by poking his own stick out there in the way. Of course, the old man wasn't alone: the other seven were in their places, out there behind him, backing him up, protecting Mom's chastity and the way things were, putting down that rambunctious boy with the big rebellious bat. But they don't always hold him off. Junior explodes one off his piece of lumber and the whole shebang is in trouble; can send the old man to the showers and upend the whole damn system. Of course, just getting his bat on it isn't enough, he's still got to make the full circuit, and it's a long run around there, lot of ground to cover, and a lot can happen on the way, but he hopes, and the minute he leaves it that old home plate starts exerting a tremendous pull on him, and the good ones, on the good days, they do get around there, they do make it back. But how, Henry, what kind of pull, you mean like this? That's right, and he's gotta keep driving, keep moving, stay awake, stay alive, no letting up, stealing what he can, digging in, grabbing for every inch, around and around, and maybe, Hettie, just maybe—but they say he can't do it, and damn it, he *must*, he *will!* Oh, come on, come on, Henry, here, come on *home!* Yes, and they're pulling for him, Hettie, and he rounds second, he's trying to stretch it to third, but I don't know, it's still a long ways to the plate, no, he just can't make it, not this time, and the second baseman, he's got the ball, and he's gonna—No, no, *I* got it, Henry, *I* got it! come on! come on! keep it up! Behind his butt, she clapped her cold soles to cheer him on. Yes, he's pushing toward third now, yes! and he's picking up, yes, that's it! he's hard to stop now, he's churning, he's pouring it on, and he's around third! on his way home! but they've got him in a hotbox! wow! third to catch! back to third! hah! to catch! to pitch! catch! pitch! catch! pitch! Home, Henry, *home!* And here he comes, Hettie! He's past 'em! past 'em! past 'em! he's bolting for home, spurting past, sliding in—*POW!* Oh, *pow,* Henry! pow pow pow pow *POW!* They laughed softly, hysterically, flowing together. She let go her grip on the ball. He slipped off, unmingling their sweat. Oh, that's a game, Henry! *That's* really a *great* old *game!*

So that was how and why it was that Henry showed up that Wednesday at the offices of Dunkelmann, Zauber & Zifferblatt, Licensed Tax & General Accountants, Specializing in Small Firms, Bookkeeping Services & Systems, Payrolls & Payroll Taxes, Monthly, Quarterly & Annual Audits, Enter Without Knocking, somewhat after the lunch hour, and there was just no doubt that the third-named and last-surviving of the firm's partners, Mr. Horace (n) Zifferblatt, Fiduciary Expert and Adjutant of Minor Industry, had his dander up. Of course, he had his reasons. Zifferblatt was a militant clock-watcher, and Henry's record of late had been none too good. And then there'd been that disturbance back during the last pennant scramble when Henry, distracted, worrying about injuries on the Keystone pitching staff, had posted to the general and subsidiary ledgers of one firm the journal entries of another. Whole quarter's worth. So: might as well expect the worst. Still, in spite of his lifelong reverence for hard work and dependability, and that letting-the-team-down guilt he'd always suffered after such lapses, today he found he just didn't care. No, Henry walked today in a perfect vault of well-being, crystalline and impenetrable, and there was nothing the wrath of Zifferblatt could do to crack it.

Following ablutions and purifications, he and Hettie had hustled out for noontime breakfast, full-blown $2.25 platters, big No. 7 on the coffee-shop menu, the kind of farmer's breakfast that pasture-keepers like Stan Patterson and Witness York liked to put away, with extra cups of coffee along the way. Odd day outside: clear one minute, pouring the next—they'd had to sprint the last block under a sudden cloudburst, had piled into the coffee shop laughingly wheezing and snorting like a pair of ruttish nags, hot for the feedbag. Hettie had played old-time country music on the juke to accompany their celebrations, and one of them had caught his imagination; like the cloudburst outside, a whole new Sandy Shaw ballad for the UBA had poured suddenly out of him. Nothing to it. Everything came easy today. He'd explained to a curious Hettie that songwriting was a kind of hobby. No, no luck so far, he'd lied. In the UBA, after all, they all sang Sandy's songs. Funny thing about both country music and baseball with its "village greens": they weren't really country, not since they got their new names anyway, but urban. Kid stuff, dreams of heroism and innocence, staged by pros and turned into big business. The "New York Game" they called the old townball version, and borough born and bred it was and is . . .

It's early in the mornin' and I been out all
night,
Bad times with my woman and I'm tryin' to git
right,
I stagger into bed but the boss calls my name,
He says, git out on the field, we got a im-portant
game!

PLAY BALL! (My head's a goddamn balloon!)
PLAY BALL! (Go 'way, don't come back soon!)
PLAY BALL! (That's what the umpire said . . .)
PLAY BALL! (But, boys, I just gotta stay here
in bed!)

Well, I'm stretched out on my cot there like an
old tomcat,
I got such a hangover that I don't know where
I'm at,
I'm dreamin' 'bout that woman when the boss
busts in the door,
Throws water on my head and dumps me out
on the floor!

PLAY BALL! (Oh no! git outa my mind!)
PLAY BALL! (Cantcha see I'm damn near
blind?)
PLAY BALL! (That's what the umpire said . . .)
PLAY BALL! (Gawdamighty, I wish I was
dead!)

Wisely, Hettie had asked no further questions about the who or wherefrom of Damon Rutherford, though, on parting, she did with a Hettie Irden wink say that if ever that boy had a new pitch he wanted to try out on an old veteran, he'd find her warming a stool at Pete's. Warming the bench, Henry had corrected her, then had pointed out she had not yet witnessed sliders, spitballs, screwballs, knucklers, or the turnover fast ball, not to mention the duster, or "purpose pitch." Hoo-eee! she'd whooped at the list, and: Purpose? What purpose?

Bean ball, high and inside, force the batter back, drop him to his knees, the pitch Toothbrush Terrigan was famous for, touch of meanness that could turn a game into a general free-for-all. Oboy, that's for me! she'd cackled, then had sent him off with a whispered: Tonight!

Well, he'd have to see. For the moment, he spread open ledgers before him on his desk to look busy and thought about line-ups for the next round of games. Let's see, the league-leading Knickerbockers had lost yesterday, so that closed the Pioneers up to just two games behind. Too bad he couldn't pitch Damon against the Haymakers again tonight; that'd finish Pappy Rooney off forever. Who then? Had to save the Ace, Mickey Halifax, for the upcoming series with the Knicks, so he'd have to go with one of the Regulars. Drew McDermott maybe. Idly, he summarized sales receipts, one eye on his boss Horace Zifferblatt, who paced in a flushed pout inside his glass cage of an office. Didn't come out, though. Henry didn't know if that was a good sign or a bad one. Probably bad.

One thing was troubling him, and he realized he had to face up to it: Damon Rutherford meant more to him than any player should. It had happened before, and it had always caused problems. For example now: Damon had already pitched over sixty innings, and he had the best earned-run average in the Association. To be classified an Ace the following year, a pitcher had to pitch a minimum of eighty innings, have one of the ten lowest ERA's in the league. It was the same with hitters: the top twenty-four batters of one season were the Stars of the next. These ratings gave them slightly better odds with the dice, gave the game more continuity. There were always a few changes each year, of course, as some of the Stars and Aces fell, usually at least a fourth of them, and newcomers moved up to take their places, but this was perfectly natural and desirable—what in fact made room for guys like Damon Rutherford. All right, here it was, just midseason, still thirty-seven games to go, and they might suddenly start hitting him. The smart thing would be to baby Damon through the remaining fifteen or twenty innings he needed, pitching him against weaker teams, using him in one-inning relief stints in which, according to the rules, he would pitch as an Ace, so as to make sure he made that all-important leap next year, without which no great career was possible. Otherwise, pitching him regularly, the bottom could suddenly fall out. It had before with other bright young Rookies, many times. So why shouldn't Bancroft do it, why shouldn't he baby him? Because Barney Bancroft didn't know what Henry knew. He didn't know about the different charts. He didn't even know about Aces and why it was the good ones often stayed good over the years. Of course, he must have sensed it, they all did: that peculiar extra force that these great players seemed to radiate. Take the Haymakers' Hamilton Craft, for example, now in a miserable slump, and yet Rooney couldn't pull him from the line-up yesterday because he somehow felt that Craft was the best man he had—he was right, but he didn't know exactly why. It was the same when a man fell from class: you could feel it, though sometimes it was hard to believe it, and you kept using the man anyway, waiting for him to bounce back. But what could you feel about Damon Rutherford right now? Only that he might be the greatest pitcher in world history, and how could you bench a man like that? No, Damon had passed up Ace Halifax, was clearly the bellwether of the Pioneer staff, the number-one starter, and unless he showed some signs of losing control that Bancroft could recognize—and even then Barney might rightly prescribe *more* pitching and not less—then he'd have to pitch at least another ten or twelve games. And could Henry sit idly by and watch the kid get powdered, lose hope of becoming an Ace? He had to. Oh, sure, he was free to throw away the dice, run the game by whim, but then what would be the point of it? Who would Damon Rutherford really be then? Nobody, an empty name, a play actor. Even though he'd set his own rules, his own limits, and though he could change them whenever he wished, nevertheless he and his players were committed to the turns of the mindless and unpredictable—one might even say, irresponsible—dice. That was how it was. He had to accept it, or quit the game altogether.

Someone, he noticed, was bulking by his desk. Henry looked up, expecting the worst, but it was only his friend Lou Engel. Zifferblatt seemed busy at his desk, working his mouth as though chewing a cud. "Henry!" Lou whispered, one eye Ziffward. "Have you been sick or . . . or something?"

Henry felt an impulsive urge to explain, to tell Lou about the perfect game, but it would have taken too long and Lou probably wouldn't have got it anyway, so he merely said, "No, no! Feel great, Lou! Just great!"

Lou looked unconvinced. "Let's talk after work," he said. Ziff reared his head, and Lou hurried clumsily down the aisle toward his own desk, kicking over a wastebasket along the way. "Oops! awful sorry!" Poor Lou.

At times, it was true, Henry longed not only to talk about his game, but to have somebody to play it with him. Often, especially during the long routine stretches with one team way out in front, or when continuity and pattern dissipated, giving way to mere accident, he felt the loneliness of his game, longed for an equal with whom to reminisce, to judge, to plan. He had invented alternate schemes for playing the game which would allow for two proprietors or more, and had hinted at the game when talking with Lou, but Lou didn't seem to have quite the right feeling for projects like that. He preferred to play chess or collect stamps or listen to classical music. Of course, now there was Hettie, and the other player didn't have to be an equal, after all. No, there was the possibility of some new arrangement based not on two competing and antagonistic equals, but rather on the relinquishment of certain, let us say, *feminine* powers and duties, the creation of a kind of vice-proprietor, as it were. But Hettie was probably too unconscious. Whatever she did, it would have to be pretty simple.

So I'm out on the field and the sun is mighty hot,
And I'm thinkin' 'bout all the goddamn troubles
I got,
Next thing I know I'm sawin' 'em off at first
base,
And this guy gits a hit and comes and stands on
my face!

PLAY BALL! (I'm gonna split if it's all the
same!)
PLAY BALL! (What the hell is the name of
this game?)
PLAY BALL!

"All right. Where were you this morning, Mr. Waugh?" Just when he least expected him, there he was: Horace Zifferblatt.

And what could he say? Playing baseball between the sheets with a B-girl? Celebrating Damon's Day in the UBA? He smiled. Looking more carefully now at his work, he saw that he had entered a whole list of figures in the wrong column. In pencil, fortunately. Zifferblatt reared before him, fidgeting in a cold yet incensed quiver, thumbs rammed into the snakeskin belt of his black-and-gray striped trousers, his third and grayest chin beetling neatly over the hard knot of his purple-and-cream tie. Henry knew he should wait until the man had gone, but he didn't. He got out his eraser and went to work.

"Is something *wrong*, Henry?" The shift in name was not necessarily a good sign. Ziff, he knew, was watching him erase.

Henry had to admit that the more carefully he figured the percentages and tabulated the records of his Association, the more mistakes he seemed to make here at work, and though he knew he shouldn't really be bothered by the fact, nevertheless he still suffered from that professional pride of computational infallibility, and so no doubt he was blushing now. He brushed eraser crumbs from the ruled paper and surveyed his work. He supposed that the whole office was watching them now, but he really didn't know what to tell Ziff. He saw Damon Rutherford down in the locker room, one foot up on a bench, lacing a cleated shoe, saw him feel a foreign presence, saw him straighten up, tall, lithe, self-composed, a look of amusement commingled with compassion arching his young brow, saw him turn to look down on this little fat man, standing there in confused rage, heard him say: "How's that, fella?"

Zifferblatt rocked back on his heels, blew out his cheeks in genuine astonishment. "Waugh!" he squeaked. "I want you to come in and see me first thing tomorrow morning—*first thing!* You hear?" The man rotated, and head bulled forward, stumped off to his private office. Henry watched him, then returned to his books. Lou dropped by cautiously, but Henry waved him off; couldn't Lou see he really didn't care?

He transcribed the misplaced figures into the right column, but once that was done, he couldn't seem to keep going. His mind kept drifting back to his kitchen table. Big night tonight. He still had to post all the action of the forty-seventh games, then write it up in the Book. Plenty to talk about. Terrific pennant chase developing between the Knickerbockers and the Pioneers, with the Pastimers and last year's champs, the Keystones, not far behind. Patrick Monday's new political party. Though, with Damon's no-hitter, he was less excited about that now; it seemed less necessary. Still, the seed was sown. Monday probably fretting about the new league mood. Wait and see. Also there was the developing slugging contest between the Knicks' Walt McCamish and the Pioneers' Witness York. Signs of a new Rutherford Era. What a season! The big story tonight, of course, was the perfect game. The boy with the magic arm. The man who knows himself. Phrases and headlines floated through his mind. Return of the Pioneers. Hopes soar for first pennant in twenty-four years. Have to remember that interview with Barney Bancroft he had in bed this morning. What about Damon's consecratory romp in the sack afterwards? Sure, why not? Somebody's virgin daughter. Maybe the Knicks' manager Sycamore Flynn had a daughter he could use. Only one? Hell, a whole stadium full! Line 'em up! Boy with the magic shortarm!

What was he doing here? He had to get out, get home! He looked at the clock: 4:21. Couldn't even wait nine minutes? Couldn't he play the horseracing game he kept in his desk drawer, for instance? He couldn't. He glanced toward Zifferblatt's office: bent over the books. Well, it would be a hard pill for the old man to swallow, but that was tough. Henry closed the books, put them away, stepped over to the hat-tree for his gray felt, raincoat, and black umbrella, and left the office. On the move. Come on, boys, let's take the field. Lot of pepper now. As he passed Ziff's office, he caught a glimpse of the old man's gray head jerking up to glare at his early exit. Well, too bad, but how could anyone take seriously, after all, a man named Horace Zifferblatt? Once in the elevator, going down, he was able to forget about work altogether. He was headed for home, returning to his league and all its players, to the Book and tonight's big story, and there weren't any Horace Zifferblatts there.

Outside, it was raining again, nostalgic fall evening, and Henry, as he stepped along under his umbrella, found it pleasant to muse about the origins. He'd always played a lot of games: baseball, basketball, different card games, war and finance games, horseracing, football, and so on, all on paper of course. Once, he'd got involved in a tabletop war-games club, played by mail, with mutual defense pacts, munition sales, secret agents, and even assassinations, but the inability of the other players to detach themselves from their narrow-minded historical preconceptions depressed Henry. Anything more complex than a normalized two-person zero-sum game was beyond them. Henry had invented for them a variation on Monopoly, using twelve, sixteen, or twenty-four boards at once and an unlimited number of players, which opened up the possibility of wars run by industrial giants with investments on several boards at once, the buying off of whole governments, the emergence of international communications and utilities barons, strikes and rebellions by the slumdwellers between "Go" and "Jail," revolutionary subversion and sabotage with sympathetic ties across the boards, the creation of international regulatory bodies by the established power cliques, and yet without losing any of the basic features of their own battle games, but it never caught on. He even introduced health, sex, religious, and character variables, but that made even less of a hit, though he did manage, before leaving the club, to get a couple pieces on his "Intermonop" game published in some of the club literature.

And so, finally, he'd found his way back to baseball. Nothing like it really. Not the actual game so much—to tell the truth, real baseball bored him—but rather the records, the statistics, the peculiar balances between individual and team, offense and defense, strategy and luck, accident and pattern, power and intelligence. And no other activity in the world had so precise and comprehensive a history, so specific an ethic, and at the same time, strange as it seemed, so much ultimate mystery. He had started out by selecting eight teams from baseball's early days in the Civil War and Reconstruction eras, and supplying them with rosters of twenty-one ballplayers each. Marshall Williams. Verne Mackenzie. Fancy Dan Casey. Barnaby North. How clearly he remembered the stars of that first year! He even recalled the precise results of those first games, how the Beaneaters won their first six games in a row and never gave up the lead, beating out the Keystones by five full games. If he tried hard enough, he could probably even remember the exact scores.

Of course, the abrupt beginning had its disadvantages. It was, in a sense, too arbitrary, too inexplicable. In spite of the almost excessive warmth he felt toward those first ballplayers, it always troubled him that their life histories were so unavailable to him: What had a great player already in his thirties been doing for the previous ten years? It was much better once a kind of continuity had been established, and when new players had taken over the league who had their whole careers still ahead of them. It was, in fact, when the last Year I player had retired that Henry felt the Association had come of age, and when, a couple years ago, the last veteran of Year I, old ex-Chancellor Barnaby North, had died, he had felt an odd sense of relief: the touch with the deep past was now purely "historic," its ambiguity only natural. Luckily, all the first-year records had been broken. And soon there would be no more living veterans born before Year I.

The rain tumbled like gentle applause on his umbrella. Under it he walked, skirting the puddles, dry in the deluge, as though glassed in under a peaked black dome. Hunched-up cars pushed through the streets like angry defeated ballplayers jockeying through crowds on their way to the showers. Henry waited at a corner for a red light. Offices emptied out, filling the streets. A policeman in a slicker stood stoically in the thick of the traffic, blowing his whistle and jerking his arms like a base coach urging a runner on. The light changed to green and Henry crossed over to his bus stop. Green. Slicker. Cop. Copper Greene. Might try it. Have to jot it down when he got home.

Everywhere he looked he saw names. His head was full of them. Bus stop. Whistlestop. Whistlestop Busby, second base. Simple as that. Over a storefront across the street: Thornton's. He'd been looking for a name to go with Shadwell, and maybe that was it. Thornton Shadwell. Tim's boy. Pitcher like the old man? Probably. But a lefty. Will he play for the Stones? No. Unless the old man gets sacked this year. His Keystones were in a slump. Manager of the Year last year, in trouble this. Life was fast and brutal. More likely, Mel Trench's Excelsiors will grab young Shadwell up. Outstanding prospect.

Henry was always careful about names, for they were what

gave the league its sense of fulfillment and failure, its emotion. The dice and charts and other paraphernalia were only the mechanics of the drama, not the drama itself. Names had to be chosen, therefore, that could bear the whole weight of perpetuity. Brock Rutherford was a name like that; Horace (n) Zifferblatt wasn't. Now, it was funny about names. All right, you bring a player up from the minors, call him A. Player A, like his contemporaries, has, being a Rookie, certain specific advantages and disadvantages with the dice. But it's exactly the same for all Rookies. You roll, Player A gets a hit or he doesn't, gets his man out or he doesn't. Sounds simple. But call Player A "Sycamore Flynn" or "Melbourne Trench" and something starts to happen. He shrinks or grows, stretches out or puts on muscle. Sprays singles to all fields or belts them over the wall. Throws mostly fast balls like Swanee Law or curves like Mickey Halifax. Choleric like Rag Rooney or slow and smooth like his old first-base rival Mose Stanford. Not easy to tell just how or why. Or take Old Fennimore McCaffree. He was "Old" the year he came up to play third base for the Knicks. And not just because he'd got an unlucky throw of the dice on the Rookie Age Chart and started in as a thirty-year-older, but because that was simply who he was: Old Fennimore. Scholar and statesman. Dark. Angular. Intense. Sinewy. Fast. Tough. Year XIX. Same Rookie year as Brock Rutherford. Fenn got overlooked in all the other excitement that year, but in XXI he stroked out a .371 to cop both the batting title and the year's Most Valuable Player Award. Determined man. But still Old Fenn. Now, just inquire of poor Woody Winthrop, who till then had been the perennial third-base All Star selection, and who, in fact, if Henry remembered rightly, had himself in that Year of the Rookie, Year XIX, won the MVP Award, if that was Player A he was getting eclipsed by. No, friends and voters, that was Old Fennimore. Shrewd, relentless, cool, reliable Fenn. When you scored against the Knickerbockers in those years, you even felt a chill just crossing third under Old Fenn's glare. Then, suddenly, he was not just old, he was too old. Great playing record, but too brief to be sure of making the Hall of Fame. And for Fenn there was no halfway house in history. A spectacular career as manager might be enough more to do the trick, he figured. So he talked Woody Winthrop, by then the champion Knickerbockers boss, into quitting his job to enter Association politics, while he himself, wily Old Fenn McCaffree, took over as manager of the team Woody had built. Something of a bastard, but he won ball games, and that was what counted in baseball. Twelve years, six championships. And so he did make it: Hall of Fame. And now he was even the UBA Chancellor. And whom did he succeed? Woody Winthrop. Looking back, it seemed all but necessary. Strange. But name a man and you make him what he is. Of course, he can develop. And in ways you don't expect. Or something can go wrong. Lot of nicknames invented as a result of Rookie-year surprises. But the basic stuff is already there. In the name. Or rather: in the naming.

The bus was late. Due to the bad weather probably. He might as well have stayed at the office. But no, he'd enjoyed this moment. It had given him time to think. Prepare his mind for tonight's activity. Exciting year, LVI. Years from now, he'd look back on it with the same nostalgia he was feeling now for Year XIX.

"Henry!" It was his friend Lou, trotting flatfooted through the puddles, holding his hat, coat undone and flapping in the rain. "Henry!" he called again, but then couldn't get his breath to continue. The bus came. Henry smiled at Lou, squeezed aboard. "I . . . guess (wheeze) I'll . . . ride along," Lou gasped, and intruded his bulk.

The bus was jammed, they had to stand. People jostled, rammed them moistly toward the rear. Rain drummed on the roof. If skyscrapers were penis-prisons, what were the buses? the efferent tubes? The driver barked orders. Passengers protested at the shoving. Lou was the biggest in sight, so everybody turned their darkest looks on him. A woman complained about getting elbowed, and though it wasn't Lou's fault, he tipped his hat in apology, dripping water from the brim onto the evening paper of a man sitting next to them. The paper spoke blackly of bombs, births, wars, weddings, infiltrations, and social events. "You know, Lou," Henry said, "you can take history or leave it, but if you take it you have to accept certain assumptions or ground rules about what's left in and what's left out."

"How's . . . that?" squeaked Lou, wrinkling up his nose. His breath was still coming in short spasmodic gulps, and one gulp broke his question right in the middle. Lou oughtn't run so hard with his weight.

"History. Amazing, how we love it. And did you ever stop to think that without numbers or measurements, there probably wouldn't be any history?" He asked it that way for Lou's sake. Really, he was thinking the thoughts he always thought on buses and subways, drawing the old comparisons—why, he wondered, at such an inherently joyful moment, was he feeling so melancholy? Was it the rain? or maybe the unspoken recognition that Damon Rutherford, wonderful as he was, would someday have to hang up his cleats like all the rest? Maybe it was only because this was Year LVI: he and the Association were the same age, though of course their "years" were reckoned differently. He saw two time lines crossing in space at a point marked "56." Was it the vital moment? Silly idea. It would probably get better next season. "At 4:34 on a wet November afternoon, Lou Engel boarded a city bus and spilled water from his hat brim on a man's newspaper. Is that history?"

"I . . . I dunno," stammered Lou, reddening before the sudden distrustful scowl of the man with the newspaper. "I (wheeze) guess so."

"Who's writing it down?" Henry demanded.

"Henry, listen, what's the matter? (Wheeze.) What was the point of that row with Mr. Zifferblatt anyhow? Where were you this (wheeze) morning? And where were you going in such a rush? Why, you left nine (wheeze) minutes early, did you know that? I had to run five blocks"—here his voice broke, and he had to gulp for air again—"almost to catch up to you. What is it, Henry? Can I help somehow? Is (wheeze) something wrong?" Once he got his wind, it came like a gale.

"No, no, like I told you, Lou, everything's fine, just fine. Wonderful, in fact." His stop. He stepped down, and Lou clumsily followed. Henry was impatient to get home, to look at that box score again, but he waited for Lou, who had no umbrella.

"I just don't understand you anymore, Henry!" Lou protested. There was an awkward silence as they walked along under the drumroll of rain. "Look, Henry, I got an idea, why don't you come along with me tonight? I found a new place, Mitch's Bar and Grill, great steaks—"

"Sorry, Lou, I'm busy tonight."

"That's what you always say, Henry. What do you do? I don't understand. Look, I got an idea—"

"Not tonight, Lou." They were at the front door of Diskin's Delicatessen. Maybe tonight was the night to show Lou the game. Yet, damn it, somehow he felt jealous of that perfect game, felt an uncommonly strong wish to be alone this evening, and besides, Lou could spoil it. His questions were almost never the right ones. "Some other time. I may want to go out and celebrate soon, in fact."

"Celebrate . . . ?"

"Would you like to use my umbrella, Lou? the rest of the way?"

"No, thanks, Henry, I catch a bus on the next corner and it's . . . but, but listen—"

"Say, Lou," Henry interrupted as he turned into the doorway of the stairs leading up to his apartment. "Is Mitch a first or last name?"

"Mitch? You mean the . . . ? First, but . . . ?"

"What's his last name?"

"Porter, I think."

"Mitch Porter." Henry collapsed his umbrella and stood at the edge of the rain, listening to the name of Mitch Porter. Might make an outfielder. Or a good third baseman. "We'll have to try it sometime. Good night, Lou."

Lou sighed. "Night, Henry." His friend Lou looked dismal in the rain, hat brim adroop, eyebrows soggy, and if it hadn't been for the recording of the perfect game that awaited him, Henry would have relented, would have taken leave from the Association tonight and gone with Lou to Mitch's Bar and Grill, try to cheer him up. And, yes, someday, no doubt about it, he'd have to show Lou the game. If he didn't get it, so what? At least let him have his chance.

The stairway always had a certain smell that quickened Henry's pulse. Like hot dogs and beer in a ball park. Probably came from the delicatessen, but in any case it always made Henry take the last ten or fifteen steps on the run. At the door of his apartment, he was often grabbed by mild panic, felt the fragility of this thing he'd fashioned: a fire, theft, even a hard wind . . . he drove the key into the lock, turned it, stepped inside.

But on the kitchen table, everything was in order, just as he had left it. Scorecard of the game, final entries scrawled a little excitedly perhaps. The dice still showed Hard John Horvath's grounder to third. In a sense, it was still that moment, and if he wanted to savor it or if he got occupied with something else, it could go on being that moment for weeks. And then, when things got going again, would the players have any awareness of how time had stopped? No . . . but they might wonder how all the details of that moment had got so firmly etched in their minds.

Of course, there were other games yesterday. The lowly Excelsiors had risen up to knock off the league-leading Knickerbockers, 6–to–2, trimming their edge over the surging Pioneers to two games. The Pastime Club, riding a winning streak, had edged the Keystones in the ninth inning, 4–to–3, to tie that team for third place and give troubled Tim Shadwell another white hair. And, in a second-division free-for-all, Winslow Beaver's Beaneaters had nailed Wally Wickersham's bumbling Bridegrooms deeper into the cellar, 12–to–8, both teams using five of their six pitchers in the hectic course of the game. The first thing Henry did after hanging up his hat, coat, and umbrella, was to bring the Team Standings Board up to date. The Board, which years ago Henry had constructed with removable wooden name-slats and numbers, hung on the wall behind the kitchen table. When he was done, it read:

TEAM	WON	LOST	PCT	GB
Knickerbockers	28	19	.596	–
Pioneers	26	21	.553	2
Pastime Club	24	23	.511	4
Keystones	24	23	.511	4
Haymakers	23	24	.489	5
Beaneaters	22	25	.468	6
Excelsiors	21	26	.447	7
Bridegrooms	20	27	.426	8

Then he put on fresh coffee and switched on the light, a hundred-watt bulb with a green metal topee, painted white on the underside, that hung directly over the table. Next, he got out the binder of running pitching statistics for this year, filled in the details from the forty-seventh round of games. Henry had the forms for these statistics, like all his forms now, printed up for him by a small-job printer. There was room on each form for a full team of six pitchers, and there, with little marks that ended up looking like railroad tracks, he recorded their Games Pitched, Complete Games, Games Won, Games Lost, Shutouts, Strikeouts, Walks, Hits Allowed, Innings Pitched, Earned Runs Allowed, and Special Remarks. There were spaces for writing in, at year's end, the Won-Lost Percentage and Earned Run Average.

The coffee was done, so he poured himself a cup, returned now to the table to post the day's batting statistics. These charts were larger, had room for a full roster of twenty-one players (pitchers had batting averages, too, of course, and a couple of pitchers in UBA history had, in spite of the odds against them, hit their way into Star categories and become right fielders in the course of time), contained such information as Games Played, At Bats, Runs, Hits, Doubles, Triples, Home Runs,

Runs Batted In, Stolen Bases, and so on, with special columns to record Injuries, as well as Most Valuable Player points, awarded after each game. Room, too, for end-of-season Batting and Slugging Averages. As for injuries, these occurred with a dice roll of 3–3–3 on all nine of the basic charts; the dice were then thrown again to obtain the details of it from the special Injuries Chart, which included everything from a hit batsman who, uninjured, took his base, to multiple injuries that sometimes kept ballplayers out of the line-up for several games, or even the season. It was every manager's headache and it was probably the worst way to lose a pennant, to have your Ace nursing a chip in his elbow or your Stars hobbling around in casts, but it was a crucial part of the whole game, and though Henry always felt a twinge of remorse when it happened, he was pleased with that detail in his system.

Finally, the dullest job—recording of fielding statistics. The trouble was, all these averages stayed pretty much the same, and worth was a hard thing to judge by them. Incompetent ballplayers just didn't make it up to the big leagues in the first place, and as for the competent ones, a couple percentage points here or there didn't tell much of a story. He had managed to bring a little color and pattern to them with small subtleties worked in over the years, such that brilliant fielders took more chances, made fewer errors, had a better chance of throwing out base runners from the outfield or setting up double plays, but except for a handful of unusually flashy glovemen, he couldn't keep his mind on it. He had thought of giving them up altogether, they took a lot of time and didn't seem worth it, but there were all those fielding records already established, and what would they mean if they had no challengers? Besides, it was, as Sandy Shaw knew, the third part of the game: ". . . *Pitchin', catchin', swingin', out on the field all day!*" So he had stayed loyal even to this, the most wearying part of his game.

This done, the posting of all statistics from the day's play, Henry turned to the job he enjoyed most—writing it up in the Book. He'd begun the logs in Year IX, feeling the need by then to take counsel with himself, though even before that, he had been writing up uncommonly exciting moments on loose sheets of typing paper (glad he did; these later got bound in). Now it consisted of some forty volumes, kept in shelves built into the kitchen wall, along with the permanent record books, league financial ledgers, and the loose-leaf notebooks of running life histories. He seemed to find more to write about, the more he played the game, and he foresaw the day when the number of archive volumes would pass the number of league years. He always used a standard-size record book, three hundred pages, good rag content for durability; he kept a shorthand point on his fountain pen and never used anything but permanent black ink, except when he underlined or boxed in extraordinary incidents or insights in a draughtsman's red ink. On the title page of each volume were the volume number and these words:

OFFICIAL ARCHIVES
THE UNIVERSAL BASEBALL ASSOCIATION
J. HENRY WAUGH, PROP.

Into the Book went the whole UBA, everything from statistics to journalistic dispatches, from seasonal analyses to general baseball theory. Everything, in short, worth keeping. Style varied from the extreme economy of factual data to the overblown idiom of the sportswriter, from the scientific objectivity of the theoreticians to the literary speculations of essayists and anecdotalists. There were tape-recorded dialogues, player contributions, election coverage, obituaries, satires, prophecies, scandals. It provided a kind of league's-eye view, since functional details of the game were never mentioned—team analyses, for example, never referred to Stars and Aces except metaphorically, and, intentionally, erred slightly. His own shifting moods, often affected by events in the league, also colored the reports, oscillating between notions of grandeur and irony, exultation and despair, enthusiasm and indifference, amusement and weariness. Lately, he had noticed a tendency toward melancholy and sentimentality. He hoped he'd get over it soon. Maybe he could do a piece on next year's upcoming rookies, boys like Copper Greene and Thornton Shadwell and Whistlestop Busby, something to spring his mind forward. He often did that: forcibly reversed his mood by a story inappropriate to it. Like the time, following a siege of minor illnesses which had left him in a deep gloom, when he had told the story of Long Lew Lydell's rape of Old Fennimore McCaffree's spinster daughter in the Knickerbocker dugout in front of five thousand wide-eyed spectators. Lew married the girl eventually, under political pressure, since the Legalist Party, which McCaffree headed up, could abide no scandals, and, so they say, he was even tamed, though whether by Fanny or by his own political ambitions, it was hard to say. Henry smiled, remembering. Sandy had a song about it . . .

. . . For believe it or not,
Though Long Lew had a lot,
Fanny had never had any!

Might have started a new Association pre-game warm-up ritual, if they hadn't threatened Long Lew with expulsion from the league. Poor Fennimore! A lesser man would have sunk away into the earth. But not Old Fenn: here he was now the Association Chancellor and his son-in-law was a party bigwig. New elections coming up this winter, but it looked like McCaffree would be reelected. Raped daughter or no.

Henry spread open the current volume of the Book, read over the previous entry, considered this one. He wrote out a few possible lead sentences on scratch paper, but none appealed to him. He stood, poured himself another cup of coffee, carried it back to the table and stood there, staring down at the open Book. He rarely copied box scores into the Book, since they all got kept in each year's manila folders, but today it seemed the right thing to do. All those zeros! He decided for the zeros he'd use red ink. Zero: the absence of number, an incredible idea! Only infinity compared to it, and no batter could hit an infinite number of home runs—no, in a way, the pitchers had it better. Perfection was available to them.

Damon Rutherford. Rutherford. Henry was sitting now, gazing through the steam off his coffee toward the League Standings Board. He recalled that vision of the boy, standing there on the mound, one out from immortality, and not one twitch or flicker. He saw the women screaming, offering themselves up, watched the surge of adoring masses, saw Damon pitch the ball out to that little kid. Who was that boy? Someday they'd probably all find out. The reporters tried to interview Damon directly, of course, but he told them he had nothing really to say. Was he excited about what he'd done? Yes. I mean, *really* excited? Yes. What was the secret of his success? No secret. But that pitch—how was it . . . ? what did he do . . . ? Nothing, just threw it. Hey, Damon, what did Ingram say when he came out to the mound? Nothing much, just helped me relax. Helped *you* relax! Laughter around. Damon smiled. Say, I guess your Daddy's proud, hunh? I hope so. Did he come to see you pitch? Yes. What did he tell you afterwards? Good game.

Henry paced the kitchen, his mind on several things at once. He poured what was left of the coffee, put another pot on. Rain splashed on the window. Getting dark already. Should be moving on, he had work to do yet tonight, but he decided first to get out the archive volumes from the Brock Rutherford Era. Yes, he was definitely calling it that now. He thumbed meditatively through those old Books, taking notes, soon found himself reliving those great years of the Pioneers as though they were happening today. Pugnacious little Frosty Young, whistling and catcalling around second base, making those picture plays: the Demonic Duo they called Young and his shortstop-buddy Jonathan Noon. And five-by-five Holly Tibbett running the bases splay-legged: ho ho! look at him go! Loose-limbed Mose Stanford hitching his baggy pants, stuffing a loose shirt-end under the belt, spitting sleepily on his hands, and shoes unlaced and socks drooping, whacking out another game-winning double: led the league in doubles five straight years, an all-time record! And Toothbrush dusting Gus Maloney—on the Extraordinary Occurrences Chart—and setting off the greatest fight in UBA history, not only all over the diamond, but even out in left field where the Haymaker relief pitchers charged out of the bull pen to gang up on Willie O'Leary! And through those years, out in center field, the Old Philosopher, brilliant Barney Bancroft, floating with that unruffled grace, pulling impossible catches out of the air, pegging the ball home on the fly. A whiplash hitter and the fastest man in the UBA in his day, Barney was the last of the great Pioneers to leave the scene, was in fact the oldest active player in world history, hanging on to his Star rating until the age of forty-five, retiring finally in Year XLIII to become a Pioneer coach and eventually their manager. The Man Who Couldn't Quit.

Year XIX: Year of the Rookie. Five eventual Hall-of-Famers in the crop. Not only the Pioneers' Rutherford and Young, but also shortstop Sycamore Flynn of the Bridegrooms, now the Knickerbocker boss; the Knicks' own great Fennimore McCaffree; and the phenomenal Edgar Bath who that year pitched his first game for the Keystones, eventually leading them to an upset pennant win over the Knicks and Pioneers in Year XXIII. "Well," said Bath, "we were lucky that year, but we were good, too. We had—" No, wait: Henry checked the deceased lists; yes, Bath was dead, thought so. Jake Bradley came up in XIX, too, to play second for the Pastimers. Didn't make the Hall of Fame, at least not yet, but a great UBA personality.

One thing that struck Henry was the optimism in his own style back then. Even a kind of jauntiness. He'd changed. He couldn't write like that now. Not even if he had the kind of story he'd had that year. Brock's great rookie season. Election of Fancy Dan Casey to the Hall of Fame just before it began. Fourteen different records broken. It was the year they formed up the first real political parties, the semi-official Individualist Party, later called the Bogglers (from Barnaby North's great speech in XXIV), and the Legalists. And it was the year the ever-impotent Bridegrooms, led by the great Woody Winthrop, who took the batting title and the MVP award, rose up to snatch the pennant from the long-time UBA powerhouse, the Haymakers and the Knickerbockers, and the surging exuberant Pioneers—the only year in all Association history that the Grooms finished first! After XIX, it was the Pioneers' league: nine pennants in fourteen seasons, and only once as low as third. Henry remembered how he himself had wearied finally of the Pioneer domination, and how, secretly, he had rooted for any and all challengers. Of course, he hadn't interfered directly in any way, and yet the Pioneers must have felt, somehow, his resistance, and in ways not really visible, he had probably in fact made it harder for them. And yet, there they were, year after year, right on top, and Brock Rutherford, the winningest pitcher in baseball, was right on top there with them. Once he lost his Ace status, he didn't stay on long, just two years, and Henry was glad for him: it was painful to see an immortal going clumsy. With Brock gone, the Pioneers collapsed, finished higher than seventh only twice during the next fourteen years. Henry graphed all this out, studied it over a fresh cup of coffee. The Brock Rutherford Era. He called down to the delicatessen and asked Mr. Diskin to have Benny bring him up a couple hot pastrami sandwiches and more beer.

Holly Tibbett was the guy who loved pastrami and beer. Of course, he loved everything edible. He was always eating. "You remember how he used to keep a pastrami sandwich next to his belly, under the guard, to nibble on between pitches?" "Do I remember!" Brock said with a grin. "I used to aim at it!" Still a husky guy, hair cropped short, graying a little maybe, dressed in a plaid wool shirt and wash pants, a bit fuller around the middle now. "Ever hit it?" That was Tim Shadwell, broad grin on his face. "Once. But I had to throw when he wasn't looking." Gabe Burdette laughed: "I remember that! He was arguing with the ump. You nearly laid him out!" Now Frosty Young and Jake Bradley were laughing, too, Young himself an umpire now and getting the hell he gave so many years. And Jumpin' Joe Gallagher and Willie O'Leary. "I heard about that," Bradley put in. "The funny thing was to see old Holly run," Gabe said. "Only catcher I ever knew who walked the same silly split-ass way no matter whether he was wearing his guard or not." "You tellin' *me!*" Bradley laughed in that soft ironic way of his, leaning on the bar. Amber light gleamed off his pate, but his shirt was a dazzling white. "It used to put me in a pea-green funk every time I saw him come charging up at me from first! It looked like he was going every which way at once!" "And standing still at the same time!" Frosty put in. "Yeah, that's right, he wasn't very fast." They all laughed to see old Holly Tibbett huffing and puffing toward second base, where bald Jake Bradley waited in a mock funk. Jake poured a round of drinks. Gabe Burdette told again the story of the clam chowder. They'd all heard it before, but they all wanted to hear it again. They stood at the bar, seven aging men, laughing to think of their old friend Holly Tibbett, who had died finally, not of gluttony, but of a brain tumor. While nostalgic music thrummed out of the jukebox, Gabe told how Holly, who avoided women with the same shy intensity with which he sought food, got talked into visiting this broad they all knew, who, they told him, made the best clam chowder in world history. So he wouldn't get suspicious, Gabe and Frosty went with him. They were just sitting down at the table, when the girl, who had been put up to it, spilled the whole mess in Holly's lap. Gabe and Frosty asked the girl if she could clean the pants a little, maybe run over them with an iron. She said, sure, and before Holly could argue (and anyway the pants were scalding hot), they'd got him into the bathroom and the pants off him. That was when, after they'd slipped out with the pants, that the girl hollered out, "Eek! my husband!"—and Brock, wearing glasses and a false nose and mustache, came storming in as the irate spouse, discovered Holly in the head and went for his gun. "My pants!" Holly screamed, but then Brock let fire a salvo, and out the door old Holly shot. "He looked just like something out of an old movie!" Gabe howled. They were all laughing. Jake Bradley had tears in his eyes. Frosty ran up and down in the barroom, imitating splay-legged Holly Tibbett in an old movie. Brock chased him down the street, firing shots into the air. "Just *mention* clam chowder to Holly after that!" Gabe cried. Brock's laughter boomed out over the others, free and resonant. "Those were the days!" Jake said. Old Holly. Their laughter dwindled. They found themselves sighing, staring wistfully into their glasses. "Another round, Jake," said Brock softly.

Henry had hardly noticed when Benny had brought the sandwiches. One of them was already gone. He looked at his watch: eleven. He closed the Book, ate the other sandwich, washed it down with beer. If he stepped along, there was still time for one round of games before turning in. He wrote out the eight line-ups, making a couple strategic changes here and there, considering each team's needs. The bottom teams, for example, were already beginning to develop for next year, while the ones near the top, fighting it out, still had to stick with the best. Unusual season, though, in that all of the teams were pretty close.

Things went routinely through the forty-eighth game of the fifty-sixth season in the UBA. The Knicks shellacked Mel Trench's Cels, and hung on to their two-game lead. The second-running Pioneers knocked off the Haymakers again, and Pappy Rooney's ulcer got worse. The benighted Bridegrooms upset the Beaneaters, and Cash Bailey's red-hot Pastimers, led by Virgin Donovan and Bo McBean, took their third straight from the Keystones, last year's champions, to move into undisputed possession of third place. Henry brought the Team Standings Board up to date, logged all the statistics, wrote up a routine report of the day's play in the Book, punched open another can of beer. It was only 2:30 and tomorrow—today, actually—would be a light day at the office. Well, there was that tiresome matter with Zifferblatt, but he could take care of that. Besides, to be honest with himself, the idea had been dogging him for the last two or three hours: *He wanted to see Damon Rutherford pitch again tonight!*

It wasn't the recommended practice to start a pitcher after only one day of rest, but it wasn't against the rules. Besides, there was an extra day of travel in there, as the Knickerbockers came by train from the Excelsiors' Flint Field to Pioneer Park. And that was the other thing that was exciting him: the Pioneers were up against the league-leading Knicks in a three-game series that could ultimately decide the outcome of the entire season! Already, phrases for the Book were flashing through his mind. He drank down the beer and opened another, took a couple minutes to quell the rebellion of his kidneys, and then, with the premonition of a great impending drama driving him, he sat down quickly at the table and wrote out the starting line-ups. He decided to start rookie pitcher Jock Casey for the Knicks to make the game an even match, although secretly he knew—in fact, he hesitated, admitted it out loud: "They should start their Ace southpaw, Uncle Joe Shannon."

Knick manager Sycamore Flynn fended off the criticism. "I'm saving Shannon to pitch against Halifax." And he was right. With a two-game lead, the Knicks could risk losing the first one, and still, by bearing down with their two Aces in the last two games, come out of the series better off than they went in. In any case, there'd be no further concessions, if in fact that was one. It was Damon's job, and he wouldn't like it if he didn't think he was doing it by himself. He emerged from the locker room with that same incredible poise, that same effortless calm. Autograph hunters, mostly kids, jammed around him. He signed a few scorecards, smiled at the other youngsters, then moved on toward the field. "Hey, Damon!" a young boy hollered. "Can I have the ball today?" And all the others picked up the cry.

The hometown Pioneer fans went wild when he appeared on the field to take his warm-up pitches. Manager Bancroft fretted about that a little, but he saw it didn't seem to affect Damon any. Barney really needed this game. He wondered if he'd done the wrong thing sending him in again so soon. The crowd was shouting: "*Rutherford! Rutherford! Rutherford!*" over and over. Henry tried to sit, but he was getting pretty excited himself. He swallowed down some beer to take the tension out of his throat. "Go out and win one for the old man, son." Who said that? Why, that was old Brock! Yes, there he was, sitting in a special box seat over near third base, up behind the Pioneer dugout. In fact, Henry realized suddenly, *it must be Brock Rutherford Day at Pioneer Park!*

Henry leaped up, paced the kitchen, sat down again. Yes, that's it! Of *course* Damon had to pitch! Over in the special bunting bedizened section, Chancellor Fennimore McCaffree, gaunt and black-suited, was shaking Brock's hand. Oh boy, the Pioneer fans were raising the roof! Yes, Brock's day, and they were all there with him: Gabe Burdette and Willie O' Leary, old Mose, Surrey Moss, who'd lost his hair and grown him a belly since the last time Henry saw him, and there was No-Hit Nealy and Birdie Deaton and Toothbrush Terrigan and Jonathan Noon, still the stringbean he always was, and Gus Maloney and Jaybird Wall and Seemly Sam Tucker! They piled in there, shook hands, clapped shoulders, waved at the crowd, laughed at each other's paunches. "Hey, look! there's Long Lew Lydell! And Cueball McAuliffe! And Jake

Bradley, blinking in the sunlight! Hey, Jake! set 'em up! And Bruiser Brusatti! And Chadbourne Collins, old Chuckin' Chad! All those great guys from all those great teams!"

His birthday maybe. Why not? Henry checked: he was, let's see, came up in XIX at—Henry's heart leaped and he nearly spilled his beer! Incredible! *Brock Rutherford was fifty-six years old!*

He paused—but no! the boys rolled in and it was alive! and there was stirring music and stunt-flying and skywriting over the Park and fireworks and flowers for all the ladies. Somebody noticed it was going to be a duel of dynasties: Jock Casey came from a noble line, too—went way back to Year I and the great Fancy Dan Casey. Henry hadn't been too happy about bringing Jock up. He was getting tired of the name Casey, and wasn't all that interested in having yet another one. But there'd always been a Casey in the UBA and habit had got the best of him. Jock wasn't a Fancy Dan, but he was a fighter and always good for a surprise. Played the game his own way, threw everything except what the catcher ordered, got along with no one (or so Henry supposed, because now that he thought about it, he couldn't recall the kid's face), and still kept winning ballgames, anyway more than he lost, was a big factor in the Knicks' flag drive. Well, now he was glad he had done it, brought a Casey up, the last touch to a great day, turned it into a history-making event no matter who won or how.

Chancellor McCaffree opened the special ceremonies with anecdotes from Year XIX, his own rookie year as well as Brock's, and ex-Chancellor Woody Winthrop, a bit doddering but still a fine old gentleman, told how old Brock nearly kept him from winning the batting title that year, and then there were more introductions and more presentations and thundering ovations and cameramen scuttling over the scene like a troupe of hopped-up monkeys; and then out came the opposing managers, Barney Bancroft and Sycamore Flynn, and arms over each other's shoulders, they told what it meant to be a part of the Brock Rutherford Era, yes, they called it that, in front of everybody, the Brock Rutherford Era—spectacular! ecstatic! It was a day to forget your cynicism, boys, your sophistication, and shed a respectable tear or two! It was *more* than history, it was, it was: *fulfillment!*

Over the loudspeakers came the announced line-ups. For the league-leading Knickerbockers:

SS Scat Batkin (Rookie)
2B McAllister Weeks
1B Matt Garrison (Star)
CF Biff Baldwin (Star)
RF Walt McCamish (Star)
LF Bran Maverly (Star)
C Chauncey O'Shea (Rookie)
3B Galen Musgraves
P Jock Casey (Rookie)

And for the hometown and second-place Pioneers (incredible ovations, almost impossible to hear the announcer):

2B Toby Ramsey (Rookie)
LF Grammercy Locke
3B Hatrack Hines (Star)
CF Witness York (Star)
RF Stan Patterson (Star)
C Royce Ingram (Star)
SS Lance Wilder
1B Goodman James
P Damon Rutherford (Rookie)

And then the game was on. Henry hastily jotted down the details of the pre-game ceremonies for later inclusion in the Book, then excitedly got the game under way. Frosty Young, Brock's old teammate and fellow rookie, and today the home-plate umpire, brought the ball, brand-spanking new and glowing white in the sunlight, over to Brock, and as all Pioneer Park—indeed the whole baseball world—roared its approval, Brock pitched the ball out to his son, waiting on the mound. Frosty jogged back behind the plate, adjusted his mask and guard, and squatting behind Pioneer catcher Royce Ingram, "*PLAY BALL!*" he cried.

Bancroft, feeling edgy, too much spectacle maybe, decided to baby Damon today. If he got in any trouble, he'd pull him out. Lot of reasons. Too little rest. Too much pressure. And he didn't want him to get knocked around in front of the collective history-maddened eye that was on them, in front of his old man on his biggest day. Of course, he grinned, forcing himself to relax, to sit down, looking out there toward the kid on the mound: who said he was going to get in any trouble?

Trouble! The first three batters to face Damon—Batkin, Weeks, and Garrison—all struck out! Oh my God! call out the cops! there's gonna be a riot! hold those fans back there! eight more innings, folks! hang on to your hats!

Casey, caught up in the unbelievable fever of the moment, pitched like his old forebear himself, giving up a walk to Pioneer lead-off man Tobias Ramsey, then mowing down the next three. In the Knickerbocker dugout, fighting manager Sycamore Flynn clapped his players in off the field. "Now, let's hit this kid!" he barked, but he didn't know if he really meant it or not.

"Oh, god*damn* you guys!" he shouted, shouted the stands,

the Pioneer players, at the Knicks. Don't bust it up! Take it easy!

"Nothin' to it, Damon baby! Buncha pansies!"

Sure, pansies! All Damon had to face in the second were three of the most formidable sluggers in all baseball: the Knicks' all-star outfield of Baldwin, McCamish, and Maverly. Bancroft sent a relief pitcher out to the bull pen—no, he didn't! Easy, boys! Easy, Barney! Here we go: throw! Hah! Well, anyway, Biff Baldwin didn't strike out: he popped up to catcher Ingram. Then McCamish lined out to left and Maverly sent a dribbler down the third-base line that Damon fielded himself—easy throw across the diamond to James: *out!* Henry, whooping insanely, danced around the kitchen, then—*FSSST!*—punched open another can of beer.

Say, wait a minute! He looked it up: yes, Damon Rutherford now had a string of twenty-three consecutive scoreless innings, just sixteen short of the world record, a string of seventeen hitless ones, only six short of the record, and a fantastic run of fourteen perfect innings, two shy! Think of it! At least two new world records were riding on this ball game!

"Okay, let's bring 'em in there, boys!"

"A little pepper now!"

"Come on, Stan baby, pop it outa the park!"

"Send that Casey kid back to the minors!"

"Let's dock Jock, Stan baby!"

Again the first man up for the Pioneers, strapping Stanley Patterson, drew a base on balls. Casey was clearly nervous.

"*Hit him! Hit him! Hit him!*" they shouted from the stands.

The old Pioneers drank from hip flasks and clapped to get a rally going.

"Knock Jock outa there!"

"Kiss her clean, Royce baby!"

"Let's chase Case to the showers!"

"Wait him out! That ain't Fancy Dan, that's Gawky Jock!"

But Ingram and Wilder looked at third strikes, and Goodman James grounded out, third to first. The dice roll for James was triple ones, which, under the right circumstances, was a triple play, and which, in any case, led now to the special Stress Chart.

Oh boy! As if things weren't already wild enough! Referral to the Stress Chart always woke Henry up—now it made him sweat. Damon was pitching to rookie Knickerbocker catcher Chauncey O'Shea. Anything could happen. Two or three back-to-back home runs. A fight. Errors. Row with the umps. Impatient and reluctant all at the same time, urged on by the shouts from the fans and the players, Henry threw the dice: 1–1–1! three strike-outs at once! Or rather: three in a row! another perfect inning! the fifteenth straight! one away from the world record!

The bleachers were in an uproar! It might be the greatest pitching duel of all time! The old-timer Pioneers and other players from the past were out of their seats. All but old Brock. He sat like a country gentleman, leather jacket open, grinning affably, hands folded between his knees, leaning slightly forward.

"*Rutherford! Rutherford! Rutherford!*"

Henry, though, had a strange tingle in his spine. His mouth had gone dry, and his heart, he knew, was racing. Damon's throw of triple ones, the second set of ones in a row, had brought the Extraordinary Occurrences Chart into play! This was the only chart Henry still hadn't memorized. For one thing, it didn't get used much, seldom more than once a season; for another, it was pretty complicated. Stars and Aces could lose their special ratings, unknowns could suddenly rise.

Rain could end the game, a drunken fan could crack a player's skull with a pitched beer bottle, a brawl could break out, game-throwing scandals could be discovered, epidemics of flu or dysentery could ravage a line-up. But as he got out the chart to look at it, Henry could see only one line:

1–1–1: *Batter struck fatally by bean ball.*

And the first batter facing Jock Casey in the bottom of the third inning was the ninth man in the Pioneer line-up: *Damon Rutherford!*

Henry was on his feet. He paced to the refrigerator, to the stove, to the sink, back to the table. He slapped the back of the chair with his hand. Incredible! He tried to swallow, couldn't. He went to the refrigerator, opened it. No more beer. Maybe Bancroft should pull the kid, repent of this crazy game, send in a pinch hitter. Don't be an idiot! No one on base and the boy's got another perfect game going. One inning from the world record.

Of course, come on now, relax, there was only one chance in 216 that he'd throw a triple one. He could just as easily throw a triple six, for example: that was a line drive that struck and killed the pitcher. Was *that* what it was? Not just a duel of dynasties, but a *real* duel, a duel to the death between Jock Casey and Damon Rutherford? He saw the sun beating down, saw the sandy space of sixty feet and six inches between the rubber and home plate, saw these two great rookies facing each other, lean, expectant, saw the breathless masses, waiting for this awful rite to be played out.

But no, of course not, they couldn't know. They could feel the rising tension, the terrific stress, the moment's ripeness, but that was all. Only Henry knew. The triple ones stared up at him from the tabletop. He looked away, tried to think of rain or flying beer bottles. Couldn't. No clouds in the sky. Delirious fans, but no malice there. Far from it.

Of course, think now, it never happened before, why should it now? You're getting worked up about nothing. He could throw a 3–4–6, for example: triple and a steal of home plate. Win his own ball game.

But, damn it, could he risk leaving him in there? No, somehow, he had to get him out of there! He sought for some excuse. Something Bancroft saw in the way the kid was exercising the bat as he moved toward home plate? A kind of slump or twitch in his pitching shoulder? Why not? look close, Barney! But who could he sacrifice in his place? Tuck Wilson? Rawlings? And listen! what if he pulled him and then—as had always been the case—Casey threw an ordinary number? The second no-hitter, which could smash nearly all the records in world history, would be out the window . . . and all for nothing. He rinsed his cup out at the sink, poured himself a cup of cold thick coffee, saw how his hands were trembling. And what about Damon, getting jerked from the game like that, what would his attitude afterwards be? What would he make of it? There was more than one risk here.

Henry returned to the table, leaned over his chair, studied the line-up. Some mistake . . . batter overlooked? He went over each throw. No, that was how it was: Casey pitching to Rutherford on the Extraordinary Occurrences Chart. There's nothing to be done about it, he said to himself. Play it out. He sat down, drank cold coffee, put the cup on the table beside him, reached for the dice.

But then, suddenly, he remembered old Brock Rutherford up there in the stands, up there where all the bunting was, up there with all the old Pioneers from the Rutherford Era, and all those other great stars, all of them sitting up there, cheering up there, on this, Brock Rutherford Day at Pioneer Park, full of joy, aware of no peril, just the excitement, this great game, wonderful boy, yes, shouting for young Damon to get a hit, and Henry leaped up and paced the floor again.

"Let's get a rally going, Damon boy!"

"Them ain't Knickerbockers, them's *bloomers!*"

"Put some wood to it, sonny! Kill that bum!"

And there was ragabag Jonathan Noon yelling for a hit, clapping his hands, on the move, never still, just like in the old days, "Come on, boy!" and everybody picking it up, Gabe Burdette howling like an Indian, Jake Bradley slapping his bald head—how small he looked outside his bar!—and that old clown Jaybird Wall pulling off his suit jacket and flapping it around and around like a flag: "Hot damn, son! Give her a ride!"

Henry clapped his hands over his ears. He stood over his chair and stared down at his papers, at the scorecard, and at the three dice, gazing up at him, *through* him, as though with fearfully constricted pupils. Brock was eating a hot dog. He was joking with old Mose Stanford there beside him. Something about his own abysmal batting record. Then he finished the hot dog, took a drink of Coke, and leaned forward in all his ignorance to cheer his son on.

Damon had stepped out of the batter's box. He was knocking the dirt out of his cleats with his bat. He glanced up at the stands, saw his dad there. Maybe he looked at the dugout, too —yes, he looked at the dugout, just in case, and Bancroft . . . did nothing, he smiled at the kid. And Damon looked away, stepped back into the box, worked his shoulders, set himself, fixed his steady gaze on Casey.

Henry snapped up the three dice from the table and worked them around in his perspiring hand, but he couldn't sit.

Couldn't swallow, couldn't think, could hardly focus on what he was doing. He wiped his face with his shirt sleeve. Get it over with, he said. Casey stepped up on the rubber, took O'Shea's signal, shook his head. Shook it again. Then he nodded.

The dice felt sticky in his hands. He got a plastic cup out of the cupboard. A glass fell and broke. He put the dice in the cup, shook it. Cold hollow rattle. Casey stretched. The sun beat down, or maybe it was just the lamp—anyway it threw a withering glare off the papers on the table, made Henry squint his eyes, and he felt somehow he was up to something sinister. That's it, he chided himself, pile it on, you'll feel like a fool when nothing—he listened to the rattle, to the roar, held his breath, pitched the dice down on the table.

He knew even before he looked: 1–1–1.

Damon Rutherford was dead.

No one moved. All stared at home plate. Damon lay there, on his back, gazing up at a sun he could no longer see.

Impossible. He blinked, looked again.

Brock sat. Head reared in shock and his face was drawn. He looked suddenly gray and old. He rose.

He stepped back until he came up against the stove. But he couldn't get his eyes off the table. Now the others, Bancroft, the Pioneer regulars, Flynn, the old-timers, were moving, they were running toward the boy, pressing around, crying out. *Do* something!

But do what? The dice were rolled.

Casey watched—

Henry was thinking, *had* to think, something, some way ...? He was at the table again, leaning over the dice, trying to stop, trying to back up, force like the clashing of tremendous gears shrieked in his mind, the fans were all shrieking, they were crying and shouting, and he reached out—but no, he let them, he let it be, he had to, he stayed his hand, because the boy was dead, he was dead, Damon was dead. Damon Rutherford! "Oh no!"

Barney Bancroft knelt by the boy, unable to believe, faced with those eyes that stared strangely past him, that lean beautiful wrist in one hand, wrist that threw the—crowding round, calling for doctors, yet knowing—"*Stand back, please!*" Right under the sun. Head cracked like an egg. Bancroft sought the communicative beat, found instead the ebb of warmth, the ebb of all warmth...

Reporters moving now. Fennimore McCaffree, ash-gray and long-striding, darkly emerged from the masses, then into the Pioneers' ball-park office, to the phone.

Bancroft let the wrist drop. It fell away. Barney stood, turned to Gabe Burdette and Willie O'Leary. He nodded up at Brock, stricken in the stands. They understood, went up there to be with him.

The rookie catcher Chauncey O'Shea sat behind the body, mouth agape, eyes damp, and had he called . . . ? But Casey had shaken him off. Twice.

Henry caught his breath, sank down into the chair, faced with the strange insistence of those staring ones.

Brock standing paralyzed. Alone. Knowing, but not knowing, his fists balled in silent appeal. Staring down at his son, where, from a crouch, an old friend's face looked up, told him: no.

"That's right," said McCaffree. "Funeral tomorrow." His long pale hand curved corroboratively out of black sleeve, white cuff, tips of fingers poised on the black phone's white dial. "We'll be there," the voice on the other end said softly.

Old Sycamore Flynn, manager of the Knicks, at home plate,

stood up. Glancing toward the stands, his eyes met Brock's. Was Brock looking at him, singling him out? Flynn looked away. He saw Burdette and O'Leary moving off. As though a shrinking. Henry felt it. O'Shea in tears there, and nobody coming near, but Casey—two times! And now quietly out there on the mound, he—

Brock saw them, knew why they had come. Neither Gabe nor Willie said anything. They stood by him, but gave him leave by their silence to do it his own way. Their coming helped him move at last. He took a breath, giving what life he could to his suddenly aged and borne-down body, and started forward toward the field. The two friends trailed. The sea of bodies parted and they passed through.

Henry sat again, chewing his fist, trying to keep the tears back. Couldn't stop them—Royce Ingram broke free, went for the mound, went for Casey. Yes! Casey hadn't moved, still stood by the mound, oddly aloof. Bancroft wanted to stop Ingram, but lacked the voice for it, crying himself and Flynn didn't know what to do either, it seemed out of their hands. It was clear now, yes, the rivalry, the secret grudge being nursed, the signals shaken off, Casey had *wanted* it, and now Ramsey and Hines were following. The Knicks stood back. Under the sun. Pupils constricted. No, wait! But then York and Patterson stepped out. Casey watched them come. He didn't seem to care. He watched them converge. Locke. Wilson. James. Wilder. "*Kill him!*" they cried, they all cried, and now the fans—but a hesitation . . . a moment . . . Bancroft stopped them, yes, no, he—Casey smiled! Oh the *fool!* Ingram hit him first. Smashed his bony face. Yes, it *was* a bony face with cavernous eyes and fat arrogant lips, mad, he was mad! Mad Casey staggered back. Hines threw one to the gut, doubling the killer forward. Patterson split his mouth with a crushing right, knocked him to the dirt. Henry wept, shredding paper, sobs racking him like insane laughter. James and Ramsey jumped on him, dragged the dirty bastard to his feet. Witness York—no! no! they *didn't* hit him—

"*No!*"

The voice stopped them, *had* stopped them all. Didn't touch him. Ingram, his arm cocked for that first blow, heard it. He held back. They turned. Brock stood over his son's body and his quiet mournful gaze shamed them all. "No," he said again.

No. The Proprietor of the Universal Baseball Association, utterly brought down, brought utterly to grief, buried his face in the heap of papers on his kitchen table and cried for a long bad time.

3

HE went out. Feeling sour. Undiscoverable sun at four o'clock in the hazy sky. But a kind of glow in the streets, mocking him. Later, he'd have it rain.

Neck and back stiff from dozing all night on the tabletop. Strange dreams there. Some high hill with ruins on it. They were playing ball up there, bunch of kids, and the ball kept disappearing over the side of the hill. He chased one, had to, thinking all the time: I'll never make it back up. There was something awful down below, but he didn't know what it was. Grabbed up the ball, but it kept slithering out of his hands. Holding it tight to his chest, climbing up with it, he discovered one leg was shorter than the other. The short one was spindly and weak and threatened to buckle under him; the long one, the left one, was thick as an elephant's leg and had to be dragged up. He was crying. They were calling him Greasy-fingers and pushing the ruins down the hill at him. Catch this, Greasyfingers! they hollered. The stones they threw had strange markings on them which they tried to read as they hurtled by.

Later they wrote on his face and rolled him up in newspapers. His tears spoiled his notebooks and a teacher pushed his face in them. The teacher looked like Zifferblatt, but had a sunburned neck like Rag Rooney. And on and on through the early morning. Not once did he dream of the dead boy.

At seven, he'd stood. Shakily. He hadn't entirely forgotten about work, it was there in the back of his mind all the time, just at seven especially, but he'd stumbled on his two odd legs directly into the bedroom, freeing himself of shirt and pants on the way, had collapsed on his rumpled bed and slept until midafternoon. Later, he'd discovered he'd torn all the buttons off his shirt.

It was a long walk to Lou's but he had a lot of time; Lou wouldn't be home until well after five. They'd all be coming, he supposed, the old and the young, all the survivors. By car, train, plane. Lot of them already in town, the old-timers anyway, because of the special ceremonies for Brock. Lot of special ceremonies for Brock. That poor old guy. Still, damn it, that's what he got for fathering more ballplayers. Rutherford couldn't be just one of the passing boys, no, he'd had to try and sanctify his own goddamn blood and name. If he'd been blessed with a name like Rag Rooney, maybe he'd have had fewer illusions. His gut ached with a surfeit of glory and history, and somehow he felt it was Brock's fault.

Well, Rooney was sorry the kid had got killed—who wasn't—but it had given him a day off, time to think, so perversely, coldly, he was grateful, too. He'd got locked in the season's pace and rituals, gone mindless in the midsummer heat, and now suddenly he'd waked up. He had to shake his boys up, shuffle the line-up, make them move, make them run, get them back into the fight. Yesterday's game with Melbourne Trench's Excelsiors had got underway before Rooney had even realized it. He'd been sure there was something he'd meant to do before, but there was the goddamn ump, hollering to get the game going, and he hadn't been able to think what it was. He'd wondered if he was getting too old maybe. Addled. His stomach had griped. He'd put one calloused hand through his flannel shirt to squeeze and soothe it, watching his Haymakers pile out onto the field.

Yes, feeling rotten. Need to eat something. Can't eat.

The Homemakers, the sportswriters were starting to call them, and Pappy's Pantywaists, Rooney's Boobies. He'd scanned the bench, trying to remember what the hell . . . ? He'd seen Swanee Law sitting there, tensed forward, not his day to pitch, but dressed just the same, popping gum and whooping it up. A pro, all right. Goddamn it, he'd be the greatest in the league if he had guys like York and Patterson to back him up. Power and control: Rag Rooney's kind of pitcher. In fact, if he had to choose between Law and the Rutherford kid, Rooney'd still take Law over the long haul. And that was what he'd been thinking about when the dugout phone rang, bringing him the news. He'd turned to Law and said: "Rutherford's dead." Why tell Law first? Rooney wasn't sure. Maybe because he'd sensed Swanee's resentment at getting beat by the kid, thought he might—but no, Law had turned white as a sheet. Rooney had called his ballplayers back in off the field to wait there in the dugout then for the official announcement before going to the showers.

Street of shops, and the one he was now passing sold flowers. For All Occasions. B. Valentine, Floriculturist & Modeler. In the window, mostly asters, chrysanthemums, and cornflowers, Indian corn in bunches, funeral wreaths. Golden-banded lilies: Chancellor McCaffree's idea. Bancroft plumped for plain old marigolds. And bittersweet. Why not? Heliotropes and nightshades. Bancroft smiled wryly, brushed his eyes. Above the heaped flowers, a conical vase of red and white carnations, disarranged, all leaning to one side as though blown by a wind. Inside the shop, in a humid showcase, there were arrangements of roses, fuchsia, blue flags, hyacinths, gladioli, and calla lilies, set off against sprays of maidenhair ferns. A few orchids. Dense vegetable atmosphere.

An old man emerged from a back room, wizened, peering dimly over bifocals, smiling faintly, gray apron down his front, holding his hands out limply in front of him. A silvery substance glittered on his fingertips. In the back room, there seemed to be something cooking. "A bouquet," he said; it was hardly a question.

"Well, I was just sort of looking," Henry said.

The old man stood beside him, looking too, peeking over the rimless spectacles into the rich damp display case. "An orchid," he said softly.

"Well, actually—"

"Extraordinary development," the florist whispered. "Highest point of monocotyledon evolution. Perfection of the imperfect."

"How's that?" Henry asked. He realized that he, too, was whispering.

"Unisexual. Utterly impotent without insects. A loner. Exquisite." Mr. Valentine plucked an aster from a counter vase. "Perfection," he explained, roughing its bright head with a sharp-nailed thumb, "is bisexual."

"Hmm," said Henry.

"Dull? Perhaps, but multifarious," the florist said with a smile. "I have some pretty comos, if you like. Zinnias, marigolds, and bachelor's-buttons. Quite cheerful in big bunches."

"I was thinking about a wreath," Henry said.

"Ah!" Mr. Valentine sorrowed. "I didn't realize." He stepped behind the counter, brought forth a prickly wreath sprayed with silver, black-ribboned. "A popular item."

Henry took it in his hands. "Why, it's plastic!" he exclaimed.

"Yes," the florist smiled, "my own work."

Now Henry noticed the flowers all over the walls. Foxglove, lilies of the valley, primrose, violets, nasturtiums, buttercups, jonquils, sweet peas, streamers of ivy, morning glories, tulips: all plastic. He fingered the wreath. "Really, what I had in mind—"

"It will last forever," the old man whispered.

"But . . . well, that's not the point, is it?"

The florist crushed the aster in his blue-veined silvery hand. "We must keep searching, we must carry on the work, we must resist to the end!" he whispered hoarsely.

"I'll take a white carnation," Henry said.

In the street once more, wearing the carnation in his lapel, he passed a newsstand.

DAMON RUTHERFORD DEAD!

TRAGICALLY FELLED ON

BROCK RUTHERFORD DAY

> *Pioneer Park*, LVI:49—(Urgent) A high inside fast ball thrown by Knickerbocker rookie Jock Casey struck and crushed the skull of Pioneer rookie pitcher Damon Rutherford today, killing him instantly, the first such death in UBA history. In the bottom of the third inning, young Rutherford, already one of the game's immortals . . .

Rooney snorted. A dead immortal! Who thought up that crap? Of course, you had to feel it: the sudden loss. Even Law felt that. As for the rest of it, the great promise unfulfilled, the history-maker dehistorified, the record-breaker busted, that was the kind of sentimental claptrap that singed Rooney's weary ass. Oh, yes, he was sick of it! He saw those news guys writing it all down, eyes crossing over their own noses, and saw them for what they were—a pack of goddamn leeches, inventing time and place, scared shitless by the way things really were. History my god. An incurable diarrhea of dead immortals. It was the one thing he and Law didn't see eye to eye on. Law knew all the records in the book by heart, thought everybody else should know them, too. To that extent, he was stupid.

Soot settled sullenly on the residential section through which Henry walked. The day's glow was gone, and a deep bitter gloom was on him. He looked out, not to sink in. A dog barked at a window. Cars passed. A child smashed ants on the sidewalk with an egg-shaped stone. No, not a stone. Plastic again. Had they finally found it after all these centuries of search? That Stone of great virtue, called a Stone and not a stone? Next thing, they'd be going off the gold standard, filling Fort Knox with plastics. The quintessence, *huantan*, the sacred stuff, though the ants might disagree. He was early; just five.

"I hear they went for Casey after," one of the boys was saying, just killing time on the train.

"Did they rough him up? The papers don't say anything—"

"Brock held them off."

"Well, that's right, it wouldn't have . . . changed things. I wonder if he . . . you know, threw it on purpose?"

Now Swanee Law joined them, leaning his big seriocomic head into their midst, whispering as though hatching some plot: "Ah called up old Fenn. Don't say nothin', but he figgers it's purty sure. Case shook Chaunce off twice."

"What'd O'Shea call?"

"He ain't talkin'. But he and ole Case was roomies, and they say Chaunce's moved out. Like as how he's skeered or somethin'."

Rooney grinned to watch the studied pucker on Law's big face. You couldn't love a sick bastard like that, but you had to admit: he was one helluva ballplayer. Rooney recalled the game against the Pioneers four days ago, when, humiliated in the eighth by those two homers and not a prayer of a chance to win, Law had come back in the ninth tougher than ever, could have pitched another fifteen, twenty, thirty innings. Nothing ever bothered the sonuvabitch for longer than an inning. He brooded sometimes, but not really *about* anything, it was just one of those mood shifts of his. Organic. He wasn't exactly stupid either, but there were some connections most people made, Law didn't make.

"Whaddaya mean, Swanee?" somebody asked. "You think Casey's a little . . . off?"

Law turned on his holy/concerned/studious/fatherly/moralizing pan and whispered: "We don't know yet."

"Ahh shee*eittt!*" griped Rooney. "You ladies are making me sick! Pitcher throws a duster, the batter don't duck. Well, hell, that's *his* tough luck."

"Behind the ear, Pappy. That's pretty far inside."

"Ole Fenn he's purty sure he's got a case," Law insisted.

"Got a case is right," said Rooney. "He's got a case of political buboes, that's what he's got." They all grinned, but Law's heart wasn't in it; that boy had real ambitions, all right. Rooney truly hated McCaffree and all his pious Legalists, and it bugged him that Law was one of them. In love with his own silly name probably. "Why, I'm surprised at you, Law. After as many guys as you've dropped to their butts!"

Law leaned back, lifting his hands in mock protest, expression of abused innocence crossed with collusive irony on his big face: "Ah pitches 'em close, Rag, but Ah don't aim tuh hurt nobody."

"Well, you're not as good a shot as Casey, that's all."

"Aw, Rag," said Law, but it was still more than an off-balance filling of shocked silence: Rooney saw by their expressions he'd got to them all with that one.

Raglan Rooney. Ragbag, they called him his rookie year, Year X. And then it was Rag. The Ragger. Coined some of the most famous obscenities in UBA history. Now in his forty-seventh consecutive year with the Haymakers. Forty-seven. Henry trembled. Played first base, coached under Gus Maloney when he got too old to play, took over the team when Gus quit to grab control of the Bogglers Party, been at the Haymaker helm ever since. And not a ball game in those forty-seven years he didn't try to win. He was the worst loser the UBA had ever known, and he was goddamn proud of it. The old Haymakers he played for won three different pennants and were always in the running—in spite of Crock Rubberturd and his goddamn Era. Oh boy, Rooney had to laugh at that one! How could guys like McCaffree and Flynn and Bancroft come up with such a dumb idea? Had they forgot how it was? Immortal deadheads.

He wondered what Flynn was going to do now. Probably ought to get rid of Casey. Otherwise, the whole damn team was in for it. Besides, Casey probably wouldn't be much good now anyhow. "Killer," they were already calling him. But Rooney knew Sycamore Flynn well enough to know he'd never do what was smart. Hell, he'd probably even start feeling sorry for that young sonuvabitch.

They pulled in. Through the window as they unloaded, he could see that Lew and Fanny Lydell had come to meet the train; darkly wrapped, somber faces, pious tilt to their heads, carrying umbrellas. Long Lew was even beginning to look like his father-in-law—silly bastard was forgetting his own immortality, wanted to be Chancellor instead. Fanny McCaffree was her daddy's girl, all right. Hadn't plumped out at all. Must be pushing fifty, and she still had that long stringy spinsterish frame she had back in XLIII when Long Lew split it for her in the Knick dugout to win a bet with Jaybird Wall. Her butt hadn't even spread much, for all the action. Not a peep out of her that day, no thrashing about, just an imbecile loll of her head off the players' bench, eyes bulging on that birdy face, and something like a soft gurgle in her long white throat. They had all laughed to watch it rip. The Knicks really packed them in for a while after that, and there were always clusters of the curious nosing around the dugout after games, hoping for a rerun. If Rooney'd had any daughters or even a wife, he would have tried to work up something like it in the Haymakers' ball park. No imitators of that boy, though. Long Lew humbled them all. Now, in an unflattering droop, he extended his hand and said: "We're glad you've come."

"Henry!" cried Lou. "Gee, I been looking for you! I just come from your place, it was all dark and I thought—Henry, is there something . . . ? I mean, Mr. Zifferblatt nearly—what's the matter, Henry?"

"I'd like to listen to some music, Lou. Would you mind?"

"Music! Well, no, but—Henry! why, what's—you look awful!"

"Nothing. A . . . a death. I—"

"Oh!" Lou's round weight sagged softly. He stared at the white flower. "I'm . . . I'm sorry, Henry. Who . . . ?"

"I don't feel like talking about it, Lou. I just thought, well, I dropped by, I thought maybe some music might . . ."

"Why, *sure,* Henry!" Lou squeaked, truly concerned. He fumbled in the bulge of his coat, panting lightly, came up with the keys, dropped them, stooped for them with a tender grunt, tried three or four in the lock before he found the right one. "Mr. Zifferblatt was in a, not a very good mood, but I explained something was wrong, that it was just, you know, seemed like something was on your mind, and—it'll be all right, Henry, you'll see, he's not inhuman, he'll—" They went in.

Dark vaults. Shhh. Musty Gothic odors. Candles. The transepts ablaze with innumerable waxlights. That's it. Stop fighting it. You loved him. You don't have to be ashamed about that. Let the ballplayers come in now. Let them fill the cathedral. Pioneers, regulars and old veterans alike, the first to enter, to pass by—

Lights: Lou switched on the overhead, bringing muss and clutter to view. Not a disorder so much as a clumsy order, everything bumped out of place, but its proper place still plainly evident. Henry closed his eyes against it, sought the dark and higher spaces.

"I'm sorry, things are kind of a mess," Lou said, his welcome ritual. "Can . . . can I take your hat, Henry?"

Henry looked up at his friend. Moonface abloom with pity. Wrong emotions. One day, he realized, they would grow apart. He gave Lou his hat. Lou plodded with it and his own hat to the middle of the room, hesitated, seemed not to know what to do with them. "Do you mind?" Henry asked, reaching for the switch of a floor lamp nearby. Get that damn overhead off.

"No!" cried Lou, then clambered anxiously forward, hat in each hand, to help: with Henry's he batted the shade askew. "I'm all thumbs," he complained, putting Henry's hat on his own head and reaching forward again. Henry backed away, but almost miraculously, the light came on and the shade was righted. Lou turned toward him, grinning sheepishly under the hat two sizes too small for him. Henry switched off the overhead.

While Lou wandered absently around the room with the hats, Henry turned to the shelves, thumbed thoughtfully through the recordings. Have to be careful, no woeful threnodes, he cautioned himself broadly, no cheap sentiment. It was welling up in him; he needed something with precision, discipline, control. Like the kid himself. Harmonious, though. Nothing cacaphonic. Just damp cool concrete, a floor—his eye fell on the *Archduke*. The aristocrat. Third movement: bottom of the third. McCaffree wanted a full orchestra, something not just for the boy but for the whole Association, but no, Bancroft had his way. It was right. He put it on.

"Can I fix you something, a drink, coffee, pop . . . ?" Lou had rid himself of the hats, but wore his coat still.

"No—well, some sherry maybe," Henry said. "If it's not too much trouble."

"No trouble!" Lou assured him, ricocheting kitchenward off a table and an easy chair, in that heedless spongy way of his.

Throughout the room, equipment hummed. Henry settled back in a rocker, waited, eyes closed, for the piano's first soft footfalls. And they entered in. The somber throng, the Chancellor and his people, friends and foes, but foes none to the spirit this boy had shown them, the majesty in the mere sweep of a pitching arm, the fulfillment in the mere acceptance of a catcher's signal. Magic, yes, yes it was, had been. Resonant strings filled the air with their solemn dialogue, violin speaking of brilliance and sensitivity, cello of maturity and might. The daily upward struggle and the underlying continuity of the—or did they really say so much, Bancroft wondered. No, no—they said nothing, they simply . . . simply were true.

Henry sipped the sherry: the moist remnant of passage, sponged from the walls of sepulchres. He smiled gently at that, watching Barney Bancroft, chin in hand, suffer mutely in the cathedral's hollow gloom. Brother to the father, Barney was a father to the son. And beautiful, yes, he was a beautiful ballplayer. Was. Murdered by the past tense and laid in a lonesome grave, the black pit of history: he was. Was beautiful. Take it easy, Barney. Just love. Forget the rest.

Tick tock tick tock: high percussive pips beat the thin truth off the stained-glass windows, while far below, the strings held long painful plaintive chords, as though trying to hold time itself back. But is it enough, Barney? McCaffree wanted to know. "This is more than one man's funeral." The piano said: "It is done." Descending. "Yes, well, you mean the *Requiem,* I suppose." McCaffree nodded. The violin objected, rose in protest against the injustice of it, but saw at last it was futile and accepted. The cello, humbly, agreed. "All right," said Barney. In the cathredral: "Amen." Lou put on the *Requiem.*

"Did he leave any . . . family?"

A son? Yes, he could have, he could have at that, and his name . . . ? "No. Only a father. And a brother." And how did Brock Jr. take it, what was on his mind?

"Henry! Is it your, your . . . ?"

Henry hesitated. The question had taken him by surprise. "No," he said finally, "not exactly."

Their urgent appeal for mercy crashed suddenly in his ears, on all sides of him, the agonized pulsing of hearts clamoring for union with his own, reaching—ahh shee-*it* now! muttered a familiar voice in the back pew, and Henry grinned sheepishly. He saw by Lou's face it had all been misunderstood.

"A . . . a child then?"

"Nineteen, twenty."

"Ah!" Lou shook his head, stared down at his feet. He was out of the coat now: it lay heaped on the table like a body. "That's awful, Henry!"

"You know, Lou, when Jim Creighton died, the boys crowned his grave with a fantastic monument. It had crossed bats on it and a baseball cap and even a base and up on top a giant baseball. Or maybe it was the world. They probably no longer knew the difference."

"I didn't know he . . . died, too. I'm sorry, Henry. When . . . ?"

"In 1862." Lou blinked. "And you know what else they put on that monument, Lou? You won't believe it!"

"No. Wh-what?"

"A scorebook!"

Lou's expression remained unchanged. He didn't get it. All he could find to say was: "He . . . he was a ballplayer, then."

"Who, Jim Creighton?"

"No, your . . . uh . . . " Bastard: that's what Lou was thinking.

"Yes." And what had Barney ordered? Barney and Brock and the Chancellor?

. . . Oh, when I die, jist bury me
With my bat and a coupla balls,
And jist tell 'em Verne struck out, boys,
If anybody calls . . .

Yes, maybe Verne Mackenzie had a big monument like that somewhere. But not Damon. The music tried to tell him what. Simple yet complex. Intricate but harmonious. The light he brought to the league. Yes, a lamp maybe, Aladdin's lamp, the boy with the magic arm . . .

But then, suddenly, the thin voice of a small boy cried out, a boy in terror, boy gripping a baseball, gift of the slain giant, boys all, hurt, terrified, the emptiness, the confusion— Henry gasped. *What kind of a world was this?* Cum . . . vix . . . iustus . . . iustus—children! sit securus! He sighed, bowed his head. No, no, even worse than that, much worse. Barney, afraid of giving way, tried to think about something else, the larger picture, the season ahead—how would he get them moving again, their minds off of it? Salva me! Salva me! "It's how Damon would have wanted it, fellows . . . " No, he could never do it that way. Maybe Flynn could. Even that old cynic Rooney could probably do it. But Barney Bancroft couldn't. He gazed across the nave toward Sycamore Flynn and his Knickerbockers—that kid catcher Chauncey O'Shea, loosed in tears again, undone by it: how many careers would be wrecked by that bean ball? Something . . . something was changed . . . somehow, inalterably, the entire Association had—Barney tried to think, but the music was too loud. I shouldn't have pitched him, I shouldn't have pitched him! He struggled against the mad crescendo. The perfect game had already sunk away into a kind of unbelievable golden age, long lost, forever inaccessible. *Where have I taken us?*

Wrong! "No, it's all wrong!" Barney cried to himself. His mind bolted ahead, racing through Mozart's creative operations, the way he chased flies, fielded grounders, threw to first, swung, ran . . . smooth, faultless, but something was wrong. Not just the words, but the music too. "Artifice! Arrogance!" The bogus hell's-better-than-nothing comfort. He realized suddenly that he hated the thing, hated the shabby neatness, the trumped-up despair, he wanted to lay into the whole damn outfit, kick them while they played, make them sing while running the basepaths until they dropped! "I hate it!" he cried out. "*Stop it!*"

Lou, lurching, sent his drink flying—needle shrieked insanely across the record, knocked against the center post with a resounding *clock!* heard through all the many-speakered system, bounced back to report one "*lux aeterna!*" then rejected itself.

"I . . . I'm sorry, Lou." What was happening to him?

"Is . . . is there something else you'd . . . ?" His friend watched him, wide-eyed. Calm down. Funny, after all. See poor Lou. His gloom runneth over. Seeping darkly into the rug's earth-brown nap. Stunned, Fenn and Barney stunned. Rooney winked.

Henry grinned. "Put on the Purcell."

"You mean the . . . the funeral . . . ?" Lou in a state of total and mournful perplexity. For the day, it would seem, was dark and troubled. "Are you sure, Henry? That's kind of . . . " He wrinkled his nose.

"I don't care, put it on." Confusion and emptiness, teehee and boohoo, get it straight from the master's whinny!

"Well . . . all right, if . . . it's really what you'd like," Lou said, and revolved irresolutely, poor old tub in an unexpected weather, to search out the record.

Henry stood, poured more sherry, drank it off at a dispreciative gulp. The sepulchral dew: ha ha! He switched to bourbon. Corn liquor, the really basic stuff. Yes, let's have a little fire, boys! And feet on the ground! The fatal hour comes on apace!

Ruefully, the sackbuts poop-poop-dee-pooped, discreetly distant. In bitter cold, through streets draped in black, slowly advanced the pallbearers. Hop, skip, and a long cold shuffle. The frozen corpse rocked in the hollow box: *whump!* tum-tum-tum *clump!* Long live the dead queen! Yes, it took a leering toper to lay it on the line! Ho ho! who left this life, and is gone to that blessèd place where only his harmony can be exceeded —*whump!* Henry drank whiskey and laughed aloud.

Lou stuffed himself, shrinkingly, in a shadow. "Henry . . . ?" he whimpered from darkness.

Trompetta! blaa-aa-att! and a mocking rumble of the tympanic gut! Man that is born of woman, woman that is laid by man! Blaa-aa-att! He cometh out! He goeth in! Raunchy giggle of trumpets. Pallbearer Rooney is giggling. Giggling hysterically. It infects them all. Oh that goddamn Rooney! Hee hee! Spare us, Lord!

"Shall I . . . take it off, Henry, or . . . ?"

"Oh no! he is much lamented!" Tee hee hee hee hee hee, boo hoo hoo hoo, tee hee hee hee, boo hoo hoo hoo, ha ha ha ha— oops! the body bounces out! they pop it in again! out! in! it's one-old-cat, boys, with the earthly remains! Hee hee ha ha ha ho ho hee haa haaa!

"Oh, Lou!" he cried, holding his sides, "why do we go on?"

Suddenly inspired, he turned to the machine, flipped it up to a higher speed. "Thou knowest, Lord!" they piped. Yes! he knew it! A tavern song, after all! The secrets of our hearts! "Tonight!" whispered Rooney, jigging along under the burden.

"Jake's!" The Hole in the Wall. Tweet-tweet-tootle and a rattle of tin spoons on a hollow hilarious bouncing skull!

He left, hatless, cold wind on his wet face, his funeral a shambles.

Play resumed. It always resumes, every dying old bastard's despair. But first, the night before, a troupe of the old-timers gathered in Jake's Bar behind the Patsies' Park. Brock wasn't there, of course, and McCaffree stayed away, but Pioneers Gabe Burdette and Frosty Young were present, and Willie O'Leary and Jonathan Noon and doleful Barney Bancroft. And there was beer-bellied Surrey Moss and Mose Stanford and Chad Collins and Toothbrush Terrigan. Young Brock Jr. was among the absent: he'd bolted for home the minute the burial was over, dragging his missus behind him, and there, pressed by an inexplicable urgency, had heisted her black skirts, and without even taking time to drop his pants, had shot her full of seed: yes, caught it! she said, and even he felt that germ strike home.

It was Rag Rooney's idea, this gathering of the grieving, and he was of course on hand, salting his ulcer with bourbonic acid, and with him came his old boss and crony Gus Maloney, blowing smoke and stoking his political machine with good humor and an occasional round of drinks. Some of the boys on the inside, too, Seemly Sam Tucker and Big Bill McGonagil, a dozen or more. Hometown Pastimer boss Cash Bailey showed up, though his Patsies were on the road, faced the Beaneaters in their park the next day, but the Beans' manager Winslow Beaver was there, too, so it was even up. The other managers came, too, why not? The Excelsiors' Melbourne Trench and the Bridegrooms' Wally Wickersham and Timothy Shadwell of the Keystones, last year's Manager of the Year but this year's most promising goat: he needed a drink. Even Sycamore Flynn. It was funny about Sic'em: they all loved the bastard, pure gold the man's heart, yet this night they couldn't get close to him. Wasn't his fault. Yet something was happening. They all felt it: his Knicks were gonna get it. Things had to get evened up. Gawky Jock had jinxed them all. Flynn set them up and left early, a relief to everyone.

Sandy Shaw brought his guitar and Long Lew Lydell his reputation. Jason (Jaybird) Wall was on the scene, dropping rubber bugs in drinks, passing out explosive cigars, and slipping whoopee cushions under couching hunkers, the only consolation being that, fairly soon, Jaybird would pass out, bringing a sodden peace to the place, the more appreciated for its contrast to the persecutions preceding. And two great player-coaches from the Golden Age of the XX's turned up: the Knicks' Whipper Will Andersen and the Bridegrooms' Puritan Ballou, both Hall of Famers. And Yip Yick Ping, the Chinese lefty, and Prince Hal Scarlet and Chin-Chin Chickering and Cueball McAuliffe and Agapito Bacigamupo. And there came Bruiser Brusatti and No-Hit Nealy and Birdie Deaton and Jumpin' Joe Gallagher and a bunch of their old teammates with them.

Intense, brilliant, but isolate Patrick Monday looked in, but Pat didn't stay long: Monday, it was remarked by all, had aspirations above and beyond the temporal kingdom of elbow-benders. No love for old Maloney either, and matters might have got touchy had Monday stuck around. Gus had squandered a lifetime building up his Bogglers Party, and knocking off McCaffree's Legalist gang was almost a sure bet, if not this year, then in LX, and now, just when the old man had a chance at last, along came Monday to chew him up. Monday was starting his new party from scratch, after all, he had to get his followers from somewhere, and where he was getting them from mostly, it seemed, was from the ranks of Boggler soreheads. Especially the young ones. Patience, young fellas, we all die, you'll get your chance. At a corner table, Gus puffed, laughed loud at jokes, and bought rounds, while Monday, with that maddening self-assurance of his, stood coolly at the bar and dropped the now-familiar phrases: the imperative of excellence, freedom through constancy, the contagion of confusion, pilgrimage back to majesty—Maloney's laughter boomed, the coins rang, but his ears quivered with attention. He slipped Jaybird Wall a buck. "The intransigent will of history!" Monday declaimed, and sat back: *blaa-aat!* moistly. He smiled faintly at the bar-wide rhubarb and pulled out.

Funny thing about real gloom, Bancroft reasoned; it had a giddy core. Made hard things soft, silly things true, grim things comic. Psyche, up against the wall, had its own defenses. Bancroft, the rationalist, disbelieved in reason. It was the beast's son, after all, not the father, and if it had a way of sometimes getting out of hand, there were always limits: it lacked the old man's cunning. And it had no hands. Re: back again, the primitive condition, the nonreflective operating thing: res. His son: if he couldn't scare the kid into submission, he could always tickle a rib and break all the connections. Rooney, sourest man in Association history, was staggering flop-limbed around the bar in an old man's fit of spittle-chinned cackling. Drunk as a skunk and he shouldn't even be drinking: "Hell, it split open hours ago, I gotta *ster*ilize it!" And a wild rattle of hysterical laughter. The point was: Rooney was afraid to die. Pushing seventy. Whole digestive tract nothing but one long raw sore. If he stopped to think about it, he couldn't keep going. So the old cerebrum got its switch flipped. But suicide . . . ?

Was he intentionally feeding that inner volcano, hoping for the dark? Maybe, maybe not. Plastered, after all, he loosened up. Bile stopped pumping. Bourbon wasn't medicine exactly, but it might be a slower sweeter poison. Barney drank his own, listened to Sandy and the boys, waxed slowly soft and barmy: he received thanks, relayed through the skittish sconce, but sent him by the other fellow . . .

I been gatherin' blisters in the bull pen,
Out here where the green grasses grow,
But you've kept me awaitin' so long, man,
The grass is all co-huh-vered with snow!

The grasses was all turnin' yeller
When our ace he got sent to the show'rs,
But ya went'n sent in some other feller,
And left me a-out here apickin' flow'rs!

I been gatherin' blisters in the bull pen,
Out here where the . . .

"It was a nice funeral, Barney," Tim Shadwell said, leaning close. Tim was the greatest pitcher in Association history until Brock Rutherford came along to wipe out all his records. How did he feel about that? That it was a nice funeral. "Fenn told me you had a lot to do with it."

"Not so much," Barney said, smiling faintly. Did rue sit so heavily on him? Tim was the fourth man to pass his bar-end perch, go glum, release a hushed lament. Guilt. The sons banded together. Old man psyche had his hands full, all right. Legalism. Was Tim a Legalist? We all were. McCaffree was in, wasn't he? Whoa, Barney! Slipping your stitches. "Slitching my stipples."

"Howzat?" Tim leaned closer, drunk, sincerely. Sincerely drunk. Looked like his eyes might sincerely cross. Not more than a week ago, Barney's pile-driving Pioneers had shattered Shadwell's crumbling Keystones, socking them out of second with a three-game swamping sweep and they were still in a full-tilt tumble. Shattered Shadwell. Tuckered Tim. Didn't he hate? Well, talk instead about the funeral. Community of pain and beauty.

"I said, can I buy you a drink?"

"You owe me one," tumbling Tim said flatly, and leaned away.

I know thet I give a lotta passes,
I know thet I ain't no more a pup,
But yer love for me is like these grasses,
Yer love fo-hor me is all dried up!

I been gatherin' blisters in the bull pen . . .

Barney caught Jake Bradley's eye, and Jake filled them up. Grieved shake of the bald pate: they grievedly shook to ratify. Tough. It was. Poor Brock. "You'll pull out," Barney said.

"I hope so, Barney," Tim replied, sucking in deeply the dark bar air. "The sinking Stones: boy, those news guys really eat you up when you're down." Words of wisdom from the Manager of the Year. Tim reached for his drink, knocked it over. Full-tilt tumble. Clunk of the year. "God, I've had enough," he said sheepishly. As Shadwell righted his glass, Bancroft saw his hand was shaking. Too-tight Tim. Called for Jake again. "Another one, Jake. And a bar rag."

I wish thet you would reconsider
And let po-hore me back in the game!

The grasses is brown and they're bitter,
And you have forgo-hotten my name!

I been gatherin' blisters in the bull pen,
Out here where the green grasses grow,
But you've kept me awaitin' so long, man,
The grass is all co-huh-vered with snow!

Well, it was some gathering, this wake, bar packed to overflowing, and what was it for? it was hard to tell. It was like they'd all been squeezed into this big retort, Jake's athanor, seeking a transformation, a way of going on with it, some viable essence unaltered by the boy's death that they could start over with, and to be sure, the heat was on.

She came up to him. He hadn't noticed her there before. She winked cheaply and asked: "How's Damon's pitching arm tonight?"

"He's dead."

"Hunh?"

"Damon Rutherford is dead."

It was as though he'd struck her in the face. He asked Jake for another. When he looked again, she was gone. He turned to Tim Shadwell. "How's the boy coming along?"

"Who?"

"Your son. Thornton. Going to be ready next year?"

It was the wrong question. Shadwell began to break. Tears bubbled out. "When I saw that boy there today, Barney . . . in that . . . that box . . . so . . . so dead . . . I kept thinking . . . I kept feeling . . . my own boy . . . I'm afraid, Barney . . . he's so young . . ."

And you're so old. Don't kid me, Shadwell. "He can take care of himself, Tim." As though to make matters worse,

Sandy struck up "The Happy Hours of Youth," and Tim and the other guys joined mournfully in . . .

Oh, rookies, come along
And hear m' sad song!
Old age is the bane o' mankind!
So enjoy while ya may
The fair spring day,
Cause the blue season ain't far behind!

Oh, the happy sunny da-hays of old!
When our feet were fleet and our hearts were bold!
There's nothin' so fine in the world to behold
As the happy hours of youth!

When the years're green
And the hits come clean,
You're honored among the ath-letes;
But they'll come a day
When they won't letcha play,
And like us, you must hang up yer cleats!

Oh, the happy sunny . . .

Glorious days, bold hearts: Barney, you're just an old fool like the rest of them. Some of the boys were snuffling, most had a sparkle in their eye, as they harmonized on the chorus. Distantly, he heard Rooney vomiting. Too much drinking—or maybe it was the cheap sentiment. No letting up, that was Rooney's success. Shit maybe, but hard shit, hard as bricks. Rooney had a lot of fire all right, but there was no real life in it. It was fratricidal. Destructive. Divisive. But are you really sure, Barney? Maybe the old sonuvabitch had the truth after all. Beside him, Tim Shadwell, all choked up, sang brokenly, soddenly, loudly. Nauseating, all right. Yet there was something human there. If Rooney did have the truth, Barney didn't want it. He entered in . . . into the *soft* shit . . .

You're a rookie jist once
And kin beat outcher bunts
While yer years still number few;
But the day will come
When yer legs won't run,
And you'll bid this League a-huh-dieu!

Oh, the happy sunny da-
hays of old!
(*Oh, the happy happy sunny sunny glorious*
days of old!)
When our feet were fleet and our
hearts were bold!
(*When our cleated feet were fleet and true*
hearts were ever bold!)
There's nothin——nn' so fine in the world
to behold
(*There is nothin' quite so fine in the wide world*
ever told)
As the happy hours of youth!
(*As the happy sunny hours of youth!*)

"Heh-*hey!*"
"Ya-hoo!"
"Oh, that was beautiful, Sandy!"
"Brings back the *old* days!"
"The happy hours of youth!" Tim Shadwell exclaimed and

blew his nose, and there were melancholic mutterings of assent around the barroom, and then a soft silence. The moment was ripe, and Sandy probably had a new song ready, McCaffree supposed, for the occasion. Rooney's retching seemed to have stopped. Maybe the old sonuvabitch was dead . . . ? Not likely. Even old Gus Maloney, stogie stuffed defiantly in his fat jowls, derby tipped down his bald pate toward his nose, seemed to have a tear in his eye, though one could never be sure, the old bastard may have worked it up for a vote or two.

The UBA Chancellor Fennimore McCaffree sat alone in his darkened and gloomy office staring morosely at the barroom scene on one of his television sets. Jake Bradley was a loyal Legalist and his bar was a popular hangout, so the installation of a camera there had been a natural for the party. He'd noticed that gatherings like this one always did something to the ones who came. Changed their politics, altered their view of reality, transformed them in subtle but often surprising and upsetting ways, and it was something Fenn had to keep an eye on. Especially since he himself functioned poorly in groups. He was a Legalist, the social construct was his central concern, group behavior was his favorite study, but he was, paradoxically, more of a loner even than Rag Rooney. He'd been lucky after all to get a gregarious son-in-law. Long Lew took on Fenn's public role.

So, he'd watched them gather, watched Pappy Rooney mix them up, watched Gus Maloney and Patrick Monday politick, seen Monday leave early (tailed, of course), watched Maloney's henchman Jaybird Wall—dentures fastened to the seat of his own pants—play his usual run of practical jokes, eavesdropping for Maloney on the side, had watched them drink and sing and wax sentimental, wondering what it was all going to come to.

Right now, Sandy Shaw was fingering his guitar lightly, tuning up. One of the old Bridegrooms, back in the days of Winthrop and Flynn and Gallagher. Fenn remembered the first time he had to swing against Sandy, his rookie year. Sandy was the ace of that championship Bridegroom team of XIX. Twenty-two wins that year, best season Sandy ever had. He looked harmless: freckled boyish face, light frame, graceful delivery, mild soft-spoken manner. But Sanford Shaw could really mix them up. Fenn had never seen so many different pitches as he looked at that day. Got called out on strikes three times, before he finally hit Shaw: double against the center-field wall. But by then, the Grooms had the game in the bag, and maybe Sandy was letting up. His major weakness. It was never Fenn's. Sandy started making up folk songs in the XX's to cheer up his teammates, those being grim letdown years for the Grooms . . . "Cellar Dweller Blues" . . . "Where Have All the Base Hits Gone?" . . . "Benchwarmer's Lament" . . . "Just A-longin' for Home" . . . "The Day They Fired Verne Mackenzie" . . . "No-Hit Nealy" . . . "Gone Down Swingin' Blues" . . . "When Toothbrush Dusted Gus in the Third" . . . fifty or sixty different songs. In his sixties now. No one like him. It'll be a great loss, when he's gone.

Sandy looked up now at the boys. They were all watching him. Hushed. They all seemed to sense he had a special number, had been waiting for it. Fenn knew, of course, what it would be, and it troubled him. On the other hand, he reasoned, maybe that was the solution: turn it into folklore. Wouldn't be in the way then. Sandy tucked his chin down into soft neck folds, going over the words once in his head maybe, and a kind of shadow passed over his face; then he looked up, and in his soft mellow tenor commenced—slowly, plaintively, syllable by drawn-out syllable—to sing . . .

Hang down your heads, brave men, and weep!
Young Damon has come to harm!
They have carried him off to a grave dark
and deep:
The boy with the magic arm!

We had gathered there to celebrate
His daddy's great career,
When an ill-fated pitch struck him down at
the plate:
The end of a brave Pioneer!

Hang down your heads, brave men . . .

Fenn watched their faces. There they were, men turned into boys, whelmed by awe and adolescent wistfulness. In a way, Sandy did them a disservice, provided them with dreams and legends that blocked off their perception of the truth. But what was the truth? Men needed these rituals, after all, that was part of the truth, too, and certainly the Association benefited by them. Men's minds being what they generally were, it was the only way to get to most of them . . .

Oh, who has it been, brought to such grief,
While pitching a perfect game?
Whose life has been so bright, so brief?
Damon Rutherford is his name!

Hang down your heads, brave men, and weep!
Young Damon—

McCaffree switched off the volume, paced the floor, one eye on the screen. This killing couldn't have come at a worse time. Just when things were looking up. Not his fault, nothing he could have done to prevent it, yet it was bound to have an effect on elections this winter. Damon had been a wonderful league tonic. The whole process had been slowing down, the structure had lost its luster, there'd been rising complaints about meaninglessness and lack of league purpose. His Legalists, for no other reason except that they were the incumbents, had been dropping in popularity polls. And then Damon Rutherford had come along. He'd captured all their hearts, Fenn's included. Brock Rutherford Day had been Fenn's own idea. The whole UBA was suddenly bathed in light and excitement and enthusiasm. Fenn had foreseen an election sweep. Maloney and his Bogglers didn't have a single new issue. Patrick Monday was a rising threat, but at least four years off. The Guildsmen couldn't find a candidate. Total mandate. And then that pitch.

He wasn't sure what he could do about it. Investigate the incident, of course. But what if he uncovered the worst possible fact: that Casey had thrown the bean ball on purpose? All pitchers threw one from time to time. All right, a new law maybe, lower the strike zone an inch or two or something, stiffer penalties, but nobody really wanted that. The only conceivable forms of meaningful action at a time like this were all illegal. Which meant, no matter what happened, he'd have to be on the wrong side, so to speak. Of course, he might be able to pressure Sycamore Flynn and the Knickerbocker management into getting rid of Casey. But then what? Monday or Maloney or somebody would probably make an issue of that. Yes, that's right, Monday didn't have to wait four years now. Boggle, boggle. And the empty Guildsmen candidacy was starting to look pretty attractive, too. Gatherings such as this one tonight in Jake's, he saw, were dangerous. He scanned the familiar faces. Gallagher. O'Leary. Stanford. Any one of them could suddenly emerge tonight as a new political figure.

And with the glamor of this ceremony attached—gilded—to him. Sandy Shaw himself, for example. Yes, they were all with him right now, to be sure. Some eighty or ninety boys there altogether, a small cut of the thousand or so living UBA veterans who made up the electorate, but enough in concert to wield a tremendous force. Yes, damn it, he ought to break it up somehow.

Sandy's song was over and they were milling about. Small groups were forming up, dispersing, reforming. They'd heard the song and wept and been released. Things would start getting noisier. Sandy Shaw was drinking over there with Shadwell and Bancroft. Jaybird Wall was up to his tiresome tricks again, and Rag Rooney, apparently revived, was back out there seeking new victims. Here and there, arms over each other's shoulders, groups of three or four men were singing together. Well, there were ways he could do it, ways he could bust this thing up and get them out of there, head them home. He reached for the phone. But he hesitated. Enjoyment. What in god's name did enjoyment have to do with people and life and running a goddamn baseball league? He stared dismally at the TV scene. Then, dispiritedly, he did call. He watched Jake appear on the screen, pick up the phone, glance up at the camera, up at him, Universal Baseball Association Chancellor Fennimore McCaffree, alone and full of sorrow, self-pityingly encased in that dark gloom that would pursue him to his grave. "Jake, this is Fenn. Listen . . . set the boys up a couple times . . . for me. Will you?"

Things were livening up. Some of the family men had left, but Jake's was still packed and there were still a good many bottles that hadn't got drunk up yet. The collective eye was on Jaybird Wall, whose own night was nearly done. He was into his old ball-chasing act, imitating himself out in left field, losing a fly ball in the sun. Wearing a ball cap over his eyes so just his big red nose stuck out, detoothed mouth agape, using Maloney's derby for a glove, shirttail out, pants sadsackly adroop, shoestrings untied, he rubber-legged around the barroom, trying to spy the falling ball. Sandy picked up his guitar and played a tremolo on a high string. Chants and shouts. "Look out!" Laughter. "I *thee* it! I *thee* it!" Jaybird gummed, scrawny arms upstretched to invoke a fair catch, and then, "*Glop!*", seemed to swallow something. He lowered his chin, pushed back his cap, crossed his eyes, staggered around clutching his throat, then stuffed one finger into his muzzle and leaned over Maloney's derby. He seemed to be prying something out . . . *POP!* (sound effects by Jake)—he smiled broadly, produced a baseball from the hat. Applause and laughter. Jaybird beamed, dropped the ball back into Maloney's hat, and with a drunken weave and flourish, grandly donned the derby: *CLUNK!* (Jake bopping the bar with a beer bottle) and over he went. Descending whistle (the whole crowd in concert): *WHOMP* (no sound effects needed)! Not to rise again. Not this night anyway. No matter how they whooped and paid him tribute.

Trench and Rooney dragged Jaybird out to keep him from getting walked on, popped him onto the back-room cot, kept there for the purpose. Who hadn't slept there? Home away from home. Had been for Trench anyway. Sandy had a song about it . . .

. . . I'm all washed up, boys,
I got the axe, I got the aches;
Now you'll find me when you want me
On the sack in the back of Jake's!

Mel Trench had ended his playing career here in this town, traded to the Pastime Club by the Excelsiors when his deep belts no longer cleared the wall so often, when they had a way instead of getting caught. Difference of ten feet maybe, but it was enough. What was the grave, but a difference of six? He'd watched them lower that boy today, put him under the sod, and he himself had had a pretty sinking feeling. Something like he felt when the Cels traded him off to the Patsies. Nothing wrong with the Patsies, great guys, but a comedown after his heyday with the Cels: five championships in seven years! Oh, they were great, and he, Mighty Mel Trench, the Terrible Truncheon, was the greatest by god of them all! Hell-born Melbourne. Look out! Home-run king and the only man in UBA history ever to win the Most Valuable Player Award two years running. Not even Brock Rutherford had done that. But suddenly he lost it. And the Cels packed him off. He didn't deserve that. All the newspapers said so. A deserving guy. A rotten deal. But he wasn't bitter. They all noticed that. Sweet fellow, they said. Swell Mel. And he'd tried like a bastard for the Patsies, hoping for just one more pennant, but the fences just kept backing off, and the Patsies those years were no real contenders. Toward the end, he wasn't much more than a pinch hitter. Benched Trench. Finally, in XLVIII, they let him go. And then, the next year, the Patsies did win the pennant. No mention of Swell Mel then. He slept back here a lot those days. Hellborn.

Finally, though, it was his old outfit that rescued him, showed up here winter before last with an offer to manage the Excelsiors. Not too much to work with, but at least he couldn't do worse: they had finished LIV in the cellar. So he accepted and gave it all he had . . . and wound up in the cellar again last year anyway. And that was where they still were today.

En-Trenched. He had to do something, but he didn't know what. Made him want to cry, just thinking about it.

But anyway he was glad he had come tonight. Helped him see the bigger picture, loosen up a little. All came out the same in the end, he saw that now. Some won, some lost, it didn't really matter; what mattered was . . . well . . . the Association, this whole thing, bigger than all of them, that they were all caught up in. When he tried to picture it in his mind, it fuzzed into a big blur, but in his heart and when they were all together like this, he knew what he meant. Yes, it was a terrific bunch of guys out there tonight. Most of them were old-timers, ballplayers he'd watched as a kid, old heroes, in their late fifties now, some of them—like Rooney and Wall here—even older. Still looked and talked and laughed like ballplayers, though. Something in the blood or the heart or the balls that made you keep going, no matter what. He heard old Sandy Shaw out there, tuning up his guitar again. In his sixties, and Sandy still looked like a freckly-faced kid. Trench felt his own thick paunch. I'll be dead before any of them, he said to himself. Didn't really believe it, though. He looked at old Rooney. Pappy. One of the greatest of all time. Lean face scarred with deep wrinkles now. White hair. Crinkled leather skin on the back of his neck looked hundreds of years old. Somebody said he had cancer. And yet look at him: still a terrific scrapper, still out there every day, giving it all he had. Wonderful old man. Hall of Fame. Trench wanted to wrap his arm around him, show the old guy he cared, and that he'd truly be sorry when he died. Tomorrow, Rooney was his worst enemy. If Trench didn't get his Cels out of the cellar, he was through, and he had to start tomorrow, *had* to knock off Rooney's Haymakers. But still, tonight, he could put his arm around the old bastard and swear blood oaths: I'm with you, man. And he knew, when the chips were down, he could count on Rooney, too. That's how it was in this game.

Now, Rooney turned to him and said: "Trench, I just wanted to mention: we're gonna knock the holy *shit* outa you tomorrow."

Trench was caught off guard, but he managed to say: "What with, sewing needles?"

Rooney grinned patronizingly, and very gently, very distinctly, said: "We're gonna *bury* you, boy. For good."

Trench felt something cold whistle clean through him. Before he could think of a comeback, Rooney had gone back out front. Trench turned, stared down at toothless Jaybird Wall, snoring on the cot. Oboy. Move over, man . . .

Ain't no more roar
In the park no more;
Down in the cellar
And cain't find the door . . .

Hot shit! Raglan (Pappy) Rooney was on his way to the final transmutation! into the land of the goddamned blessed! yes! grind, grind without slackening, first law of the game! soak it up, blow it out! Those first shots tonight had burned Rooney's belly like salt and vitriol and had brought on a bloody purgation that scared the hell out of him; but then, taking a deep breath, he'd discovered that the old tubes had somehow been fritted by the fire, and the rest of the night it was all sublimation. He'd revivified himself with a long rosy piss, then gone back out to slaughter the innocents. He really got a bang out of drinking with these guys. He didn't give a golden chamberpot full of solid silver turds for buddyship, so-called, but Rooney loved to drink and he hated to drink alone. He liked to hear them laugh and bitch, liked to hear old Sandy sing, liked the racket, the meanness, the tension, the heat, liked it all filled up and boiling away. And above all, he loved to rag 'em. Ho ho! fat Trench had nearly popped his cork: fffooOO! They were going to beat him all right, Trench was through. Dead. Rooney cackled. Bathe 'em in blood, boys! Give 'em the truth! And the truth? It was raunchy and morbid and arid, but it was all there was and worth a passing celebration!

Yeah, you're down and you're out, boy,
All the playin' is done,
You tried and you failed, boy,
And you ain't anyone . . .

This was Rooney's party and nobody was enjoying it more. The wake's at Jake's! He sang and hollered and whipped it up. It tickled his best rib to see them all show up, they couldn't stay away, afraid to come, more afraid not to come. Too bad Sick Flynn was gone, he'd had a few more things he'd like to jab him with. Like shotgunning poor Damon for jumping his virgin daughter. But Flynn was scared. And he'd better be. They were going to needle him and that kid pitcher of his right out of baseball. The great-grandson of Fancy Dan Casey. End of the line! Mad jocks get off!

No-hit Nealy, ho ho ho!
When they pitched high, he swung low!

"Hey, Gooney! Stop garglin' and get rid of it, man!"

"Aw, you guys ain't got no appreciation!" He laughed with them, though. When they stopped ragging him, they'd bury him.

He caught Bancroft on the way to the head: "Hey, Philosopher, can I interest you in a coupla pitchers?"

"What kinda pitchers?" Barney asked. He was smashed.

"*Dirty* pitchers!" Rooney howled with delight. "Things're gonna get tough, Philosopher!"

"The Rutherford spirit," Bancroft slurred, "will carry the day!"

"Oh yeah? What's your spirit's E.R.A.?" Rooney cackled, oh hey! that's a beauty! "E-R-A, get it?" He dug Bancroft's ribs—the Old Philosopher my ass, a lotta puff and blow, but he'll never make it—then spun on the others. "Hey! It's the new Rutherford Era!" he hollered. "The *Spirit E-R-A!*" He roared with laughter, but laughed alone. Nobody got it. "Pour 'em out, Jake! Keep 'em alive!"

While the house was picking itself up again, he soft-shoed over to Shadwell, got old Tim yakking sentimentally about the old days. Rooney and Shadwell had come up as rookies the same year—Year X: who the hell said XIX was the Year of the Rookie?—and Tim had dusted Rooney more than once over the next fifteen seasons. Then, once he'd got Tim waxing eloquent and blubberish, Rooney leaned close and whispered, "Now, honestly, don't that Brock Rutherford Era crap twist your balls, Tim?"

Shadwell flushed pink as a punched virgin. "Well . . ." he said, squirming, looking around. His hands shook and the cubes rattled in his glass. "Of course, uh, Brock had his faults, but . . . I mean, it's not exactly the, you know, right time to . . ."

"Crock Rubberturd."

Shadwell, uncontrollably and no doubt shocking his own lily-white self, commenced to giggle. "Rooney, you're worse than death," he allowed.

"Hey, Sandy!" Rooney bawled out. "Give us 'Long Lew and Fanny'!"

Lew Lydell protested, but the rest of the boys picked it up. "*Long Lew and Fanny!*" Sandy stroked a chord and loose laughter rattled in the bar. "Give her all you got, Sandy!" some wag shouted.

"Too late for that," Sandy drawled, and they whooped again...

Come, boys, give a cheer,
And buy me a beer,
And sit down beside me a spell,
While I tell the uncanny
Tale of Miss Fanny
McCaffree and Long Lew Lydell!

Oh, who can ever forget
That day the Grooms met
The Knicks on the Knicks' home diamond?
Long Lew'd made a vow
That they'd win somehow
Or Fanny would forfeit her hymen!

Now, this much is true:
The first was Long Lew,
Though later there may have been many;
For, believe it or not,
Though Long Lew had a lot,
Fanny had never had any!

After nine innings of play
On that hot summer day,
The Grooms lost, nothing to six;

So Long Lew went and caught her,
The long-legged daughter
Of McCaffree, the boss of the Knicks!

"Excuse me, Miss Fanny,"
Said he, "don't take any
Offense if I must tell you true
That this will hurt me
More than you, for you see
Here the reason they call me Long Lew!"

Oh yes, this much is true:
The first was Long Lew,
Though later there may have been many;
For, believe it or not,
Though Long Lew had a lot,
Fanny had never had any!

Now, when all of Long Lew
Came into full view,
Miss Fanny collapsed in dismay—
She fell on the bench,
Did that long-legged wench,
With her skirts tucked neatly away!

There was wrenching and pounding,
The noise was astounding,
And still he had only begun!
But he banged and he bored
Till at last he had scored,
And Fanny cried out: "HOME RUN!"

No, I'm sure this is true:
Number one was Long Lew,
Though later, perhaps, there were many;

For, I swear on this spot,
Though Long Lew had a lot,
Fanny had never had any!

How he managed to pin her
And get it all in her
Remains an eternal league mystery;
But the crowd round the pit
All had to admit
That Long Lew Lydell had made history!

As for Fanny, though fallen,
She said: "Stop your stallin'
Long Lew, and prove you're a pro!
I've seen your muscle,
Now show me some hustle:
You still got eight innings to go!"

Oh yes, I'm tellin' you true,
Her first was Long Lew,
Though later there were probably many;
For it's true, is it not,
That Long Lew had a lot,
But Fanny had never had any!

Well, Old Fenn came upon her
In total dishonor
And Long Lew in a state of fatigue;
He'd've made Long Lew shorter
But was stopped by his daughter,
Who said: "Daddy! I've made the Big League!"

So the Knicks won the game,
And Long Lew his fame,

And Fanny had fun in her fall;
McCaffree was furious,
The fans merely curious,
And the moral is: don't win 'em all!

Yes, this much is true:
The first was Long Lew,
Though later there may have been many;
For, believe it or not,
Though Long Lew had a lot,
Fanny had never had any!

Well, yes, it was a great wake, and as they joked and shouted, he saw that it was good, but yet it wasn't enough. Something was missing. "Hey! All you old pissers! Over here!" Rooney shouted.

"Whatsamatter, Pappy?"

"Get over here!"

"Pappy, if I take this bar out from under my elbow, I ain't got nothin' left to hold me up!"

But he kept insisting, and finally they all came, he gathered them all together, and when he'd got them all over, they looked back toward the bar, and there she was, nobody'd noticed her before, but now, there she stood, alone, at the bar. They wasted no time. They rolled the cot out from the back room. Old Jaybird Wall still snored there, biting his ass with his own dentures; they dumped him off and her on. No time or words wasted. They'd had enough of the putrefaction phase, they'd passed through the dissolutions and descensions and coagulations: what they wanted now was union. And oh yes, they seeded her well, they stuffed her so full it was coming out her ears, it was a goddamn inundation . . .

"Well, it's a funny world," said Jake.

"Yeah . . . yeah, it is. You said it."

His name will shine down through all time,
Shine like an eternal flame,
For though he has died in his youthful
prime,
His spirit lives on in the game!

Hang down your heads, brave men, and weep!
Young Damon has come to harm!
They have carried him off to a grave dark and
deep:
The boy with the magic arm . . .

Going into exile, heartsore, Sycamore Flynn stared out on the night, seeing nothing there, not even his own pale reflection, staring dispiritedly back into the coach. He had no thoughts, any more than a drowning man had thoughts, just anxieties, and his mind in trouble pitched here and there, rocked by the wheels' pa-clockety-knock, jogged loose from the continuum, sloshing here and there, the green and the gold, the suns and the shadows, the sons and the fathers, the sons and the fathers—and the piping cries of the sandlot boys, the leaping and throwing and running and swinging, all the games won and all the games lost, balls came bouncing at him, were thrown at him, flew by him, arched over him, and he was running back, and running back . . .

He looked away. Running back. Tomorrow's game. Which was yesterday's. Pa-clockety-knock, pa-clockety-knock, nearer and nearer. Well, there was pattern maybe and legend and graphs and prophecies—but there was something else, too, and it came at you and it was hard and it was tangible, yes, to say the least, and sometimes you could field it and turn it to glory, but sometimes it hit you right in the teeth, and no, you couldn't stop it, you couldn't even duck. You couldn't even give it a name! He was afraid. Not only for himself. Not just for his team. For everybody. They'd all be there. Brock Rutherford Day at Pioneer Park . . . plus two. Resumed. Substitution announced: *for the Pioneers, pinch-running for . . .*

He'd thought of every possibility. Getting rid of Casey. At least benching him. Quitting himself. Withdrawing his Knicks from all further games this season. Proposing they call the rest of the season off, give the pennant to the Pioneers, who were anyway in second place behind them. Even: that they close down the Association. Why not? Because what would all the past mean then without the present process? Nothing at all, but so what? No answer: only dread. And everything less than that fell short or looked cheap. Finally, he supposed, it would resume, and he would simply have to play out his part. But he dreaded that, too.

His daughter had disappeared. She'd left no note. Hadn't been necessary. He knew what she was telling him and there was nothing he could do about it, nothing he could do that would bring her back. Harriet was as dead to him now as her Damon was to Brock. Even more so, because Damon died and left no hate behind. In a way, Flynn envied Brock. No, that wasn't true. You're just trying to smooth it over, ease the guilt. You can still love her even though she hates; but what does Brock have to love? You can't love a corpse.

Brock the Great. His Era: yes, yes, it was. It had hurt Sycamore to say so in front of all those people—like he'd been tricked or something, and it had made him sore, sore at Mc-

Caffree, sore at Bancroft, and sore at Brock Rutherford. But it was true. Sycamore Flynn, age 57, Hall of Fame, all-star Bridegroom shortstop Years XIX through XXX, Most Valuable Player in XXVIII, Knickerbocker manager since LIII and twice a boss of champions, knew it was. He was there. He'd come up with Brock in XIX, and his one personal triumph had been his selection—over Brock and all the others—as Rookie of the Year. Brock had got back at him. Oh yes, many times over. Like at the end of the season three years later when Sycamore and Brock's teammate Willie O'Leary were fighting it out for the batting title. The Pioneers were taking the pennant in a walk that year, and they even got a little sloppy in the final games, but not when Sycamore Flynn came to the plate. Brock personally struck him out seven straight times in the final series—and once when there was a man on second, no outs, and first base open, when he should at least have passed him, but no, it was Get-Flynn-Year, and get him they did. Finally, he finished up fourth. Brock the Great. Oh yes, damn it, damn him, he was!

The train pulled in. Sycamore was alone; his players had returned ahead of him. The depot was only a block from Pioneer Park, the hotel where the Knicks were staying just another block or so beyond that, so he decided to walk. Loosen up. Anyway, he wasn't all that confident about getting in a cab here in Damon's hometown: he might be recognized and that might not be so good. Though it was a warm night, he turned up his collar, chose the dark sides of the streets. What was hounding him? That he didn't feel guilty *enough?*

He passed under the stadium. It bulked, unlit in the dark night, like a massive ruin, exuding a black odor of death and corruption—no, no, just that modest stink of sweat and garbage all old buildings had, and ball parks especially. It caused an unreasonable dread in him, a stupid dread; to purge it, he crossed over, touched it, felt the solid stone, just plain ordinary lifeless matter. A ball park. Like any other. The arched entranceways, he noticed, had no gates. How did they keep the crashers out? Just a passageway, maybe; other doors and gates inside. He peered in. Couldn't see anything. It was pitch black in there.

Inwardly, he laughed at himself. Crossing a street to see if a building was real! Funny what funerals could do to the mind. If anybody saw him, they'd take him for a complete nut. He glanced about furtively, but he seemed to be alone. He rapped a wall, skinning a knuckle, as a kind of self-punishment, and set off for the hotel. But then he hesitated. Silly thing, but those gateless entrances bothered him. Forget it. What you need is a night's sleep. Or a night's rest anyway—he wasn't sure he could get to sleep with tomorrow's game to wake up to. Well, that's right, so what's the hurry? He turned back.

No, no gates. Not even the hinges for one. And inside: it shouldn't be that black in there. Was it the streetlight out here, dim as it was, that made it look that way? He stepped inside. Still couldn't see anything, but once inside, he realized it was more like a tunnel than the entrance to a ball park. He edged to his right, hand outstretched. Yes, a wall. Rough and damp. He traced it a few paces. Peculiar. Construction work maybe. Excavations. Have to come look at this in the daytime. He turned, half afraid that—but, no, there it was, the dimly lit street. But something new now. Voices. Indistinct, but not far away. Better wait. They'd take him for a thief.

As time passed, he grew impatient. A couple guys standing on a street corner describing conquests, no doubt. Of course, they could also be cops. Better stay put. To take up the time, he explored a little further, left hand stretched out in front of him, right hand tracing the contours of the wall. Earthen. Sweating. It seemed endless. Finally, he gave it up, turned back. Now, in fact, there *was* no street! Moment of panic, but he made himself think. The wall he was tracing must have been curving. He stepped out away from it. Still couldn't see a thing. Better go back the same way you came. He reached out for the wall, but couldn't find it. Then he did panic. Wheeled around, scrambling in every direction at once, not afraid of the voices now, but afraid to cry out. Why? he didn't know—ah! the wall! But which one? He was breathing heavily, ashamed. He'd lost his head there for a minute. And now what, right or left? He decided to gamble on its being the same wall, so followed it now with his left hand. But after a hundred paces or so with no sight of the street, he realized he'd guessed wrong, was just getting deeper. Turned back. Keep calm. It'd be easy to break. Count. At one hundred, he paused. Must've started about here. Another fifty or a hundred paces, and he ought to see the street. But after twenty, the wall curved suddenly to the right. He swallowed, licked his lips. Keep thinking, keep cool. Could put your back to the wall, then strike straight out on the perpendicular—have to find the opposite wall sooner or later. But he had a grip on this wall and didn't want to let go. And when he did find that other wall, which way would he go? Besides, if these were excavations, there might be drops: he could fall, hurt himself, have to spend all night here. No, consider. This tunnel must go somewhere. Some other exit probably. Better stick with it, keep moving. He was afraid of the right turn he'd come on, so he went back over the same ground again, right hand out in front, left hand tracing the rough passage wall. Hundred paces and that wall curved, too, sharply to the left. Too soon. But maybe he was taking bigger steps now. No point in going back. Better keep moving. Don't think. Just lead to panic. Move, just move, hustle. In his mind, he kept up a little pepper. That's it. Lotta action. Hup, two, three. Every hundred paces or so, the wall again bent left. Going around in circles. Or maybe a spiral. What kind of a goddamn ball park was this anyway? Don't question it. Keep going. Seemed to be climbing now. Lift those knees. Come on, Sic'em baby, cover ground! He was sweating now, his clothes felt sticky on him, the air heavy—heart going too fast! He dropped his right hand to feel its beating and smacked up solid against a sudden right turn in the wall.

Face stung. Felt dizzy. Greasy. He paused there, in the corner, half ready to quit, getting his breath. Then he saw where he was. In his own dugout. Visitors' dugout near first base. Still dark, no shape to things, but no longer pitch black. He stepped through the dugout, out onto the field, to get his bearings, get some fresh air. As he did, as he passed through the dugout, he saw them there, but he looked away. No, that would be too much. Even out on the field, the night air was oppressive. He stared off toward where, more or less, home plate was, must be; but his back tingled. Another trick of the shadows, he supposed. Night. Always did that. Irrational. But he was pretty sure they were there, pretty sure he'd seen them. Sitting on the bench. Didn't know who. But they were there behind him. Imagination. Go back and check. No, don't be an idiot, that's how you've ended up here in the first place, remember? He recalled an exit behind home plate. Head for that. Get outa here. Yeah, boy. Walk, don't run. Control. But speed, too. He sighted on the bag at first, only thing he could see out there. Finally he was running.

But at first base, he pulled up short. Figure lurking there. No turning away from that. Flynn was all alone out on a darkened ballfield, behind him that dugout with its goddamn spooky benchwarmers, the tunnel back of that—and something even worse ahead. The figure stood about six paces off first base, down the baseline toward second. Flynn's baseball habits made him think instinctively: he's playing too close to the bag. Or maybe he was moving toward first. Someone coming up from home? Base on balls? Or . . . ? aha. Oh no.

Damp dank wind curled around his ankles, crept down his back. Made his clothes tug and tremble on him, and the first baseman's pants fluttered around his motionless knees. Flynn felt rooted to the spot. "Matt?" he whispered. No answer. His mouth was dry, tongue thick. Almost didn't hear himself. "Matt, is that you?" Face in shadows, no features visible, but the body, the shape, looked like Matt Garrison. Cap tipped forward like he always wore it, jaw out-thrust. Just fixed there. Flynn, keeping his eye on the immobile first baseman, circled, then backed away. Toward home. Toward the exit. Oh man. You gotta get outa here. This is something awful.

But then he paused. Felt the turf under his shoes. Not the baseline. He'd got off it. Must be near the . . . the mound. Yes. And he knew: there was somebody behind him, all right. Didn't have to look. Didn't have the nerve anyway. "Jock?" Could still faintly make out Matt Garrison's figure, and beyond Matt, the black mouth of the dugout from which he'd come. McAllister Weeks over toward second. "That you, Jock?" Turn around and look, you ass. Can't. Sorry, just can't. "Jock, if you don't want to pitch it out . . ." He could imagine Casey's face. The hard thrust of bone against the lean flesh. The scooped-out shadowy loner's eyes. That set cold stare. Couldn't turn and look, though. "Just let me know, I can . . ." The night wind. The lifeless field. His own heart which was going to fail, going to break, going to quit. "*Why've you done this to us, Jock?*" he cried out. Flynn was near tears. Behind him, he realized, past Casey, past home plate, there was an exit. Maybe it was a way out, maybe it wasn't. But he'd never make it. It was all he wanted, but he'd never make it. He couldn't even turn around. And besides, he wasn't sure what he'd find at home plate on the way. "I quit," he said.

But then the lights came on.

4

FLYNN had his back to the mound and was staring probably out toward his bull pen where he had two relievers working and at the same time watching Matt Garrison shift over there toward first as the Pioneer pinch runner came down the line to take his—but who was that? who'd those guys have? Tuck Wilson maybe: Bancroft sent Wilson in to run for Rutherford, okay. Henry stared woozily down upon those three ones on his kitchen table, trying to put all that scene back together again, get some order in this damn operation, men, and he was Old Fennimore McCaffree in his black suit giving orders and Barney Bancroft urging the boys how they had to win this game and all the old Elders sitting like a panel of enraged titans up on the Elders Bench and the catcher Chauncey O'Shea blubbering there behind the plate all broken up by this thing and he was the umpire Frosty Young hollering out they had to play ball no matter what and thinking how hard it was going to be to call them straight though he had to and he was also each of the old-time Pioneers who'd come there for Brock

Rutherford Day at Pioneer Park and now a little awestruck but back there to see this thing out . . . but mostly he was only J. Henry Waugh, pooped and plastered Prop., thinking that this was sure a helluva thing for a grown man to be doing at dawn on a working day, and how was he going to face up to old Zifferblatt two hours from now?

But Flynn finally turned to Jock Casey and asked him: "You sure you feel like staying in this game?"

And Casey said, "Yeah, why not?"

"Because I can always—"

"Forget it." Casey was impatient. "Let's just get going."

Well, old Flynn shook his head, as though to say it was out of his hands, and he left the field, Casey being essentially right: finish it out. See what happened. The stands were dead still. Jammed, though. They had all come back. They wanted to be there. Who could tell? might be the last game in the UBA.

Henry wrote in Wilson pinch-running for the hit-and-now-buried batsman, R.I.P., but his gloves made his fingers so clumsy he could hardly read it afterwards, so he pulled them off and threw them over on the shelves, then traced over what he'd written; it was still pretty hard to read. Henry considered the situation, that it was the bottom of the third, Pioneers batting, Wilson on first, no outs, Ramsey swinging against Casey on the Rookie-to-Rookie chart, and even managed a dim picture of how it was down there to start this game up again, how it must be, no matter what anybody was saying out loud; then he picked up the dice, scrambling the bean ball in his fist, and rolled for Toby Ramsey, and things were moving again: *GO 1B/R Adv 1 if F*, which meant that Garrison took the play unassisted at first, Ramsey out, but Wilson now down on second, and it suddenly occurred to Henry, now thinking like Bancroft, or maybe like one of the old Pioneers, Willie

O'Leary perhaps, that Ramsey should have been ordered to bunt, but it really didn't matter, came out the same way anyhow, and also: why did Bancroft send an old tub like Tuck Wilson in as a pinch runner? he must have meant to use one of the younger boys, and in the confusion—but, hell, that was no damn way to run a ball game. Henry, feeling oddly suffocated, realized then he still had his coat on, so he took it off and dropped it over the back of the chair. So now it was Grammercy Locke, one out and a man on second, which meant Casey should give Locke an intentional pass and try for the double play, and even though Henry personally wanted to see Locke swing away, wanted to see them all swing away, he gave in to the logic of it, and that put Locke on first, Wilson on second, and Hatrack Hines at the plate: action on the Rookie-to-Star chart now for four straight Pioneer batters. He supposed there was probably a little chin music down there now around the base paths and in the dugouts, and maybe even some gathering hoopla up in the stands, but he couldn't hear it. He rolled for Hines, who got a walk, loading up the bases, with home-run champ Witness York coming to the plate, and finally he was able to smile, and, scratching his head, he wondered where he had left his hat. He rolled: *FO RF/R Adv 1*. Well, a fly-out to right, pretty disappointing, but at least it brought old Tuck Wilson waddling in from third after the catch, put runners in scoring position on second and third, two outs, Star hitter Stan Patterson at the plate, but Patterson, trying too hard maybe, struck out, and that was all. Struck out! Henry was standing, curved over his table, supported by both stiffened arms, gazing despondently down upon his Universal Baseball Association. It was as though nothing had happened, Casey was still burning them in, and even though it was now Pioneers 1 and Knicks 0, nobody had got a hit yet.

Henry tugged off his scarf, tossed it over on the drainboard by the sink, and sat down heavily. Should go to bed. No, then he'd never get up and he'd be out of a job. Today was Friday. If he could just get through the day somehow, there was the weekend to recover. All right, who was up? oh wait, that's right, the Pioneers needed a pitcher in there, and who was it going to be? better use their ace, Mickey Halifax: they had to win this one, didn't they? they did. And so he sat there, leaning on one elbow, fighting sleep, vaguely worried about Zifferblatt, one of Sandy's tunes wandering through his sodden head, rolling the dice, and not much happened for a couple innings except that Chauncey O'Shea, the Knicks' rookie catcher who was supposed to be blind with tears of remorse, tripled in the fifth to spoil the Rutherford-Halifax no-hitter. Luckily, Halifax got the side out, O'Shea dying on base, but meanwhile the Pioneers were doing just nothing at all.

Okay, so now the sixth, the game was officially a complete one, even if it got called, and as of now the Pioneers would be the winners, 1–to–0, so surely it was a temptation for Frosty Young to see clouds in the sky, but on the other hand, Casey still had a no-hitter, and there would be a lot of resentment if they didn't let the Pioneers have another chance or two at busting that up, and besides, it still wasn't time to go to work, and he had to do something. Henry put fire on under the day-old coffee sitting on the stove and tried to talk himself into a little of the old excitement. He even said out loud: "All right, fellas, a little pepper now, let's wake up!"—but he heard himself talking to a wooden kitchen table all too plainly, and he thought: what a drunken loony old goat you are, they oughta lock you up.

But he sat down anyway, just to see what the dice would bring, because it was clearly on his mind, either something happened—something in short *remedial*—or into the garbage bag with the whole works, and with that the Knicks started laying into Halifax. It was Killer Casey who started it appropriately enough with a line-drive single, and then after a couple outs, Garrison doubled, Baldwin singled, and McCamish homered, and so suddenly it was a 4–to–1 ball game, the Mad Jock and his Knicks out in front. There was still time for the Pioneers to fight back, and Henry barked irritably at them, or maybe just at the dice, as he threw for them in the bottom of the sixth, but grim Casey cut them down, one-two-three. A hard-bitten cold-blooded sonuvabitch. And then the seventh, the old *lucky* seventh, there was Crybaby O'Shea kicking things off for the Knicks with a double off the left-field wall and Musgraves walking and Casey doubling them both home and Batkin singling to score Casey. And were they laughing about it, for god's sake? Weeks struck out, but Garrison singled and Baldwin got a base on balls, loading up the bags. "Aw, get your Ace's ass to the showers!" Henry grumped disgustedly at Halifax, and called in Drew McDermott in relief. And so McCamish knocked the ball down to Hatrack Hines at third, who fumbled it, and a run scored, and Maverly singled and a run scored, and O'Shea singled, his third hit of the ball game, and a run scored. Henry, chin in his right hand and rolling with his left, watched them prance around the bases, having a damn picnic. Musgraves, the only Knick in the whole line-up so far without a hit, singled home McCamish, which brought Jock the Jerk to the plate for the second time this inning, and now with the bases loaded and the game a goddamn rout. Henry supposed, in his morass of gloom and nausea, that Casey would probably tear the cover off the ball, but he didn't. Against every rule in the book and contrary to Flynn's signals, he bunted, a squeeze bunt under the awesome circumstances, and Maverly scored from third; Pioneer catcher Royce Ingram's throw to first was wild, Casey was safe, and on the error O'Shea came sliding in for yet another run. Insane, but there it was. Nor was it all. Batkin popped up to Hines, but Weeks singled home Musgraves and Matt Garrison doubled, scoring Casey, before Biff Baldwin finally lined out to center to end the massacre. Knicks 15, Pioneers 1. Henry couldn't see much down there in Pioneer Park, but he did notice that just about all the fans had got up and walked out.

By now the coffee had been boiling for some time and the kitchen stank of it. Henry pushed himself up out of his chair, turned off the burner, dumped pot and all into the sink. Outside, the sky, starless, was graying toward day. A few neon signs burned in the half light, proclaiming names and wonders: the new and wearisome order. He looked at his watch: still more than an hour before he had to confront the old man. What could he tell him? This was probably the end, all right: got the axe, boys, got the aches. The most he could hope for was a terrific chewing out, and bad as he was feeling this morning, that was really nothing to hope for at all. It was autumn, but Henry felt plunged into the deepest of winters. But no, it was the middle of a baseball season, remember? Green fields and hot suns and shirtsleeved fanatics out on the bleaching boards, last to give it up and go home: he turned back to the table.

Who was up? Ingram. Damon's old battery mate. Damon's old battery mate struck out—for the third straight goddamn time. Then Wilder singled to spoil—at last—Mad Jock's no-hitter (and oddly he felt regret, because not even punishment then was total), but Goodman James bounced into a double play. Why am I murdering myself like this? he wondered, but he went on pitching the dice, and in the top of the eighth, the

Knicks' Walt McCamish drew a base on balls, Maverly whacked a fly ball out to Witness York, who dropped it, and Shook-up O'Shea belted out his fourth hit of the game, bringing in McCamish. Musgraves walked to fill the bags, and Casey knocked a ball out to the mound, busting McDermott's finger, two runs scoring on the error. That was too much. Henry threw the dice across the kitchen, took a cold shower, put on fresh clothes, pulled the chain on the lamp over the kitchen table, and went out for breakfast.

His bus was already overloaded when it arrived at his stop, and Henry was tempted to walk, getting out in the air was already doing him some good, but he couldn't risk arriving late, not today, so he squeezed on with the others, joining the sour community on its morning pilgrimage. Din of coughing and snuffling, here and there a sneeze exploding from a buffed nose: assailed by microbes, his head uncovered, he felt anything but invulnerable. He pressed rearward, pushed out a couple stops early, the bus exhaling as though with profound relief, and bought a newspaper at a stand on the corner there, obeying some old impulse which, he realized, he'd nearly forgotten, the giving of the coin, the snapping up of the paper, taking the world to heart and mind, or some world anyway.

In the coffee shop, he looked around for Lou: not here yet. He waited for one of the small tables in front of the counter to clear, glancing the while at the headlines. Some priest who quit and got married. Gold and silver shortages. Orgy that the cops broke up. Rapes and murders. Makings of another large war. A table opened up: Henry claimed it, looping his scarf over the second chair. War seemed to be a must for every generation. A pageant to fortify the tribal spirit. A columnist plumped for bloodless war through the space race. Henry sympathized with the man, but it could never work. Mere abstraction.

People needed casualty lists, territory footage won and lost, bounded sets with strategies and payoff functions, supply and communication routes disrupted or restored, tonnage totals, and deaths, downed planes, and prisoners socked away like a hoard of calculable runs scored. Besides, war was available to everybody, the space race to few: war was a kind of whorehouse for mass release of moonlust. Lunacy: anyway, he sure wasn't inventing it. The dishes on his table were cleared with a hard clap and rattle that hammered on the bare raw lobes of his brain and made him wince with pain. Don't give up, he cautioned himself. The waitress sponged the table with a rag that smelled like something between an old goat and a dead fish. He ordered a muffin and coffee, hoping he could keep it down.

New customers wheezed in, questioned the scarfed chair: "Sorry, taken." Henry ducked from their scowls into his paper, sipping the hot coffee, and thankful for it.

Finally, Lou showed up, spare hat—Henry's gray felt—in hand. "Henry!" He huffed and puffed excitedly down the aisle between the counter and the tables, smashing toes and jogging elbows, brandishing the hat on high, flushed face openly smiling: man without disguises. "You left your hat yesterday, Henry!"

Henry cleared the spare chair of his scarf, accepted the hat —"Thanks, Lou"—and held on to his coffee and the table until Lou could come to complete rest across from him.

"I was worried, I mean, I didn't know where you'd—what're you gonna do today about . . . ?"

"I don't know. I suppose I'll just have to—"

"I went by last night, thought you'd be home, I asked down in the delicatessen, I was afraid you might have, I don't know, left town, or . . ."

"I went out for a drink."

"A drink? Oh."

"Your order?"

"Anyway, I went by again this morning, just in case. I thought you'd need your hat, and I thought I'd maybe go up just to, well, I mean, I didn't know what you might have, how you might have—but Mr. Diskin told me he'd seen you leave this morning, so—"

"Lou, the girl's waiting."

"Hunh? Oh! Uh, number four, please, easy over, and tea. And a Danish on the side." He glanced at his watch, tongue between his lips.

"*Four over tea'n Danish!*"

"Oh, uh, Miss . . ." Lou blushed when she turned back on him, then smiled shyly. "Could you make that . . . *two* number fours?"

"*Double up that four!*"

"Say, he certainly has wonderful pastrami!"

"Who's that?"

"Mr. Diskin." Lou smiled. Well, anyway he didn't waste his trip. Holly Tibbett himself.

"You know, Lou, I was just thinking, what if we divided up the world into eight clubs, split the wealth more or less among them, and let them, taking turns, choose space teams from all the present available talent—"

"What're you talking about, Henry?"

"The space race. See, I was thinking, if you could just work it out so that statistically it was more exciting—and see, you might make a rule where the teams could buy, sell, and trade personnel, and then for rule infractions, you could bench key scientists and pilots—"

"Henry, are you . . . ?" Lou leaned forward, studying

Henry's face quizzically, as though discovering something horrible there. "Do you feel okay? You look, I don't know . . . changed."

"Just a little tired, Lou. I didn't get much sleep."

"Oh." Food arrived, several platters of it, erasing some of the anguish on Lou's big round face, and making him wonder: "Say, Henry, are you sure you've had enough to eat?"

"Sure, plenty." Lou eyed the empty muffin plate disdainfully, then stared again at Henry's face, while scooping the eggs in. Well, Henry thought, I *have* changed. "Don't worry, Lou, it'll be all right." He was very tired, and it was making him restless. He shifted in his chair, took a couple deep breaths. "Anyway, it doesn't matter." It was amazing to watch Lou when he got really attuned to his eating. All clumsiness vanished and his fingers played over the food as upon a musical instrument, his face flushing with pleasure and mild exertion. And yet there was something demonic about it, too, something destructive: as though, if given the chance, his mountainous bulk could consume all there was. "I figure the best thing is just to go tell Ziff I was sick and hope he buys that."

Lou looked up from his eggs in shock. "But"—he dabbed yolk from his mouth with a paper napkin—"why don't you tell him the truth?"

"The truth?"

"The, you know, your . . . I mean, the relative, the one who, the funeral . . ."

"Oh, that!" Inwardly, he smiled. True, he could . . . "I don't know, I guess I didn't feel that . . ."

"Nobody goes to work when there's a death in the family, Henry. I'm sure Mr. Zifferblatt will understand that, he's not inhuman, you know."

"I suppose not."

"Is it that you're, that you don't want to, you know, talk about it?"

"Something like that, I guess."

Lou smiled broadly around a jowlful of half-chewed pastry and pointed at himself. The advocate. "I'll go up first," were his Danish-muffled words of amity.

And true, two's opposition, three's a coalition, for after Lou's preparing of the way, Horace Zifferblatt's welcome on behalf of the firm of Dunkelmann, Zauber & Zifferblatt was perhaps still something less than open-armed, but he twitched his old head in what was no doubt intended as a commiserating nod, and paid his respects to the deceased with an embarrassed grunt and floorward scowl, glancing then at the clock which showed that he recognized Henry had arrived not only on time, but five minutes early; then returned to his glassed-in office to clock the rest of the arrivals.

Of course, Henry, in his condition, had only one available strategy for the day, and that was to bluff with his empty hand. He had nothing left but will power, and was running short of that. He pursued methodically each ritual, the hanging up of his coat and hat, the gathering and sorting of ledgers, the sharpening of pencils and filling of pens, the shuffling of drawers, clearing of throat, opening of books, search for eraser, stroking of jaw, loosening of collar, adjusting of self in chair, inspection of faulty penpoint, replacement thereof: all for a gain of seventeen minutes out of a total day's play of seven-and-a-half hours. You're not going to make it, boy, he advised himself and winced as though trying to read an illegible entry in the book open before him . . . and it *was* illegible, he couldn't see a thing.

He opened the drawer to search for his magnifying glass,

came upon his horseracing game in a set of manila file folders. When last he'd played it, there'd been a three-year-old named Ramshorn causing a sensation, though the big horses were still Saturday's Exile and Portent. Yes, and there was Muffin and Saddlepoint and Annie Oakley: he flicked hastily through the folders, waking up a little. Jacinto Abril, who'd tried and failed as a UBA ballplayer, was developing into one of the greatest jockeys of all time. Henry glanced around: heads down and working. Well, it was a temptation. But no, not yet. Had to get some work done first. Ziff would be watching him this morning. Save it for the afternoon. Need it more then anyway.

He turned back to the journal he'd opened. Who was it? Meo Roth's Skylight Protection Company: Repairs, Waterproofing, Replacement, and Screening. A sad case, because the firm was dying. Purchases had dwindled to almost nothing; inventory was constant, but through obsolescence, had become a storage liability rather than an asset; gross trading profit had sunk below selling, administrative, and general expenses; and, on top of it all, there were rents, mortgage payments, and taxes to be paid out. Old Meo Roth was reeling toward the ruin level. "Join the company," Henry said, then glanced up guiltily; a head or two turned his way briefly. He cleared his throat and lipped a few numbers to cover what was becoming an incurable and stupid habit.

Exit from competition: true, that was both his prospect and his problem. Roth had a bin full of glass and junk that was only costing him money to keep; Henry had a kitchen full of heroes and history, and after heavy investment, his corporate account had suddenly sunk to zero. Accretion of wasting assets. No flexibility. Roth had blundered in his inventory scheduling: if he could dump that glass and steal a load of plastic or fiberglass skydomes, he still might, with drive and imagination, make it. But what was Henry's solution? There must be a way, he thought—but then he remembered that absurd ball game back on the table that the bad guys were winning, 18–to–1. What did he mean, "bad guys"? Because, damn it, they killed the kid. And it was the kid who'd brought new interest, new value, a sense of profit, to the game. You mean, things were sort of running down before . . . ? Yes, that was probably true: he'd already been slowly buckling under to a kind of long-run market vulnerability, the kind that had killed off complex games of his in the past. What had happened the last four or five league years? Not much. And then Damon had come along to light things up again. And maybe that was it: Casey had put out the light and everybody was playing in the dark. An 18–to–1 ball game, they *must* be playing in the dark! He watched them down there, playing in the dark, running around, tripping over bases, there in the dark, wallowing around in heaps of paper, spilling off the table edge—

He jerked his head up so fast, he got a crick in his neck. He rubbed it, peeking around at the others, but afraid to look over toward Zifferblatt's office. He took some deep gulps of air, flexed his fingers, stretched his legs under the desk, concentrated on the figures. The clock on the wall, which somehow in its fat white roundness and hard black numbers always reminded Henry of Horace Zifferblatt himself, told him: thirty minutes down, seven hours to go. He sighed. Don't think about the whole day, that'll kill you, just try to make it to lunch break. One inning at a time. But he was beginning to get pretty nauseous, which the idea of lunch only aggravated. He rubbed his neck, and with extreme concentration, managed to post his first entry of the day. Shaky, but legible. In the right place, too, he was sure of it. He smiled at his victory.

But five minutes later, he was snoring on the books. So loud he could hear himself. When Zifferblatt woke him by a violent shaking of the ledgers under his face, he was dreaming he had just signed a contract with old Meo Roth that would save the firm and his own as well, and Roth/Ziff had tears of gratitude in his eyes. "That's all right," Henry said, rearing up, "think nothing of it."

Bulging above Henry's desk, thick thumbs rammed in his belt, face white with astonishment and rage, and this time it was no act, certainly not, choking as though he'd just swallowed something big and heavy as a headstone, Zifferblatt was able only to open his mouth and close it. He jerked his jowls in the general direction of his office. Henry rose and followed. Watched by all.

Even in his office, Zifferblatt could not find his voice. He sat down abruptly behind his desk, glared once at Henry, then pulled out the company checkbook, proceeded to write out a check, his dewlaps and chins aquiver with energy and conviction.

"I'm sorry, Mr. Zifferblatt," Henry said. "I haven't been getting much sleep."

"I can understand personal problems," Zifferblatt sputtered, "but—but to disturb an entire office!"

"I know. It's inexcusable. I shouldn't have come today."

Zifferblatt grunted, worked his soft mouth back and forth, stared down at the check he had just written out, then dropped it on the desk in front of him and leaned back in his swivel chair. "Sit down, Mr. Waugh." Books with blood-red or pale green backs lined every wall but the one behind Zifferblatt's head. That one was hung with diplomas, certificates, photographs, mottos, clippings, charts, clocks, travel souvenirs, and a map of the city on which a red blot pierced by a green arrow indicated the house of DZ&Z. Under black-bordered photos of the late lamented Abe Zauber and Marty Dunkelmann, the inscription: *They are with us still.* "A young man, Mr. Engel said."

"Yes."

"An athlete."

"Yes, a baseball pitcher."

"Oh yes, baseball." Zifferblatt pressed his stiff spatulate thumbs together over his round belly and pursed his lips as though to blow a kiss or spit. "The great American game." He paused, smiled—or perhaps it was only a gas pain, a tic just below the nose: "After business, of course." The pictures of his children were all taken in infancy . . . as though he hadn't let them live past that. "And, tell me, what do *both* baseball and business need, Mr. Waugh?"

"Somebody to keep the books."

"Well, humph, yes, but I was going to say hard playing, and above all, *teamwork!*" He socked his padded palm with a rolled fist, then squeaked forward in his chair. His eye fell on the check; he tore it up, saying: "One member not pulling his share, and the whole operation can be forced to liquidate. A lot of individual stars aren't enough, you've got to have organization and discipline, as well. You do see that, don't you, Mr. Waugh?" Henry nodded, though the movement intensified his headache and the crick in his neck. Ziff stood to make a point: "You're a man now of mature years, forty, fifty—"

"Fifty-six."

"Fifty-six! Nine years from retirement! And I'm asking you, do you wish to keep your job here, or *do you not?*"

"I do, but—"

"Well, then, accept a little advice, my friend. Accounting

like baseball is an art and a science and a rough competitive business. Some make it and some don't. The ones who make it keep their heads up, their eyes open, their minds on their job, and pull their part without belly-aching. Wages are based on *performance*, Mr. Waugh, and what we want around here at DZ&Z is *professionals!*" He paced the room, getting worked up. "What we expect, we give. This is the *American* way, Mr. Waugh! Why, old Marty Dunkelmann here never quit till the moment he died! I can still remember how I came to the office that morning and found him in here, bolt upright in his chair, eyes rolled back, and one finger on an error in a column of accounts receivable. He'd showed me that mistake just the night before, the only one I've made in fifty years of accounting; we were partners but we expected just as much out of each other as we did from any employee; he must've died while I was walking out the door! I'd been sitting right where you—Waugh! *Mr. Waugh! Wake up!*"

Henry's head jerked up, but it was all he could do to open his eyes. "I'm sorry, Mr. Dunkelmann—Zifferblatt. I'd better—"

"*I'll* tell you what you'd better, Waugh, you'd better be here at 8:30 *sharp* on Monday morning and *every* morning hereafter, not one minute later, and not *one single* exception, and prepared to put in a full day's *work*, or your position with us is *terminated!* Have I made myself *clear?*"

Henry nodded and stood. Woozily. "Yes, sir."

"All right, you can go now. You're no good to anybody here today anyway—though I hardly need mention, you can't expect us to pay you for not working."

"I understand."

Ziff softened, lower lip fluttering forward in a kind of senile pout. "Now, get rested up, Mr. Waugh, and try to get over this other thing. We all suffer losses, but we must learn to live with them. Let's see if we can't make a fresh start next week. You used to be a great asset to our team here at DZ&Z, and I would like to believe you soon will be again."

"Yes, sir."

At his desk, putting away his books and materials, Henry realized his hands were shaking, his knees weak. Not anger really, just felt shot down. Ziff was right: he was getting disorganized. The old menace.

Lou in a passing whisper: "Henry! Is everything, are you . . . ?"

"Yes. I'll be back Monday. Going home now to sleep. Thanks, Lou."

"Oh." Lou watched him close things up. "I was thinking maybe about, well, like I been saying about your eating, Henry, maybe Mitch's . . . ?"

Lou's cure-all. "I don't know, I—"

"I was planning to go there tomorrow night . . ."

"Well, all right."

"Shall I come by?"

"I'll meet you there. About nine."

"Do you know where it . . . ?"

"I'll find it."

"Monday morning!" lipped Horace Zifferblatt from his glass office, shaking his stubby index finger, then aiming it clockward, as Henry left.

Some people would look on his game, Henry realized, as a kind of running away. Lou, for instance, could not understand why he didn't see more movies or visit museums or join an interesting club or something, and though he could accept the idea of taking on outside work for extra money, he'd probably be astonished to learn about the game. But descending in the building elevator, urethra of his world prison, dropping dejectedly into a kind of private sinkhole, having to return to all that commitment and all that emptiness, Henry was aware that you could see it both ways: Roth's skylighting problems were, in a way, a diversion for him from his own. Sometimes, true, in the heat of a pennant chase, for example, his daytime job could be a nuisance, but over the long haul he needed that balance, that rhythmic shift from house to house, and he knew that total one-sided participation in the league would soon grow even more oppressive than his job at Dunkelmann, Zauber & Zifferblatt.

The elevator door yawned open, discharging him into the lobby, and thence, past the building directories and signs, into the street. A bright day, after all, though the sun's light was hard and cold. The streets, as always, were full of moving people, going going going, the endless jostling flow. They gave him somehow a vague and somber sense of fatality and closed circuits. Motion. The American scene. The rovin' gambler. Cowpoke and trainman. A travelin' man always longs for a home, cause a travelin' man is always alone. Out of the east into the north, push out to the west, then march through the south back home again: like a baserunner on the paths, alone in a hostile cosmos, the stars out there in their places, and him trying to dominate the world by stepping on it all. Probably suffered a sense of confinement there in the batter's box, felt the need to strike forth on a meaningful quest of some kind. Balls hurled down to him off the magic mound, regularly as the seasons: his limited chances. Or rather: not to him, but just to earth, passive, faintly hostile, deprecatory, masked—while he interposed himself heroically to defy the holy condition . . . not knowing his defiance was merely a part of it.

So what were his possible strategies? He could quit the

game. Burn it. But what would that do to *him?* Odd thing about an operation like this league: once you set it in motion, you were yourself somehow launched into the same orbit; there was growth in the making of it, development, but there was also a defining of the outer edges. Moreover, the urge to annihilate—he'd felt it before—seemed somehow alien to him, and he didn't trust it. And yet: what else could he do? That 18–to–1 deformity waiting for him on his kitchen table was like a special message for him, a self-revelation, the clang of an alarm: wake up! get out! shuck it off! insane! Traffic zim-zoomed through the sunny streets. Of course, there might be more alternatives than just two.

Passing a newsstand on his way to the bus stop, he bought another newspaper. What am I buying all these damn papers for? he asked himself. Different paper, different headlines, different stories, even different horoscopes. Must be some other world. Reflecting on his Space Race League, he realized it was no solution to war, but only an enhancement of it. Like Zifferblatt said, professionals earn their pay on performance in a competitive milieu, and you couldn't expect them to abide by any gentlemen's agreement. And what code could hold in an association of total power? No, you'd have to expect bribes, double-crosses, coalitions, information exchanges, and, sooner or later, a bomb or two. The old McGraw-Cobb syndrome: cut 'em up! If you're the only one left standing, you just gotta be the winner—the way Rag Rooney and Frosty Young played ball, and it got them into the Hall of Fame, didn't it?

Waiting for the bus, he saw that storefront across the street—Thornton's. Well, that's right, Barney surely had the right to bring up a replacement for Damon. Injuries were one thing, but a dead ballplayer was another. Unprecedented, but the Association was bound to approve it. So why not Thornton

Shadwell? The thought cheered him some, and then on the bus, he had other ideas. First of all, that the circuit wasn't closed, his or any other: there were patterns, but they were shifting and ambiguous and you had a lot of room inside them. Secondly, that the game on his table was not a message, but an event: the only signs he had were his own reactions; if these worsened, it might be best, after all, to close down the Association, maybe invent some new game, or in fact go join some club or other. But first he should finish out this season. He had this weekend to get it done. Then he'd be free to do as he wished. Maybe some kid pitcher would pick up where Damon left off. It was possible. And besides, it was irrational, but in spite of that game on the table, he felt certain the Pioneers were going to take the pennant. Why not? First, though, he thought, alighting from the bus, let's hit the sack, team.

POWER and control. In and out. The old eagle, Swanee Law, just reared back and burned them in. In across the knuckles: zip! Zap: skimming the outer edge! Now winging in across the letters, then plunging past the knees: the Law Special. Pappy Rooney was again using nearly everybody he had today, even pinch-hitting a couple pitchers. All his Haymakers got out of all the going in and coming out was one run, but it was enough: Law gave up just two scratch singles to the Bridegrooms and struck out fourteen to win, 1–to–0, Swanee's sixth straight victory. Pappy clapped them in, ragging them about the puny hitting, but they all felt good: it was their thirteenth win in the last fifteen games, and eight of them had been by one run. As for Swanee, not only was it his sixteenth win of the season and his fourth shutout, but the fourteen strikeouts brought his season total up to 219, giving him an outside chance still to hit the magic mark of 300, attained by only five pitchers in UBA history. Law knew what he had going for himself: whenever sportswriters interviewed him, they were shown large charts he kept tacked to his wall, indicating his own game-by-game progress in comparison with that of the five men in history—Hokey Lancaster, Fancy Dan Casey, Timothy Shadwell, Brock Rutherford, and Edgar Bath—he was challenging. Brock had the record: 341, set in Year XXVII. Rooney had to laugh at Law's prostrating himself before the tired and filthy feet of history, but as long as it helped win ball games he couldn't care less. The newsboys, bored, troubled, or revolted by what was happening—or not happening—in the rest of the league, fed on Law as the last hope for revival. You were pretty mean out there today, Swanee. Yuh, he'd say, gazing thoughtfully up at his charts, but we kin be meaner. Gotta be. Photos of him: narrow eyes reflecting concern, determination, square jaw solidly set . . . a tough old boy.

Elsewhere, the action in the UBA was confused and bewildering. Moreover, Law was a false hope; they'd need more than he could give. In his private offices, high above the day's play, Chancellor Fennimore McCaffree sat with vexed spirit watching it on four television sets going at once, aware that his Association was undergoing a radical transformation, the kind sprung only from situations of crisis, extremity; his worries now were no longer merely political, but ones even of survival. With him sat his old coach and mentor and only surviving ex-Chancellor, Woodrow Winthrop. Squawk boxes, receiving from ball-park spotters, computer rooms, and special agents, chattered out their several messages, creating a low-keyed cacophony, and McCaffree missed none of it; his phenomenal powers of concentration were already a league legend. Used to be, in his day, the quality Woody Winthrop was best known for, though age had loosened his wits some in recent years. He sat now, studying Fenn, amazed as always, wondering who was the protegé of whom.

"You see, Woody, it's one thing to say that each of these players and each of these teams is interested in maximizing its expected utility, and another to know—even for *them* to know—what that utility really is."

"How's that, Fenn?" Went right by him. Conversations with Fenn McCaffree these days got pretty one-sided. He was forever yakking about distribution functions, the canonical form of M, compound decision problems, relations of dominance; like Fenn had somehow forgot the game was baseball.

"Law shouldn't have pitched today."

"Oh." That Woody could understand. Rooney was pitching Law too much, wouldn't have anything left for the stretch.

In his trademark swivel chair—party symbol for the coming campaign—Fenn pivoted from set to set, his long legs crossed, spine curved, left elbow sharply out-thrust and hand gripping the chair-arm where his intercom buttons were rigged; blacksuited, string bow tie in the high collar, pants cuffs hiked high above the bony ankles and exceedingly long and narrow shoes; high-domed bespectacled head dipped forward, leaning against the pipe held clamped between under-slung jaw and right fist, as an old man might lean on a cane. On the Haymaker-Bridegroom screen, the game was over, and Law and Rooney were being interviewed by reporters; on the other three, the Knickerbocker-Pastimer, Excelsior-Keystone, and Beaneater-Pioneer games were in their final innings. Beaneater left-fielder Bartholomew Egan poled a homer into the center-field bleachers off the Pioneers' Thornton Shadwell, and Fenn punched a button: "What did Ingram call for?"

"Low and outside." One crackly report muddled with all

the others. Woody heard it because it came in over his own right shoulder.

"Where did he get it?"

"Down the slot."

"Feed it in."

"Check."

Watching his own hand-picked successor in office, Woody realized that he himself had probably been the last of his kind. He'd thought of himself as a rebel, but in reality he'd only brought the old ways to consummation. Under McCaffree, politics, the Chancellorship, even the game had changed. Fenn fooled you. He looked old-fashioned, but he had an abiding passion for innovation. He was the most relentless activist ever to take office, yet he never seemed to move a muscle. He was coldly calculating, yet supremely loyal to old comrades, and what else was it but sentiment that was making him, against all logic and advice, support his son-in-law as the next chief of the party? "You mean," Woody ventured, "Rooney oughta be giving Law a little more rest between games."

"No, I mean he shouldn't be using his best pitcher against inconsequential teams like the Bridegrooms."

"Well, Fenn, it don't matter much who you beat, what Rooney wants is to win ball games—"

Fennimore McCaffree pivoted slightly, almost imperceptibly, to glower witheringly upon the only surviving ex-Chancellor of the UBA, and said acidly: "Well, goddamn it, Mr. Winthrop, I *know* he wants to win ball games, that's *just the point!*" Then he turned back to his TV sets, where the Cels had a rally going in the ninth: a long belt up against the screen in right, scoring two runs, and that was the game, Cels 4, Keystones 3. Poor old Tim.

"I'm sorry, Fenn. I don't get you."

McCaffree sighed impatiently. "What if, Woody, we have passed, without knowing it, from a situation of sequential compounding into one of basic and finite yes-or-no survival, causing a shift of what you might call the equilibrium point, such that the old strategies, like winning ball games, sensible and proper within the old stochastic or recursive sets, are, under the new circumstances, *insane!*"

"Hmmm," said Woody Winthrop. Only word he was sure of was the last one. Above the television sets, electronic score boards, hooked directly to those of the separate ball parks, recorded the surface data of the games, blinking their messages in a slow burn, left to right. Partridge was throwing gopher balls and his Pastimer teammates were fielding like a bunch of bush-leaguers, turning what was supposed to be the game of the day, if not of the year—Knicks *vs.* the Patsies, with both teams once again tied for the league lead, Jock Casey pitching against Sam Partridge—into a circus. The Patsies' infield, supposed to be the UBA's greatest, had made four errors so far, and the Knicks were winning, 5–to–1, with another rally going in the eighth. The Pioneers had just lost to the Beaneaters, 8–to–4. Young Thornton Shadwell's third loss; Tim's boy just wasn't going to make it. Woody didn't know exactly why, but he felt things were not going well in the Association. Ever since that boy's death. Like the soul had gone out of it or something, as if Sycamore Flynn's Knicks had stolen it somehow and wouldn't give it back, or couldn't, and the whole balance of things had got thrown off. Feeling antiquated and stupid and disconnected, Woody sighed and said: "I don't know, Fenn. Maybe you're probably right."

But Fenn was talking to somebody on one of the squawk boxes and wasn't listening to Woody. In adjoining rooms, machinery, looking like big eyeless monsters conjured up from the depths, hummed and clicked, sucking up the information being fed to them from scorekeepers, scouts, official monitors, and even a set of special camera devices that McCaffree had invented to time runners, spy out jittery fielders, register variations between what the catchers called for and what the pitchers really threw, million different things. Made Woodrow Winthrop's old head spin. "You see, given this shift and the fact that it seems to be out of our hands, some built-in flaw or gap which doesn't allow us to cope with it directly," Fenn continued, apparently speaking to Woody again, though still studying the TV sets, "it would almost be better for the whole league if the players were all incompetent and irrational."

"Is that so?" said Woody.

"Mmm. The way things are going, we're apt to get a payoff *no*body wants." Young Chauncey O'Shea was at the plate for the Knicks with runners on base. Fenn asked for a close-up of O'Shea, then leaned forward to study his batting stance, grip on the handle.

Whenever Fenn did something like that, it made Woody wince, and he winced now, feeling instinctively sorry for O'Shea under that kind of scrutiny, though in fact he didn't even know the boy, only knew he was the one calling the pitches when young Rutherford got killed, and so had no reason certainly to feel any special warmth for the man. But Woody suffered the intrusion of all this machinery, this detailed information gathering, the dossiers, the intense pattern studies and close-ups, the projections, the cumulative files which Fenn called CUMS—in Woody's day that was a dirty word— didn't like it at all, found it suffocating and unfriendly, thought there were too many people playing a functional part without asking themselves what they were doing there. And now Fenn was even using the same methods to gauge and manipulate the political picture. Of course, even if people did start asking themselves about the roles they played, that wouldn't necessarily change things. And as Fenn always said: people'll get used to it in a few years and wonder how they ever got along without. "Besides, people are narcissistic: they *like* being studied and stared at." And you certainly had to hand it to Old Fenn, he never missed a trick. Agents operating inside the other two parties and at least one on every ball club, filing the data that Long Lew Lydell and the computers tabulated. He wondered what the payoff Fennimore was talking about could be, but he didn't worry too much about it, since he figured it couldn't concern him, and above all, he didn't want to risk getting put down again.

O'Shea doubled, scoring two runs. Fenn leaned back. Casey knocked the Patsies off, one-two-three, in the ninth, giving the Knicks a lopsided 7–to–1 win. "And there's not a goddamn thing I can do about it," Fennimore McCaffree said softly. Glumly, the seventh and eighth Chancellors of the Universal Baseball Association watched the League Standings Board suffer its daily transmutation.

TEAM	WON	LOST	PCT	GB
Knickerbockers	37	26	.587	–
Haymakers	36	27	.571	1
Pastime Club	36	27	.571	1
Pioneers	31	32	.492	6
Beaneaters	28	35	.444	9
Bridegrooms	28	35	.444	9
Excelsiors	28	35	.444	9
Keystones	28	35	.444	9

Disappointing. It was. Henry glanced back at the board, then left, pulling the door to. Down the black stairs he went, across the pale threshold and into the street, trying to forget about it, get his mind on a good meal. Surely he needed one, and moreover, Lou was right, he had to restore some order to his life, especially now. He'd just played sixty straight games, the most he'd ever done at a stretch: his kidneys ached, his neck hurt, and his eyes were so tired he could hardly see, yes, he needed this break, relax the mind, indulge the lower spheres, find some stability for himself, if he couldn't find it for the Association. But try as he could, he couldn't shake it off; discontent, like a dark improper bird hatched in his own injured breast, attended Henry Waugh on his Saturday night walk to Mitch's Bar and Grill.

He'd risen after dark last evening and had done nothing since but play the game. Normally, it took him about six weeks to play out a season, not counting the week or two it took to accomplish all the midwinter blue-season summarizing, analyzing, and record-keeping, but in these twenty-four hours he'd driven himself through fifteen days of play, sixty games, nearly a quarter of the season. To accomplish it, he'd had to hold his log entries to a minimum and finally leave off keeping statistics altogether, planning to catch up at the end of the season, if he still wanted to. For all Fenn McCaffree's pretense at efficiency, the truth was the books just were not being kept, and no one knew exactly anymore what was happening. The only exception was the pitching records, he had to keep up with those in order to know what Jock Casey was doing, for Casey had become, through his own peculiar intransigence, the key to the whole mess—cooler than ever, winning games, even dusting batters on occasion, now owning the fourth or fifth best ERA in the Association. And his Knick teammates were still hanging onto the league lead, while the Pioneers, losing eleven of their last fifteen games, had dropped out of the picture. Yes, the Spirit's E-R-A wasn't worth much, to be sure.

But what more could he do about it? Henry walked the dark streets weakly, possessed by impotence. Twenty-one games to go, how could he stop them? Rooney's pitching staff had got all unbalanced and was sure to fall apart sooner or later, the Patsies were stumbling all over themselves, and the Pioneers showed no signs of pulling out of their dive. The Knicks may have become the hunted, but there were no hunters. Henry had juggled the other seven teams' pitching schedules so as to pit the Knicks almost exclusively against Aces, had under one pretense or another—personal problems, minor illnesses, obscenity on the field—shaken up the Knick line-up, even briefly benching a couple Stars, and still they kept managing to win more than they lost. There was, in effect, as Fenn McCaffree would say, a hidden coalition structure, but no rules permitting correlated strategies, and worse, an almost total and necessary league ignorance of the way things truly stood. As for Casey, Henry had thrown him in at every worst moment, even sometimes tossed the dice in advance to make sure he was going to get hit before actually writing in his name—and somehow Casey had usually made the best of it. If he didn't know better, he'd suspect the dice of malevolence, rather than mere mindlessness. And it was Henry, not Casey, who was losing control.

Food smells alerted him: he'd nearly passed Mitch's by. Over his head, a three-phase neon arrow pointed the way to the quarry: through a door strung round with red lights, giving it a carbuncular effect. Lou was in the anteroom, peering out the window. "Henry!" he squeaked, and plunged forward like a giddy seal. "Come on! I was afraid you'd got lost! Did you have any trouble . . . ?"

Henry smiled, shook his friend's hand. "I'm starved," he said. "I just followed my nose."

They bundled in, warm odors assailing them gently, past a sign that read: *Go thy way and eat thy bread with joy!* Piped-in radio music floated over the kitchen noises, the whump of doors, rattle of cocktail shakers, the bubble and buzz of underwater voices. Walls in a lush green with gold sparkle, cedar wainscoting, soft glow throughout, yet at the same time, linoleum floors and tawdry leatherette booths. Frilly lamps at the tables like little flowers, massive paintings and prints of whaling ships and dead pheasants on the walls. Elegant bar of carved wood in the romantic style, but the tabletops were cheap speckly formica. Dark-suited business types were conferring in one booth, young kids necking in the next. Yet somehow it all hung together okay.

A plump little man, tuxedoed, bobbed up beside them: "Good evening, Mr. Engel. Two?" The owner, of course: Lou always knew the owner, wherever he went.

"Evening, Mr. Porter. This is my friend Mr. Waugh I've told you about." Mr. Mitch Porter, not quite smiling, surveying Henry's slack condition and obvious need, dipped his head in recognition of this wondrous encounter, then led them primly to a table in the center, underneath a pillar. A little like Frosty Young, but better mannered. Not a third baseman, though. Second maybe, like Frosty. Or a catcher. Yes, that was it, put him back behind the plate, guarding home. "He won't believe, you know, that the food's so, as good as I say, so he's finally come to find out for himself."

"I hope you won't be disappointed, Mr. Waugh," the owner said politely, discreetly nodding them into their places. He bestowed menus upon them with his right hand, his left discharging a practiced and imperial command kitchenward. Henry saw no one there to receive it, yet a moment later a waitress was headed their way with table linen and silverware. Mitch Porter knew he was good. Poise: no really great star was ever without it.

"Lou's kidding you, Mr. Porter," Henry assured him. "He's what they call in baseball a real swinger at the plate, and I have complete faith." The waitress, bellied over the table, spreading the fresh white linen as though preparing a marriage couch, smiled at that. The worm stirred . . . yes, balance, let the dark forces rise. Plop! plop! the napkins, and long silver instruments—the better to fork you with, my dear, as Willie O'Leary would say, but she was gone.

Henry picked up the menu to read it, but Lou had already pushed his aside, was leaning sideways in a bulky list to confer with Mitch Porter. "I was thinking about . . . the steaks," he said softly, as though making confession.

Mitch Porter gazed thoughtfully toward the kitchen, then around to be sure there were no spies, bowed slightly forward. "I'm just not entirely pleased with them this evening, Mr. Engel. They look good, but they're—I wouldn't tell anyone but you, Mr. Engel—but they seem cut a little too green from the tree, if you know what I mean." Lou, knowing well, inched forward, ears cocked for the word. "But the duck," Mr. Porter whispered, puckering his lips and touching them with the tips of two fingers and a thumb: a soft insinuating kiss blessed them and the hand opened like a blossom.

"Duck!" announced Lou firmly, leaning back.

"Me, too," said Henry.

"And before?"

"He makes a wonderful seafood cocktail, Henry."

"Okay by me."

"Two cocktails," beamed Mitch Porter. "And to drink?"

"Right now, I'd like an Old Fashioned," said Henry, having seen that the menu plugged them, and Mr. Porter smiled, raised his brows to Lou. Lou nodded. Mr. Porter slipped away then, passing unheard instructions to barman and waitresses: whump! gaped the kitchen doors, and swallowed him up.

Lou, following Henry's gaze, turned back and whispered: "He makes the duck himself!" The kitchen, having inhaled Mr. Mitch Porter, now exhaled a waitress, exiting in a handsome breech delivery, bearing aloft a tray heaped high with silver-canopied dishes. "Henry, your eyes look all bloodshot! What have you been doing?"

"Working." And though hard, not hard enough. He'd wanted to start Monday clean and fresh, his decision made, but he doubted now he could finish the season tomorrow.

"Are you still taking that extra work home, Henry?" Lou shook his head. "Just what I thought. You come dragging into the office at noon—you're gonna end up losing your steady job at DZ&Z just for the sake of a few extra dollars, it's not worth it, Henry. What do you wanna be a millionaire for? Who're you gonna leave it to?" Lou clucked disapprovingly as the drinks came. Who was he going to leave it to? The dark bird flapped in his breast again and beaked his throat. At another table, under a storm at sea, the youngsters blew kisses at each other over their plates, and across the way, a navy officer leaned over a young woman's bosom . . . "No, really, Henry—"

"What I do, I do because I want to," Henry said, and lifted his glass in a toast, then drank. In one corner, two old men played chess beside an aquarium of goldfish, and somehow neither they nor the fish seemed out of place. Maybe he could move his Association over here. Might rescue it. He smiled.

Lou twisted around to see what he was smiling at, saw the chinless cod-faced woman who slouched dumpily back of the cash register, under a pair of lovebirds, reading a movie magazine. "Mrs. Porter," he explained. "You wouldn't believe it, would you?"

"Of course, I would!" Henry laughed. "Couldn't be anyone else!" Lou laughed blankly, not getting it. An old hand came down and touched a crown, veered past it to elect a seahorse, white as death: it leaped forward, but currents carried it slantwise. To be good, a chess player, too, had to convert his field to the entire universe, himself the ruler of that private enclosure—though from a pawn's-eye view, of course, it wasn't an enclosure at all, but, infinitely, all there was. Henry enjoyed chess, but found it finally too Euclidian, too militant, ultimately irrational, and in spite of its precision, formless really—nameless motion.

Lou asked about the interview with Zifferblatt and Henry told him, all the while watching the chess players, the excited youngsters, all the paintings and dour Mrs. Porter, the people at the bar, the waitresses, that girl with the navy officer—who was he? seen him before . . . young Brock Rutherford Jr. maybe . . . "So when I told Ziff that the Greek god of commerce was a thief and led the dead to hell, Ziff said: 'Yeah? well, look what it got the Greeks, all they got's a few restaurants!' "

Lou wheezed with giggling, his round face pink with the thought of a foolish Zifferblatt. "Did he really say that, Henry?"

"No, I'm just kidding, Lou. To tell the truth, I don't know what either of us said, because I fell asleep."

Still giggling, but shaking his head at the same time, sipping the Old Fashioned, Lou seemed to find that harder to believe than the dialogue. "I couldn't fall asleep in front of Mr. Zifferblatt," he confessed, "if they gave me ether!"

Pink sea monsters, washed up on a shore of lettuce leaves and parsley, arrived, iced, their pungent sauce piercing through the present aroma of the Old Fashioneds' bitters like an arrow: *zingo!* right to the nose! and to the palate! terrific!

While the waitress was still at hand, Henry, munching a cherry, asked for another round of drinks, then with a wink at the lady, forked the earthly remains of a once-proud crustacean. The whiskey was having a wonderfully balsamic effect; he was glad he'd come. Lou, like any artist in confrontation with the raw stuff of his vocation, fell silent, but for barely audible mumbles of judgment or bliss. The waitress, under-belly apron white, floated by, deposited fresh drinks like a lay of eggs, then flipping her rosy tail, drifted on, starched apron strings waggling in her wake. Others watching her, too. That officer, even while sounding other knees and thighs below the table. One's not enough for him. Never is. What was the mechanism? Maybe those little buggers had eyes, after all: we got that one already, dad—move on! Long Lew apologizing to Fanny McCaffree: *I'd* like to get married, Fanny, it's a wonderful idea, but what am I gonna do with *this?* Holding up that old sea serpent that dragged him under every time.

Impotent? not really. But sometimes total power was worse. Message of the Legalists: without law, power lost its shape. That was what kept Casey proud: born into a going system, he judged himself by it, failed to look beyond, look back: who said three strikes made an out? Supposing he just shipped Casey to the minors and to hell with the rules? He could at that. If he wanted to. Could explain it in the Book. It wasn't impotence. Still, it might cause trouble. What trouble? The players . . . What players? *Some* kind of limit there, all right, now that he thought about it. He might smash their resistance, but he couldn't help *feeling* that resistance all the same. Their? mine; it was all the same.

Brock Rutherford II, who had failed in the UBA, was making it in the back booth of Mitch's, having gotten his pitching fist well under a sea-blue skirt. The mystic ship of life, sail on, sail on! Elsewhere, a black queen flew south, answered by a coalition of bishops. On a far wall, red-coated horsemen leaped hedges in pursuit of . . . of something, a fox maybe, just a dark blur on the canvas there; maybe it was poor Sycamore Flynn. The youngsters beneath the raging sea had themselves grown suddenly still, eyes locked, oblivious to everything, hands chastely gripping napkins, lips meeting—Mr. Mitch Porter materialized: with his left, he ordered the youngsters out, while his right hand summoned the waitress with the bill. Down the aisle plowed her proud white breast, then back up again, outstrutting the young cock, who left doubled over his arrowing desire, face lit with shame and anticipation. Mr. Porter apparently didn't notice the navy officer who, while chatting amiably above table, had bared everything beneath. Matter of interpretation, no doubt. And why haven't you ever married, Henry? Who asked that? Lou? Henry glanced up, but Lou was ingesting neat brown slabs of duck, a jewel of orange rind glistening on his plump chin. It was really good, all right, had a wild original taste all its own, a genuine creation: Mitch Porter could play on anybody's team. Hall of Fame.

Now he passed with a bottle of rosé on ice. With a whirling flourish of wrist and fingers, he conjured out the cork, poured a finger into each of their glasses. They tasted: "Mmm, good!" said Lou. "But—?"

"My pleasure," said Mr. Porter with a slight bow, and filled their glasses, then disappeared before they could really thank him.

"Gee, that was nice, wasn't it, Henry?"

"Mmm. Great duck, too."

"I told you."

The waitress pecked disparagingly in the gravel of small coins left her by the banished teen-agers, then click-click-clicked back up the aisle with dirty dishes, swishing her ample tail; the officer, still fishing, watched benignly. The gaze of his young prey, however, fell on Henry; she started, flushed, pushed the officer's hand out, then, feathers ruffled, pranced off to the ladies' room, the door of which, Henry noticed, was upholstered in the same cheap leatherette as the booths. Left-over piece. The officer, grinning, said something to the waitress. Jauntily, she arched her hips, peeked back over her shoulder at her apron strings, flicked one hand loose-wristed at the officer—he laughed aloud—and switched on back to the kitchen, marvelously pleased with herself.

Why? Maybe it was Hettie who asked. Or Mitch Porter, dropping by on the quarter hour to receive, solemnly, their homage. Or Mrs. Mitch, yawning cavernously over her movie magazine. Yes, young Brock was handsome, elegant in his way, but it was easy to see that in a real ball game he just didn't have it. Something vital missing. How would his son—Henry assumed it would be a boy—turn out? Grandpa's genes dominating probably, and that was okay, he'd need some of that raw power, hopefully a touch of his uncle's grace—and on the mother's side? Henry watched her emerge from the ladies' room, handbag clutched front and center. She fired one angry glance Henry's way, then homed for the officer; too much temper and a little baggy in the britches. Have to wait and see. Might be worth twenty more seasons just to find out. A man like Brock Jr., with nothing else to do, could marry; Henry couldn't. That was all. A family, beautiful wife tender and loving, children with their special hurts and happinesses: great comfort, great pleasure. But Henry had chosen the loner's life, the general pain, because . . . because . . . he couldn't help himself.

Aw, shee-*it* now! cracked old Pappy Rooney, bachelor himself but suitor of no pain, except that which served to prove to him he lived still. Some like it, some don't. Rooney pinched the lady's bottom for luck, drew a dark ace in the hole: That's it! he chortled, *that's* what they're for!

"Henry, if you don't mind my saying so, I, well, I've noticed you've been talking to yourself sort of lately sometimes . . ."

Henry gazed up at the plump perspiring face of his friend, now anointed with orange sauce. "I've been talking to myself all my life," he said, and crossed his knife and fork on the plate.

The waitress, clearing, stretched out over their table, hips outthrust, full breasts aquiver—wonderful how she did that, excessive but communicative, style all her own. Willie O'Leary tucked a toothpick in his teeth, and lifting his right hand in a benediction upon that bosom, said: "When he stretched forth his hand, the mountains trembled." And, reflexively, they did.

"Oh, you!" the waitress said, cuffing him gently with a damp hand, and O'Leary tweaked a rib. Abdomen muscles flexed, bouncing her back off the table; she grinned, flicked her tail to his view—there was an instant, just time for a pinch, but this was Mitch's, after all, not Jake's, and O'Leary's hand in motion abruptly stopped and its fingers snapped—the waitress flinched, good as the real thing, then giggling to herself, swished kitchenward with dishes.

"Why haven't you never got married, Henry?" Lou asked, cheeks brightly flushed from such proximity to license. Maybe it had been Lou asking all the time.

"I don't know, never thought about it much," Henry lied. "Probably the same reasons you didn't want to."

"Didn't *want* to!" After big meals, Lou's squeaky voice mellowed. A kind of coo. You could hardly hear it. Lou scrubbed his face with a napkin, pressed forward. "Henry, I'd get married tomorrow, if I knew where to start. You always know how to say the right thing, but me—Henry, I've never even gone, you know, on a, out with a . . ." Yes, it was Holly Tibbett, all right, in the flushed and floundering flesh. Up from the ashes, a magical event.

"Shall we start then with the waitress?" O'Leary suggested. Willie was modestly but marvelously drunk, while back of the pillar, Gabe and Frosty and the boys were egging him on. They took Holly up to Molly . . . He signaled.

"*No!*" gasped Holly, looking for some place to run, but too full to squeeze out.

O'Leary saw the others splitting their sides, but with effort kept a straight face, which seeing, the approaching waitress grinned at broadly. In on it. In on everything. They took Holly up to Molly/And she said she'd like, by golly/To eat a hot tamale in the shower . . . Willie O'Leary lit up one of Holly's cigars, and admiring a navel-high splotch of shrimp sauce on the white face of the moon, said: "Molly, my girl, what can we do, you and I, to relieve a poor lad in direst distress?"

"A lad . . . ?" A little slow; she was.

"Yes, our friend here, the vice-president in charge of talent-testing for All-American Symphonies Consolidated; he's on the quest of a respectable and compassionate—and of course talented—lady companion to go, uh, round the world with him on an unlimited expense account, and who do you think we can find for him?" The brogue was a little rusty, but he saw she liked the music of it.

"Who, ya mean Mr. Engel here?" Molly said. "Ya must be kiddin'!" Slow as they come.

Henry grinned. "Sure, I'm kiddin'," he said. They all knew Holly wherever he went, too—the backside of shyness. O'Leary winked. "He's really the president."

She smiled, rubbing her nose with one hand, stroking her big round butt with the other, looked down on poor Lou, near to tears with shame and desire. Well, that tamale was a folly /For melancholy Holly/Cause that dolly stole his jolly little flower . . . "Get me back in time for work Monday?" she asked.

Holly, the crimson flush congealing suddenly into brilliant splotches, giggled hopelessly. The boys, concealed, whooped it up.

"So, what'll it be, boss?" O'Leary asked, and blew smoke on the excited birds that fluttered around them. "Round the world or two lemon sherbets?"

"Same for me!" Holly squeaked, and that made them all laugh.

"And coffee," said Henry, shifting to make room in his

pant leg for the old rahab who rose and hungered in his lap.

Molly winked gaily at O'Leary and left them. Slow, but a heart of gold, sure as sin.

"Henry! you must be drunk!" Lou gasped, reduced to a hoarse squawk.

"I am feeling pretty good," Henry admitted. Felt light, head swimming a little, shedding his duties like an old skin, rising up . . . "Glad I came."

Mitch Porter, spying a favored customer in discomfort, bobbed up once more to inquire into their well being and was reassured, but Henry was chastised with a brief suspicious squint, and Molly, too, received ample admonitions. No funny business when she brought the sherbets, but Lou went scarlet again just the same. Henry, watching, realized: why, he loves that girl. Simple as that. How many did Holly love in truth, and which did he, going out with that mushroom that bulged in his brain, dream of? Just one, maybe. It was often like that. The naval officer, Henry observed, had gone, the lady as well. Over their empty booth, ducks rose from a lake in alarm—shot rang out, feathers flew, and that pretty one, head reared: *ahh!* always glorious. Second-rate ballplayer, slack-waisted backstop: still glorious. "Let's go to Jake's."

"Where?"

"Bar I know."

The bill appeared, and then Mr. Mitch Porter, kindly assisting with coats. Henry found coins approximating a seventh of the bill, which he lay beside the saucer, but Lou, impulsively, plunged an extra dollar to the pot. The waitress, arriving too late to catch more than a glimpse of the great red-necked seal, fleeing cashierward, her penguin boss in stubby-legged pursuit, still trying to help with the coat, like a mating pair, surprised, trying to run away still hooked up, gathered up the offering with bemused care. "He's a nice man," Henry said.

"He is," said she.

At the cash register, Lou hesitated, dropping bills all over the floor, but Gus Maloney, stoked up, paid. Party's money and none a my own. "More where that came from." Old Gus, one of the great old-timers, and a classic case of the single inscrutable ego rising up to have his own way at all costs. Henry never liked him but he couldn't stop him. He'd even finally grown fond of the corrupt old bastard. Big Daddy Boggler.

They went out, huddled around cigars—Good evening, Mr. Waugh! Good evening, Mr. Engel! Night now! Thanks again! Come again soon! We shall! We shall!—and found the night had chilled a bit. Hot-stove league weather.

"Winter's coming on," Lou remarked.

"Seems like it." Would there be a winter? Probably. He'd want to tie up all loose ends. But why? once it was over, it was over, wasn't it? Well, curiosity. See if Thornton Shadwell made it into the big leagues or not. What Stars and Aces fell and who came up to take their places. Whether or not Swanee Law set those records he was aiming at: ho ho! what a surprise for that big arrogant fart to have history end as soon as he made it! He saw old Swanee's jaw set into the storm: "Ah ain't quittin'!"

"Quitting what, Henry?"

"Nothing, it's a line from a song," Henry alibied. "I was trying to think of it, just remembered it."

"Henry, you listen now, you have to stop that extra work, it's—"

"It's not really work, Lou. It's a game."

"A game?"

"A baseball game I play with dice."

"A baseball game!" Lou mulled that over. "Mmm." Which meant a certain dim light was beginning to dawn. "But then . . . ?" And now the history of the last few weeks. "With dice . . ." Reflecting on the bloodshot eyes, the office absences. "Is that really what . . . ?"

"Like to see it?"

"Well, I . . . sure! I mean, is it something, uh, something two can . . . ?"

"I don't see why not. Why don't you drop over tomorrow night? Pick up a pizza on the way. I've got plenty of beer."

"Sure!" More enthusiasm now. Two could. Yes, this might make it work again. And while Lou was learning it, suppose he had the Knickerbockers . . . might give the others just the edge they needed. "Why don't we go to the movies first, and then—"

"Well, no, thanks, Lou. I've got to clean the place up a little." That's right, Lou always went to the movies on Sundays.

"Oh, I don't care how things look, Henry. Come on, we'll—"

"No, I'm not much of a moviegoer, Lou." Had to be careful. Couldn't let it degenerate into nothing more than a social event.

"I, I didn't know you kept up with baseball, Henry, how . . . ?"

"I don't."

"But . . . ?"

"Oh, sometimes I like to read about it. But the real action was over a century ago. It's a bore now."

"You don't go to games, real ones?"

"Not for years now. The first game I saw, Lou, the league's best pitcher that year threw a three-hit shutout. His own team got only four hits, but three were in one inning, and they won, 2–to–0. Fantastic game. And I nearly fell asleep. I kept going back for a while. There were things about the games I liked. The crowds, for example. I felt like I was part of something there, you know, like in church, except it was more *real* than any church, and I joined in in the score-keeping, the hollering, the eating of hot dogs and drinking of Cokes and beer, and for a while I even had the funny idea that ball stadiums and not European churches were the real American holy places." Formulas for energy configurations where city boys came to see their country origins dramatized, some old lost fabric of unity . . . act that never quite came off. "But I would leave a game, elbowing out with all the others, and feel a kind of fear that I could so misuse my life; what was the matter with me, that I could spend unhappy hours at a ball park, leave, and yet come back again? Then, a couple days later, at home, I would pick up my scoreboard. Suddenly, what was dead had life, what was wearisome became stirring, beautiful, unbelievably real . . ."

"But why did you stop . . . ?"

"I found out the scorecards were enough. I didn't need the games."

Lou puffed his cigar and pondered that. "Did you ever want to be, you know, like a ballplayer, Henry?"

"I don't think so. Oh, sometimes I wished I could do something heroic, something tremendous and legendary, a testing of the very limits of the record systems, something that gave the sportswriters heart attacks at the very contemplation of what was happening. But, no, I never wanted to be just an ordinary ballplayer, stooping for grounders and waiting out bad balls. I never even wanted to be a manager. Of course, being manager of every team in the league at once, that might not be so bad."

"Oh, I don't think they'd let you, Henry."

"No, you're right," Henry smiled, "they probably wouldn't let me. Here we are."

Lou squinted at the neon light. "Pete's. I thought you said Jake's."

"Goes by both names."

"Evening, Mr. Waugh."

"Evening, Jake." Hettie over there with some guy. Too late. Too damn late. At the bar, he said: "My friend Lou Engel, Pete."

"Always pleased," said Pete, and Lou agreed.

"Usual for me, Jake," Henry said, though the night fell short of the celebrative. Still, a great meal like that . . .

Pete reached for the bottle, and Lou, seeing it, nodded a second. Pete seemed more reserved tonight than usual. Well, no doubt for good reason. Hettie, too, had cast a suspicious glance his way. The guy she was with was a younger man, but not all that young. Fortyish. Seedy. Ruddy. Farmer type. But younger all the same, admit it. Age. It got them all. Began at thirty, a little slower, harder to steal, harder to stretch that long ball into a triple. Injuries tended to be more serious. A little slower afoot out in the field. The slowdown accelerated at thirty-five. All of it worked into the charts. It was something the players had to live with. Some of them understood it, accepted it, developed sinkers and sliders as their fast ball slowed, learned new positions, later became coaches, managers, even club owners, as they aged. Others fought against it, kept trying to act the bright young star. Frosty Young was like that. Usually made the end, when it came, as it always did, more grotesque. Frosty finally fractured a hip trying to steal one base too many, five years too late. He later became an umpire, a good one, but he still carried a bitter chip around, as though somehow he'd been particularly and uniquely condemned to grow old. That kind of romantic sourness tended to rub Henry the wrong way, but he understood it. In fact, some wonderful league personalities needed this excess to complete their characters. What would the UBA be if they were all Brock Rutherfords or Jake Bradleys?

Jake now dropped by to fill them up again, and Henry said: "I don't remember much of what happened the other night, Pete, but I hope I didn't make too big a fool of myself."

"Oh no, Mr. Waugh," said Pete, but his face was momentarily darkened by what could only have been a grim remembrance of it. "We all have to go on a bender from time to time." He hesitated, then smiled. "Enjoyed that song about what's-his-name with the long, you know . . ."

"Long Lew and Fanny. Was I singing?"

"Oh yes." Again he smiled, winked at Lou. "More or less."

They all laughed together, though Lou clearly had only the merest inkling as to what it was all about, and that inkling was enough to make him give Henry a funny look. Well, now it would be forgotten, Henry supposed. After all, as best he could figure, he'd dropped over a hundred dollars in here that night, so Pete couldn't be too sore about it.

One of Jake's cats curled by Hettie's leg, and she reached down to stroke it. Her suitor leaned away, focusing badly, signaled for another round. A fire-red tie, pinked cheeks, ruby nose, and sparse red hair on a freckly pate made him look like he was about to boil over. Then, as though pulled by some magnetic force, they drew together again, hands in each other's thighs.

Who could do it for him? O'Leary maybe. Or young Thornton Shadwell; still a virgin probably. Or Mighty Mel, the Terrible Truncheon. No, Trench was having a bad time, probably worrying too much to get it up. Flenched Trench. Henry stared into his snifter, saw the bar and all its people squeezed into its amber sphere, lights ablaze on it, and he himself—he looked away. How about Hamilton Craft? Big rebound, must be feeling good. Or maybe . . . "Would you like to go with that one over there?"

Jolted Lou at least six inches off his barstool. "Not so loud, Henry!" he choked.

"How about it?"

Lou didn't even look, just stuck his nose in his snifter. "Not, uh, not my type, I guess."

"Not your type! Why, she's *everybody's* type, Lou!"

Lou sipped cognac oppressedly.

"Then you don't mind if I . . . ?"

"Oh no, *no!*" Lou squeaked. "Don't mind me!"

The suitor, withdrawing momentarily from her valleys, pitched around and weaved away, heaved hotly past them, bruised a table, and disappeared through a door in the rear. Sack in the back. No, not here, not really, just a font or two; Pete didn't care for the subtler needs.

"Evenin', ma'am! Whatcha say we git us up a bawl game!"

"*Henry! Ssshh!* Cantcha see I'm busy?"

"Ain't no batter up there, baby. He cain't even *find* you!"

"Maybe not, but it's you he'd better not find here when he comes back, or he'll pop a rib!"

"Aw, he kin wait. Put him off till tuhmorra, baby. Ah need you *tonight!*"

She softened, trying to figure his pitch. "That boy come back from the dead, Henry?"

He winced, but was able to hang in there. "More'n one pitcher in this here bawl game, lady." He unfolded a handful of twenties to widen her sleepy eyes, but it was her knees opened apart instead.

"Well, let's get out before he comes back," Hettie hissed.

Henry nodded a farewell to Lou. "Tomorrow night."

He shouldered out behind her, feeling good and mean. Earthy. Crude, in fact. Won't be the same, he realized. No magic. But it had its good side. Right to the point, no fancy stuff. In and out, high and low. Just rear back and burn it in.

NOT once, in the Universal Baseball Association's fifty-six long seasons of play, had its proprietor plunged so close to self-disgust, felt so much like giving it up, a life misused, an old man playing with a child's toy; he felt somehow like an adolescent caught masturbating. Year LVI, in spite of its new crop of rookies, in spite of the excitement of a new team's imminent rise to power, in spite of the records being set and the giants being toppled and that boy being killed, was a complete bore. Or so it seemed as he stared out his kitchen window on a world going to winter that Sunday afternoon. Lou was coming soon. He was afraid, but he was glad, too. Lou could save it. Or him from the game. He felt waterlogged with it. He'd played too much, too hard, since Damon died. Have to ease up. He considered writing in the Book for a while, but the weariness of it paralyzed him. So he just stood and stared.

Bad start that morning. Awake to a bed full of Hettie's odors, broken dreams about a zoo or a circus or something, all too pertinent. "That Swanee's really a good old guy," she said, getting up with an old lady's grunt, then commenced a whinnying laugh that mutated into a phlegmy cough. But he didn't feel like Swanee Law, felt more like old Woody Winthrop, senile and gravebent, or luckless Mel Trench, down in the cellar and fat in the head. Hettie padded out and into the bathroom. She'd be in there a while, he knew, so he allowed himself to doze off again. Dreamt he was in some far-off impossible place. Italy, maybe. Or Spain. It seemed like he'd been telling Lou about Hettie, how good she was, the old brag, but now they were only admiring the countryside. Soft rolling hills, vineyards, wooded valleys, blue river trickling by, stone farmhouses, almond trees in blossom. You're only kidding yourself, somebody said, didn't seem to be Lou, but might have been. Anyway, he ignored it. Distantly, a mule hitched to a two-wheeled cart creaked up a hillside, a man walking beside. It was steep, and sometimes the mule slipped backwards or stopped altogether. Then Henry and whoever was with him, if somebody still was, were helping to push. It was hard work and they were getting nowhere. If only I had an ass, the farmer said. It was true, there wasn't any animal, he'd been mistaken. If you can't find one, Henry told him, make one. He'd meant it as a dirty joke, but the man didn't get it, just stared at him blankly. Henry tried to explain, he changed it to: Did you say *an* ass or *some* ass? but there was no communication. Language problem. He felt crude and stupid, like a beast himself. A great weight pressed down on him and he was thinking, as Hettie reached under the blankets to pinch his butt a lot harder than she needed to, that today would be the hardest day of all.

He dressed and went out for sweet rolls, while Hettie made coffee. Returning, he opened the door just in time to catch her in the middle of an enormous bovine yawn, soft neck flesh folded and teeth showing their gaps. Her face wrinkled into the agony of suppressing it, and she asked: "Cold out?"

He yawned himself, unable to hold back the reflex, and replied: "Pretty cold."

Sometimes she made the bed of a morning and straightened up the room a bit, but a glance in there showed him only the rude disorder of old. He heard himself asking himself: why won't someone help? She poked sleepily into the package he'd brought, and said: "They look good." She shoved back the papers on the kitchen table and put the rolls there.

"Careful! My work . . .!"

"Just a corner, Henry."

They sat there at the cleared corner, taking rolls and coffee, used to each other and therefore comfortable, but not especially cheered by the other's presence. Conversation openings occurred to him. He projected them out. Some would lead back to the bed, some to the door, some just in circles. On occasion, his eye fell on the Association and he felt depressed, not so much by Hettie's thoughtless rumple of it, as by the dishevel his own haste yesterday had created. Take a good while to get it all straightened out. Couple weeks just to get the data posted. More work than it was worth.

"I think I'll go to church," Hettie announced.

"Which one do you go to?" he asked, hardly caring.

"Don't matter. First one I come to." She sighed, spraying crumbs.

"Absolve your sins?" he asked, feeling a little contentious, but meaning no sarcasm.

"Sins? No, I ain't got any feelings about that," she said. "I just want a place where I can go and mope in company without bothering nobody." She stared glumly into her coffee at the brown reflection of herself. "Let's face it, I'm getting old and ugly, Henry."

"Listen, Hettie," he said. He dug in the billfold, found another twenty. "Here. Go buy a new hat or something. Flowers on it."

"Flowers are for spring," she argued.

"Well, old dry leaves then. Anything. A new girdle or some fancy drawers, I don't care. I just want to see you happy."

She smiled, patted his hand gently. "Ain't that easy," she said. "But thanks, Henry. That's nice." She tucked the bill in her handbag. Putting the bag back on the table, her eyes fell on the dice. She stared at them quizzically. She glanced up at the Team Standings Board, at the bronze Hall of Fame plaques, at the bookshelves, adding machine, heap of papers full of names on the table. "What's these for? You a gambler, Henry?"

"Sort of." Caught him by surprise.

"I don't get it. Whadda dice got to do with your work?"

"Well, in a way," he said recklessly, "they're my employer." He realized his hands were sweating.

"I still don't get it." She turned an inquisitive head-tilted pressed-lips stare on him.

He sighed. "It's a game, Hettie. The baseball—not a real job in the plain sense."

She blinked. And then she laughed. Opened her baggy jaws and whooped. "A game!" She looked back at the table, a light dawning. "You mean . . .? Then that's . . .! Hey!" She jumped up to paw heedlessly through the papers. "I'll bet old what's his name, Swanee's here, ain't he?" She cackled, rummaging and clawing. "Lookit these names! We can have a *orgy*, Henry!" Her laughter tore clean through him. She turned on him and tweaked his nose: "Henry, you're a complete nut!" Laughing, grinning, she looked down on him, sighed. "But you're awful sweet, just the same." She leaned down and deposited a spongy sour-sweet kiss on his forehead.

He watched her pull her wraps on, unable to rise from his chair. "Come on!" she laughed. "Don't take it so hard, I'm only kiddin'!" She tongued a wad of sweet roll out of one of the gaps in her teeth and, standing in her coat, took a final sip of coffee. "Anyway, who ain't crazy? I sure ain't got no sense!" She stared out the window, preparing herself, then turned back to him. "Listen, ain't every man can still please a woman old as you are, Henry." Everything she said was wrong. Just, maybe, but merciless. All he could do was sit there, dumbly taking it. Now she paused thoughtfully, then dredged up from last night's blowzy doubleheader to drop horribly in the morning kitchen: "*Ah'm pitchin' to ya, baby!*" And, head thrown back, yakyakked doorward.

When she realized he wasn't following her, she turned. "Come on, Henry, say good-bye." He only stared. Ugly and old. She was. They were. Her smile faded. "Don't be a sorehead. We had a good time, didn't we? I don't wanna leave without . . ." She meant the benedictive slap on her bottom. She always thanked him for it, said if a man didn't give her one on the way out, she always felt somehow she'd failed. "Henry, I'm sorry, I didn't mean . . ." He shook his head. Suddenly, astonishingly, she burst into tears. "*Ah, go to hell, you loony bastard!*" she cried. She dug agitatedly in her purse, pulled out his money, and, hands shaking, threw it into the room, then, still bawling, slammed out the door and down the stairs. He heard her heels smacking down the wooden stairs and scrape-clicking out into the world, and for a long time he just sat there.

Then, mechanically, he cleared the breakfast away, re-ordered all the papers, and began, once more, to play the game. Now, at sunset, it was four full series, twelve days of play, forty-eight ball games later. He didn't remember the scores or who had played. He knew the Knickerbockers had lost every game but the first one, he'd seen to that, but the rest of it was just so many throws of the dice. He was destroying the Association, he knew that now. He'd kept no records, hadn't even logged a single entry in the Book. Didn't know if all the players had their required at-bats or innings-pitched, didn't know who was hitting and who wasn't, didn't know if any pitchers were running over the legal limit of innings-pitched, didn't even give a damn who was winning the pennant. He'd been obsessed with a single idea: to bring Casey and the Knicks to their knees, see them drop behind the Pioneers in the standings, if only for a day. But, in mocking irony, the more he crushed the Knicks, the more the Pioneers fell away. He tried to reach them, Bancroft especially, tried to find out what was the matter, but it was strangely as though they were running from him, afraid of his plan, seeing it for what it was: the stupid mania of a sentimental old fool. And now they'd run as far as they could run . . .

TEAM	WON	LOST	PCT	GB
Pastime Club	44	31	.587	–
Haymakers	43	32	.573	1
Knickerbockers	38	37	.507	6
Beaneaters	37	38	.493	7
Keystones	37	38	.493	7
Bridegrooms	34	41	.453	10
Excelsiors	34	41	.453	10
Pioneers	33	42	.440	11

Bump up against the door! "Henry!" Suddenly afraid: a mistake! "It's *hot*, Henry!" *Whump whump!*

Take it easy, he cautioned himself, but his heart was beating wildly when he opened the door. Lou plummeted into the room bearing garlicky perfumes and a great disk of wrapped pizza. "It's dripping!" he cried and made for the kitchen table.

"*No!*" Henry cried. "*The game!*" He grabbed Lou's elbow roughly, pulled him up short. "Here! the stove!" He swept away the coffee pot as Lou brought the platter swooping down.

"*Whoo!*" gasped Lou. He looked at his dripping hands, then around the kitchen for something to—

"Here, wash in the sink there," Henry said. "I'll get soap and a towel."

In the bathroom, he dropped the soap. Why was he so nervous? Lou alone in there, careening around, he could do anything. "It's a good one, Henry!" Lou called.

Lou charged forward to meet him halfway, dripping water. Henry lunged forward, bound Lou's hands in the towel. Lou's eyebrows arched in astonishment. "Henry, is something . . . ?"

"No!" Henry forced a loose laugh. "It's just that I was dozing sort of when you came, and you know how a sudden noise can make you jump, I'm still sort of . . ."

"Oh," Lou smiled. "I'm sorry, Henry, only it was hot and—"

"Say, it does look good!" Henry said, unwrapping it. Oregano and burnt cheese odors rose up and pleased him greatly. Must be hungry at that. Nothing since those sweet rolls. "Do you want to play a round of the game first, or . . . ?"

" Better eat it while it's hot," said Lou, looking for a place to throw his overcoat. Henry reached forward, but too late.

The coat went sailing over the back of a chair, sent a hurricane ripping through the league on the table. Lou leaned hugely over the pizza to breathe it in, eyes tracing its contours, judging its parts, studying its limits, as though deciphering a treasure map. "Boyoboy! Am I hungry!"

"I'll get a knife."

"Where'll we . . . ?" Again his eye fell on the table. "Do you think we can make a space?"

"I've got it all set up," Henry said. "Do you mind using a couple extra chairs for tables instead?"

"No!" he smiled, rubbing his hands. "Getting cold out," he remarked, "but it's good for the appetite."

Henry sliced the pizza into segments, obeying its special geography. Oils and juices oozed and bubbled. Herbs spackled the surface. A rich one with onions, sausage, mushrooms and a St. Andrew's cross of pepperonis. Lou Engel: the ubiquitous special customer. He placed half of it on the middle chair arranged by Lou, opened beers. "Ah!" said Lou, reaching for a slice. "Mmm!" said Henry, sinking his teeth in. They both laughed slyly, chewed appreciatively, drank beer, ate some more. "Great!" "Mmm!" "Feast!" "World of flavors!" "A symphony!" "Ha ha!" "Banquet, Henry!" "Mmm!" "Should've bought two or three." "Still another half." "I'm ready!" "More beer?" "You bet!" "Work of art!" "You said it!" "Out of this world, Lou!" "Those mushrooms—mmm! Can't stop!" "Why try? Be merciless!" "Onions, too—sweet!" "Paradise!" "Mmm, that's right—wonder if Adam and Eve could get pizza?" "If they couldn't, Lou, they were right in getting out!" "Ha ha! you (licking fingers) said it! Is there (tipping back to drain)—ah!—any more beer?" "Lots of it!"

It was a large pizza, enormous in fact, Henry had never

seen one as big, and as they neared the end of it, they ate more slowly, drank more steadily. Should get to the game, but an animal satisfaction was on him like a thick blanket, and it seemed criminal even to move. It was Lou, in fact, who brought it up: "What's that up there on the wall, Henry?"

"The Team Standings Board. It shows where the teams are. I made it myself."

"The teams?"

"Well, it takes a little while to explain, Lou." He belched, drank beer, trying to remember how it was he'd practiced it. For one thing, he hadn't meant to begin with the Team Standings Board. "See, the game, well, it's a whole baseball league. Eight teams. Rosters, twenty-one guys—"

"Guys?"

"Players. Names. All the teams play each other and I keep the—"

Lou looked disappointed. "I thought this was a game that two could play, you know, like pinochle or Monopoly or something."

"No reason why not. You take one team and I take another."

"Okay," he said, popping suddenly up out of his chair like a blimp cut loose. "Let's go! Batter up!"

"You sure you don't want to know more about the . . . the rules?"

"I'll pick it up as we go along." At the table, he stared down on the heaps of paper, as though not quite perceiving what all that had to do with a mere game.

Henry washed at the sink, feeling uneasy. It was the way he wanted it, wasn't it? Not exactly: inexperience was one thing, complete and disinterested ignorance another. "Don't you want to wash your hands?"

"They're all right." Lou wiped them absently on his pants. He'd found the different charts and was shuffling through them.

"They're not as complicated as they look," Henry said with a weak laugh, drying his hands.

"I hope not." Lou picked up the dice, fingered them, then tossed them down. He searched the chart. "*S if PR/LO; Others Ret S 1B.*" He scratched his head, looked down at the dice.

"That's the special chart for stealing second base," Henry explained. "If the runner trying to steal is a pinch runner or the lead-off man in the line-up, he makes it. Otherwise, he returns safe to first. Here, these are the charts for—"

"I don't know if I'm going to be able to figure all this out, Henry," said Lou frankly. He seemed ready to drop the project, but instead he sat down and began patiently to read more of the charts. He rolled again, compared the result on the different charts. "How do you know which one to use?" he complained.

"Well, see, there's nine charts because there are six different player categories. A pitcher can be an Ace or a Rookie or a Regular, and so can a hitter. I mean, he can be a Star—"

"How do you know that?" Lou was staring at him as though to say he must be kidding.

"There's a mark by his name. The Rookies come up, well, see, each year—"

"Year?"

"I'll explain that, Lou. Just wait a minute. Each year, at the end, the eight pitchers with the worst earned-run averages get retired or sent to the minors—they can come back—sometimes, I mean, if they're not too old—"

"Too old!" Lou blinked. "You know how old . . . ?"

"There's a chart for that, see . . . here it is. That's for

Rookies when they come up, tells how old they are. When they're forty, they have to quit, or before if they drop into the twenty bottom batters or eight bottom pitchers—I mean, unless they're still a Star or an Ace at forty—" He could see Lou wasn't with him any more. "Look, don't worry about that part of it now. There's three kinds of batters, three kinds of pitchers. Rookies have a few advantages over Regulars, and Stars and Aces have advantages over Rookies. So there's nine charts, one for every possible combination, Ace-to-Star, Ace-to-Rookie, Ace-to-Regular, and so on, for the Rookie and Regular pitchers. Anyway, pretty soon you get it all memorized and you don't have to worry about this part of it."

"Memorized! You know all this stuff by heart, Henry?" Lou squeaked.

"Most of it."

Lou shook his head. "Where's the playing board?" he asked.

"Well, you sort of have to imagine it," Henry said. "I used to have a mock-up of a ball park, but it only got in the way."

Lou stared gloomily at the heap of papers. "Well, let's see what happens." He looked up at the Team Standings Board. "Who am I?"

"The next game is between the Knickerbockers and the Pioneers. It just happens that way."

"You mean that team at the bottom? Why don't we play with those two at the top? Looks like more fun."

"It isn't just one game, Lou. It's a whole season. Each team plays eighty-four games. There's an official schedule, just like in the big leagues. We're at the seventy-fifth round of games, and they've all been played but one, and so it's the Pioneers against the Knicks."

Lou shrugged and smiled generously. Forcing it, though. "I don't care. Who've I got?"

"You can have the Knicks." Twinge of guilt, but he shook it off. Poor Flynn buffeted by a fat confusion. Henry brought out the scorecard, the line-ups already filled in.

PIONEERS

2B Toby Ramsey (Rookie)
LF Grammercy Locke
3B Hatrack Hines (Star)
CF Witness York (Star)
RF Stan Patterson (Star)
C Royce Ingram (Star)
SS Lance Wilder
1B Goodman James
P Mickey Halifax (Ace)

KNICKERBOCKERS

SS Scat Batkin (Rookie)
2B McAllister Weeks
1B Matt Garrison (Star)
CF Biff Baldwin (Star)
RF Walt McCamish (Star)
LF Archie Moon
C Chauncey O'Shea (Rookie)
3B Galen Musgraves
P Jock Casey (Rookie)

"These are the teams, and here's the roster with the rest of your players, in case you want to make substitutions or anything."

Lou admired the scoresheets. "Say, these are nice. Where do you buy them?"

"I have them printed."

"Aha! Those trips to the printer!"

"Yes." Henry laughed sheepishly. Had Lou come to play the game, he wondered, or only to smoke him out? Have to be careful. He sat down beside Lou, rearranged the charts so Lou could see them all, pointed out the differences between them. "These here are for special strategy plays or when there's an error or injury or something, and these are the ones we use most of the time. We only need six of the nine, since we have an Ace and a Rookie pitching." He felt miles away somehow.

"Aha!" Lou said, studying the scorecard. "So that's what this R's for by my pitcher?"

"Yes," Henry admitted, feeling suddenly guilty: didn't look fair at that. Now he'd have to explain about the rotation of pitchers, rules about when they can pitch and when they can't . . .

"And your pitcher has an A. Isn't that better?"

"Well, there's a small difference, but—"

"Don't my team have any Aces?" Lou squinted at his roster.

"Yes, but, you see—"

"Yes! here's *two* of them!" Lou looked up and grinned, wagged an accusing finger. "Henry . . . !"

"But it was Casey's turn—"

"Aw, come on now, can't I pitch one of these other boys? How about this fella Whitlowe Clay?"

"I suppose so, but he pitched two days ago—"

"Yeah, but he's tough," argued Lou, grinning. I'll start with ole Whitlowe." He erased Casey's name and wrote in Clay. "Where'd you get these names from, the funny papers?" The whole thing was fast becoming pointless. "Now, these little stars, they're for . . . ?"

"Yes, the batters, they . . ."

Lou winced studiously at the heap of charts and rosters. He

counted the R's. "Two for me, one for you. But here, you've got four stars batting, and I've only got three. What if I put that Casey fella in as a hitter instead of a pitcher, then we'd be almost even up."

"The Rookie status for pitchers only helps them as pitchers, not hitters."

"Oh? why not?" Absent question, spurred by vexation more than curiosity.

"Just the rules, Lou. It's what I was saying, maybe you ought to let me explain more before we start, see, there's a lot of special things about errors and injuries and relief pitchers and pinch hitters and lead-off hitters and pinch runners and clean-up hitters and—"

"Hey, wait!" Lou exclaimed. "There's *four* stars here! You musta left one out!"

Henry felt his face go hot. "Bran Maverly," he said. "He's been in a kind of slump, and Flynn thought—"

"Aha!" Lou found him on the roster. Left field. He erased Moon from the scoresheet and wrote in Maverly. Moon had hit 6 for 8 in the last two games: how did Flynn explain it? "We'll just see if he don't snap outa that slump," he said, and winked at Henry.

"Listen, Lou, I wasn't trying to be unfair. It's just that there's a whole history here, I mean, there's been a long season already, and you're getting in sort of in the middle. You'd understand better if—"

"That's okay, Henry, don't apologize," Lou said with a grin. "I'd do the same thing." He shook his beer can. "Is there any more?"

"Sure, I'll get some." From the sink, he watched fat Lou Engel, sitting where he himself usually sat, poking through the charts, tossing sample throws, humming some baroque melody. How has this happened? he wondered.

"Who goes first?"

"I'll go first, give you last bats." The game was in the Knickerbocker ball park, couldn't be any other way, but it seemed like the easiest way to explain it.

He sat, took up the dice. He tried to get his mind down into the game, but Lou's bulky presence seemed to blank him out, and all he saw was paper. He didn't seem to be playing with Lou, but through him, and the way through was dense and hostile. "Toby Ramsey batting," he announced, but self-consciousness made him keep the announcement brief and hushed.

"What's he?" asked Lou, poking his nose in front of Henry to peer down at the lineup. "R. Rookie. Which chart . . . ?"

Henry showed him. "We only need these three, now that we've both got Aces in," he said.

"Ace to Star, Ace to—yes, I see," Lou said, then pursed his lips in an undisguised imitation of Zifferblatt.

Henry threw. "Fly out to center."

"Wait a minute, wait a minute. Yes, FO CF—but what's this?"

"Runners advance one. But there aren't any runners."

"Oh yes. I see. Okay. Just want to get it all. What's that now? One out . . . ?"

"That's right." Henry marked the scoresheet, threw again, this time for Regular batter Grammercy Locke. Single. He waited for Lou to find it.

"Single, advance two," Lou read. "How can you advance two on a single?"

"That means the baserunners, if there were any, would advance two."

"I thought it was a disadvantage to be a plain type."

"It is. Only about eighteen per cent of a Regular's possibilities against an Ace are hits, while for a Star, for example, it's over twenty-five per cent."

Lou showed surprise. "You really got it all figured out!"

"Yes."

"Still, those aren't very good averages," he reasoned.

"Well, there are other parameters: walks, errors, injuries, different combinations and charts—"

"Per a *what?* Whew!" Lou leaned back, shook his head, picking his nose absently. "I'm never gonna catch on to this, Henry."

"You're just not used to it yet. It gets simple when you play it awhile." He rolled for Hatrack Hines.

Lou drank beer. "That was a good movie today, Henry. You should've come."

"Was it? Look. Hines is a Star and he struck out. See, Lou, you never know."

Lou watched carefully as Henry penned a K on the score-sheet. "There was this guy who kept bees. He was making tape recordings of the sounds they made, see, because he wanted to see if he could communicate with them."

Witness York sent a line-drive single into left center, moving Locke around to third. "Way to go!" Henry said.

"What's that?" Lou put down his beer to take a closer look. He read the numbers on the dice, searched the chart.

"That's the one for Rookies, Lou. Here, this one." This was going to take all night.

"Let's see, 4–4–6: that's that single-advance-two again."

"Right. Puts York on first, Locke on third."

Lou stared down at the table, trying to see it. "I'm already lost, Henry."

"Oh, for God's sake, Lou," Henry cried, losing patience, "it's not that hard. Look, two out, men on first and third, forget who they are. A Star batting. Watch." Infield fly, shortstop. Rally choked off. Somehow he felt it was Lou's fault. In a way, it was. On Casey's chart, it would have been a base on balls, bases loaded. Of course, Locke wouldn't have got his—forget it. "Well, what is it?"

Lou frowned, looked on the wrong chart again. "I don't—"

"*This* one, Lou!"

"Don't get mad, Henry, I'm only trying—here it is: what's that?"

"Infield fly."

"He's out, hunh?" Henry nodded. "How many is that, Henry?"

"That's three."

"I'm up now?"

"Yes." Henry handed him the dice.

Lou livened up, studied the line-up, saw he had a Rookie batting, put his finger on the Ace-to-Rookie chart, and threw the dice. Strikeout. Lou's finger ran down the chart. "Aw," he said, "that's a strikeout." He threw for McAllister Weeks. Another strikeout. Anyway, Halifax was on the ball today. "Base on balls."

"You're on the wrong chart again, Lou."

Lou winced despairingly. He found the right one. "Strikeout. Heck." He rolled again. Three in a row. "Infield . . . no, wait: I remember, Henry, he's a Star. Ummm: strikeout! again! It sure seems awful easy to get a strikeout in this game," he grumped.

Henry took the dice. While Ingram and Wilder popped up and James flied out to center, Lou told about the beekeeper. "So, anyway, see, he's finally got so he can translate a few of the things they say and talk back to them, you know, things about going back to the hive, danger, and so on, and—oh, I forgot to tell you about this woman—"

"You're up, Lou."

Lou droned on about the bees while taking his turn, Henry helping him find the result of his throws to speed things up a little. Biff Baldwin popped up to the pitcher and Walt McCamish fouled out, but Bran Maverly doubled off the right-field wall. "Now, what'd I tell you about that boy!" Lou gloated, and Henry had to grin in spit of himself: fattening Flynn and his Daffy Dillies, new image of the Knicks? Lou pumped the dice in his puffy fist. "Seven come eleven!" he piped meaninglessly, and tossed them down. Triple three: injury.

"Now you throw again," Henry explained, after Lou had found the meaning of his throw, "and use this chart. See, the injury can be on either your team or mine. Some are more serious than others, and it makes a difference how old the player is. Your man O'Shea, for example, is twenty, came up this year, Year LVI—"

"Year *what*—!"

Henry felt the flush come again. Hadn't meant to go that far tonight. "I'll explain all that later Lou. Just go ahead and throw."

That cold Zifferblatt-like expression of incredulity and distrust crept over Lou's wide face, but he picked up the dice and pitched them again. Henry tried to watch it happen: O'Shea's line-drive sailing out to right center, Witness York drifting over for it, Stan Patterson calling for it, Knickerbocker fans raising a howl, drowning them out—but all he could see was Lou running his stubby greasy finger down the chart, lips in a skeptical pucker: "*RF Inj Collision w/ CF: D Adv 3, RF out 4 G.*" Lou sighed deprecatingly. "What's it mean, Henry?"

"It's a double, your other man is home, my right fielder is out of the game." He wrote Tuck Wilson's name into the line-up, replacing Patterson. Out of action for four whole games! What a mess.

"I got a run?"

"That's right. Man on second and two outs."

"What about stolen bases? Can I have that man steal third?"

"You can try." Oh boy. Steal third with two outs. Way to go, Flynn. "If you want to."

"Okay, why not? Try everything." O'Shea made it. Caught Halifax and Ingram napping. He always thought of catchers as slow, but there were exceptions. Maybe O'Shea was one of them. "I still haven't found it."

"There. He made it. He's safe."

"Look at that! Say, I'm beginning to like this game. Who's up?"

"Your third baseman. Galen Musgraves."

"He's just a plain type, hunh? Maybe I oughta pinch-hit somebody. Is that a good idea?"

"Well, pinch hitters have a slight advantage. But it's only the second inning, Lou. And then you only have one other third baseman."

"Oh, that's enough. How about this fella Sycamore Flynn here?"

"That's your manager."

"Can't bat, hunh?"

"No. Anyway he's in his fifties."

"Oh, the poor guy. Well, how about, uh, Kirk Abalon?"

"If you want." When Lou pronounced them, they *did* sound like comic book names.

"Okay, write him in there." Lou rubbed the dice between both plump palms. "Come on, big Kirk!"

"Abalon's a little man," Henry said.

Lou cast a glance of total wonder Henry's way. "Okay then," he said with a bemused shake of his head, "come on, little Kirk!" He threw the dice. Incredible. Henry sank back into his chair and drank off his own beer. "Hey, how about that, Henry! That PH means pinch hitter, don't it?" Henry nodded. "So it's a single, advance one, if pinch hitter, and otherwise fly out to right field, runners advance one." Lou clapped his hands. "Way to call those plays!" he congratulated himself. "Listen, where is everybody now?"

"Two runs in, two out, man on first, your pitcher at the plate."

"Not too good a batter, hunh?"

"Odds for him are a little less than those of a Regular hitter, but—"

"Okay, that's what I wanted to know. Who can I put in there? How about that Moon fella? He missed out there at the start, so I'll run him in now. Don't want any bad feelings."

"That's okay, Lou, but there are still seven innings to go, and your Ace—"

"I got another one. Is this Archie Moon big or little?"

Six foot two, 168 pounds, thirty years old, seven years in the Association. Dazzling fielder out in center, good throwing arm. Smooth-swinging choke hitter who sprayed to all fields. One big year in LII when he punched out a .281, just missing Star status. Hair sun-bleached blond, skin tanned, cigarette-ad smile. Played pro tennis in the spring. "He's . . . pretty big."

"Okay, come on, pretty big Archie!" Lou piped cheerfully. He belched and threw. "What's that?"

"Extra base hit."

Lou found it. "You're right. Now what . . . ?"

"Throw again. Use this chart."

"Boy, this game takes forever." He threw and Moon tripled. "Hey!" Lou exclaimed when he found the place. "By golly, I think I've got this game figured out. What would've happened if I'd left the pitcher in there?"

"Same thing."

"Oh?" Lou's enthusiasm sagged. He drank beer. "You want to bat for a while?"

Henry smiled. "You still only have two outs. Keep going." He probably ought to pull Halifax, but he didn't have the energy for it.

Lou shrugged, rolled the dice. Scat Batkin went down swinging. At last. "Maybe I should've had that fella try to steal home," Lou said.

"Three to nothing, your favor," said Henry. "Who's pitching and playing third?"

"Well, that other Ace there, Shannon, Uncle Joe Shannon, and then, let's see, this man Holden Chase—"

"He's an outfielder. Koane's your other third baseman."

"Okay," smiled Lou agreeably, settling back, "Koane."

Mickey Halifax bounced one down to Koane, who threw him out. Lou looked it up and Henry explained it. "I think that was a good idea, putting that boy in there," Lou said, a bit drunkenly. He should have stopped to think about Halifax. But then who would he have pitched? Lou went to the refrigerator for more beer. "Do you mind, Henry?"

"No, help yourself."

"Want one?"

"Mmm." Ramsey struck out. Impatiently, he threw again, and Locke fouled out, McCamish coming in from right to haul it in.

"Hey, wait, what's happening?"

"You're up. My lead-off man struck out and the next one fouled out to your right fielder."

"You should've used a pinch hitter, Henry. Works every time. Listen, I wanted to tell you how this movie ended. This woman, see, was really a queen bee, trans—how do you say?"

"Transmuted."

"That's right." He drank beer. "See, these bees knew a lot more than anybody had guessed. They had scientists and all, and they had figured out how to—how did you say . . . ? Well, you know, cross over, sort of. They were just putting this man on with his little experiments, but they were really planning a big take-over. Well, the point is—did I tell you about this guy's wife? No? Well, I gotta back up. See, his wife—"

"Listen, Lou, why don't you roll while you explain it?"

"Just take a minute. His wife didn't like this girl right off. Woman's intuition, you know. The girl, I mean, the one who came to be the secretary, the one who was really the queen bee—"

"It's getting late, Lou, and we won't have time—"

"By golly!" exclaimed Lou, glancing at his watch. "Almost ten already! Can't stay too much longer." He rolled the dice. Weeks singled, but Garrison, Baldwin, and McCamish hit successive groundballs to the infield and were thrown out, leaving Weeks stranded on second. Lou patiently looked up the significance of each throw, getting deeper and deeper the while into the plot of the movie he'd seen. "So this girl—but there was this man who came, the wife had asked him to come because—are you still following?"

"Not very well."

"Let me go back. This guy was keeping bees, trying to talk to them, when one day this girl comes to ask for a job as an assistant, sort of, and he—that reminds me, that woman last night, was it, did everything . . . ?"

"What?"

"You know, I mean, work out okay?" Lou grinned sheepishly, going pink in the cheeks, or maybe it was just the beer. "I mean, is she, did you, do you like her?"

"Well, sure, but she's just a B-girl, Lou, nothing—"

"Yes, well, I only meant, I mean, she seemed . . ." He paused, took a drink of beer. "So anyway this girl comes and the wife sees something peculiar about her right off. Sense of smell or something."

"Maybe she got a good look at her in the can," Henry suggested sourly. Hines had grounded out to the first baseman, unassisted.

Lou giggled, belched softly. "That's right, if she was really a bee . . . " His mind pursued the possibilities. "But, no," he decided in all seriousness, "if she'd crossed over and got human eyes and teeth and so on, well, she'd probably got . . . everything else."

"Hines is out, Lou. I'm batting now for York."

"How . . . ?"

"Your first baseman, unassisted."

"Good boy," said Lou blowzily. "Of course, maybe not . . ."

"Maybe not what?"

"Well, the eyes and teeth and all, that's kind of on the outside, but the, you know, what we were talking about, the other, that's more like on the inside and that would be harder to change over—"

"Oh, hell, Lou!" He rolled. "York singles, line drive into right center!"

Lou frowned skeptically, looked it up. "Single, all right," he agreed. "I don't see the rest."

"York's a left-handed batter and pull hitter," Henry explained.

"Oh," said Lou. He rubbed his cheeks, staring at the chart.

"I'm going to have Wilson try a sacrifice bunt," Henry said.

"Why'd you take that fella with the star out?"

"That's the man who got injured, don't you remember?"

"Mmm. Guess I'd forgot." Lou sighed. "Care for one more?" He got up.

"I've still got some, thanks. But help yourself." Chauncey O'Shea fielded the bunt, cocked his arm toward second, but York was way ahead of him. He threw to first, barely getting old Wilson. "York is safe on second, Wilson out, catcher to first."

"Just a minute, let me see," Lou said. Perfunctory offer, Henry sensed. Fffssst. Fffssst. He brought two beers back. "What chart's *that* now?"

"Sacrifice bunts. See, here's—"

Lou grunted, looked away. "What inning are we in, Henry?"

"The fourth."

"And there's nine innings?" He looked at his watch. "We'll never make it, Henry."

"Well, damn it, let's try anyway. I usually play four or five games in the time it's taken us to get this far. York's on second, two outs, Ingram at the plate." He rolled the dice. "Extra base hit! Now we're moving, team!" he shouted. Lou ran his finger down the chart, but long before he'd found it, Henry had rolled again: "Home run! Hey *hey!* It's a 3–to–2 ball game!" He marked the scoresheet.

"I haven't even got to the part where this girl falls out the window," Lou said disconsolately. "You should see that movie, Henry."

"Wilder up . . . and he grounds out to short. Three down. But it's a new ball game."

"You really oughta go more often. Makes you think about things. There's a real good one next week—"

"You're up."

Lou took the dice absently, tossed them down. "It's down in the south. There's these two brothers, and this one gets murdered."

"Your man Maverly just flied out to left."

Lou watched pensively, as Henry inked in the out. "Everybody thinks the other brother did it, but there's a surprise ending."

"Go ahead, throw."

Lou rolled. "Listen, Henry—"

"Base on balls. Now your man Koane is up."

Lou perked up a bit. "Koane? That's the one I . . . ? Mmm." He threw. "How'd he do?"

"He struck out, Lou."

"Take him outa there."

"You can't, he's the only third baseman you have left."

"What's wrong with these other fellas? Here, put Casey in there." Lou was getting a little testy with the beer.

"He's a pitcher, Lou."

"Who's bossing this team, you or me?" Lou squeaked petulantly, then regretted it just as quickly. He smiled apologetically and drank some beer. "Oh, I don't care. Who's up?"

"Your pitcher."

"Pinch hitter."

"You don't have any more Aces—"

"That's all right, what's the difference? Let's see, this Chase fella . . . " He rolled, as Henry dutifully inked the name in. "Where'd he hit it?"

"To the pitcher."

"You mean, he's out?" Lou sighed wearily, looked at his watch.

Before he could remark the hour, Henry asked: "What's the surprise ending?"

"Surprise . . . ?"

"The movie next week."

"I don't know, they never tell you. I think there's a girl mixed up in it."

"There usually is. Who are you pitching now?"

"Pitching . . . ?"

"You used a pinch hitter."

"Oh! You jump back and forth so much, Henry, I can't keep up. I don't care who—who've I got? How about this Casey now?"

"Okay, Casey." A crazy game, but anyway he was where he wanted to be in the first place. Of course, he probably only had a couple innings before Lou used another pinch hitter. Too bad the bottom of the line-up was at the plate. "James batting. Rookie-to-Regular. Infield fly. Second baseman takes it." He showed Lou the place on the chart, though Lou really didn't seem to care any more. Halifax up again. Needed the Ace in there, but they had to hit Casey. "Axel Rawlings batting for Halifax." Barney Bancroft wouldn't have done it. Or maybe he would have. He'd be so bewildered by this game by now, he'd be apt to do about anything. But Rawlings struck out. "Oh, goddamn!"

"What's the matter, Henry?" asked Lou, starting up, suddenly concerned.

"He struck out."

"Oh. I thought you were, that something . . . well." He settled back with his beer.

Come on, Ramsey, damn it! A little pepper, boys, we gotta get a—Ramsey, waiting Casey out, watched a third strike go by. "You're up."

"Are you mad about something, Henry?"

Henry sighed. "No, go ahead and throw."

"Listen, let's go out and get another one of those pizzas."

"Ate too much already. Throw."

"Henry—"

"*Throw*, Lou, for crying out loud!"

Lou looked blearily disturbed, but he threw the dice just the same. Wait a minute. Get a new pitcher in. Who . . . ? Shadwell. No, he pitched yesterday. That's okay, the Knicks —no, it isn't okay. McDermott. He'd made mistakes like that before, pinch-hit for a pitcher then forgot he was out of the game and gone on using him, and it had been hell each time to get everything straightened out after.

They played in silence, except for Henry's reading of the significance of each throw, as he pointed the place for Lou. Batkin and Weeks walked, putting McDermott in trouble right off. Garrison flied out to left and Baldwin to right, Batkin advancing to third and then on home after the catches, Baldwin getting the RBI. McCamish walked and then Maverly singled, loading the bases and getting an "I told you so" peep out of Lou, but O'Shea struck out. Four to two. Casey'd be up at bat next inning and Lou would no doubt use another pinch hitter: it was now or never. Unless Lou was too sleepy and forgot. Couldn't take that chance. Barney sent Rusty Palmers in to bat for Locke. Locke had one for two in the ball game . . . ? That's all right. Play percentages. Bancroft's style, wasn't it? Didn't work. Palmers grounded out, second to first. The boys clapped him in, though. Don't lose the spirit. Remember who this guy is out there. They all knew. Barney didn't have to spell it out. Damon's killer. And then it happened! Hatrack Hines leaned into one and sent it clean out of the park: 6–6–6! Boy, were they pretty! "Now, we're going, men! we got him on the run! whoop it up! on your feet! chin music! It's the Mad Jock out there, boys, old Poppycock! And it's York up there now, come on, Witness baby—hey, Lou! where are you going?"

Lou already had his coat on. "I kept trying to tell you, Henry, but you weren't listening." Lou was a little unsteady; you couldn't really tell it with Lou, except that he planted his feet a little wider apart than usual. "It's after midnight. Tomorrow's a working day. We gotta be there—*you* gotta be there, Henry. It's your last chance—"

"Lou, wait a minute! I just rolled a home run—"

"We can finish it next week, Henry."

"Next week! I'll be into the next season by next week!" he cried.

"Henry, remember what Mr. Zifferblatt—"

"Oh, to *hell* with Zifferblatt, Lou! Listen, I just rolled a triple six. That moves the game to the special Stress Chart!"

"Well, that's nice, Henry, but—"

"That only happens twice in every three games, Lou! Don't you see? Anything can happen now! Come on, play out this inning anyway."

"Aw, Henry . . ." he whined, but he came over.

Henry flung the dice: "*Hah!*" he bawled at them. But all they gave him was a 2–6–6, a lot less than he'd hoped for.

Lou yawned: "Hee-oooff!" and slapped his hat to the table —*bop!* the beer can somersaulted and rolled, bubbling out over charts and scoresheets and open logbooks and rosters and records—

"*Lou!*" screamed Henry. He leaped for the towel, but Lou,

in shock and drunkenness, stood up suddenly, and they collided. "*You clumsy goddamn idiot!*" Henry cried, and shoved around him. He snapped up the towel, turned back to the table to find Lou there, dabbing pathetically at the inundation with a corner of his handkerchief.

"I'm sorry, Henry," he mumbled tearily.

"Just get outa the way!" Henry shouted. He toweled up the beer as fast as he could, but everywhere he looked ink was swimming on soaked paper. Oh my God! He separated sheets, carried them into his room and spread them out on the bed. At some point, he heard the door close, Lou's heavy footfalls descending the stairs. When he'd got up the worst of it, he sank into his chair, stared at the mess that was his Association. The Pioneer-Knickerbocker game lay before him, damp but still legible. It's all over, he realized miserably, finished. The Universal Baseball Association, proprietor left for parts unknown. A shudder raked through him as he sighed, and he felt ill. He propped his elbows on the table, folded his hands, and leaned his head against them. Great moments from the past came floating to mind, mighty old-timers took their swings and fabulous aces reared back and sizzled them in; he saw Marsh Williams belting them out of the park and flashy Verne Mackenzie and Fancy Dan the Keystones' Man, watched Jumpin' Joe Gallagher go hurling himself up against the ivied wall in center and shy Sycamore Flynn making impossible leaping snags of line drives, saw the great Pioneers drive for flag after flag and watched the wind-ups of Sandy Shaw and Tim Shadwell and old Brock and Edgar Bath, and there was the great Cash Bailey cracking the .400 barrier and Hellborn Melbourne Trench socking them out of sight, Uncle Joe Shannon, and Wally Wickersham, and Tuck Wilson, and Winslow Beaver, and Hamilton Craft . . . and Damon Rutherford. Finally came down to that, didn't it? All week, he'd been pushing it back any way he could, but it just couldn't be done. Damon Rutherford. He wiped his eyes with the beery towel, stared down at the game on the table. That was what did it, it was just a little too much, one idea too many, and it wrecked the whole league. He stood, turned his back on it, feeling old and wasted. Should he keep it around, or . . . ? No, better to burn it, once and for all, records, rules, Books, everything. If that stuff was lying around, he'd never really feel free of it. He found a paper shopping bag under the sink, gathered up a stack of scoresheets and dumped them in, reached for that of the night's game. He saw the dice, still reading 2–6–6, and—almost instinctively—reached forward and tipped the two over to a third six. Gave York and Wilson back-to-back homers and moved the game over to the Extraordinary Occurrences Chart. Easy as that.

He smiled wryly, savoring the irony of it. Might save the game at that. How would they see it? Pretty peculiar. He trembled. Chill. Felt his forehead. Didn't seem hot. Clammy, if anything. No, it's too crazy. He reached again for the night's scoresheet, but again hesitated. The three sixes stared up at him like thick little towns. Who was up next? The catcher Royce Ingram. Damon's battery mate. Poetic. Indeed. He snorted, amused by it in spite of himself. He sat down. Of course, he could throw triple ones again, and Casey'd have two notches on his throwing arm. He wasn't really thinking about the bean ball though. Now, his eye was on the bottom line of that chart:

> 6–6–6: *Pitcher struck fatally by linedrive through box; batter safe on first; runners advance one.*

He penned in York's and Wilson's home runs on the scoresheet, watched Royce Ingram pick out a bat and stride menacingly to the plate. Now, stop and think, he cautioned himself. Do you really *want* to save it? Wouldn't it be better just to drop it now, burn it, go on to something else, get working regularly again, back into the swing of things, see movies, maybe copyright that Intermonop game and try to market it, or do some traveling, read books . . .

He stood, paced the kitchen idly, feeling lightheaded. Yes, if you killed that boy out there, then you *couldn't* quit, could you? No, that's a real commitment, you'd be hung up for good, they wouldn't *let* you go. *Who* wouldn't? aren't you forgetting—never mind, never mind. He was growing dizzy, contemplating the consequences. He decided to forget it for tonight, go to bed, make up his mind tomorrow. But on his bed, he found the Association all spread out like defenders of the gates . . . oh yes, the spilt beer. He stacked them up, but didn't throw them in the bag, left them neatly on the table. Anything could happen still.

He undressed, crawled into bed in his underwear, too woozy to change into pajamas or brush his teeth. But in bed he felt worse than ever and he couldn't get to sleep. He kept seeing Jock Casey, waiting there on the mound. Why waiting? Who for? Patient. Yes, give him credit, he was. Enduring. And you had to admit: Casey played the game, heart and soul. Played it like nobody had ever played it before. He circled round the man, viewing him from all angles. Lean, serious, melancholy even. And alone. Yes, above all: alone. Stands packed with people, but faceless, just multicolored shirts. Field full of players, but no faces there either. Just a scene, sandy diamond, green grass, ballplayers under the sun, stadium of fans, umpires, and Casey in the middle. Sometimes Casey glanced up at him—only a glance, split-second, pain, a pleading—but mostly he watched the batter Ingram. Get to sleep. There'll be time tomorrow. And a fresh mood. But he couldn't sleep. Casey waiting there . . . But he was too sick to rise. Just can't —but still Casey waited, and his glance: come on, get it over, only way, and still Ingram swung his bat, and still Chauncey O'Shea crouched, and still the stands kept their awesome silence. "Somebody—!" Henry gasped. Sycamore Flynn broke it, yes, he walked to the mound. But he didn't say anything either. Just a faint jerk of the head, asking the question. Casey shaking his head and Flynn going back. A terrible silence. And Casey looking—

Henry got up. He stumbled to the kitchen in his shorts. He picked up the dice, shook them. "I'm sorry, boy," he whispered, and then, holding the dice in his left palm, he set them down carefully with his right. One by one. Six. Six. Six. A sudden spasm convulsed him with the impact of a smashing line drive and he sprayed a red-and-golden rainbow arc of half-curded pizza over his Association, but he managed to get to the sink with most of it. And when he'd done with his vomiting, when he'd finished, he went to bed and there slept a deep deep sleep.

STRANGE how that season ended. Some blamed it on the heat, some on the humidity, but they all knew better. Players hit balls, moved around bases, caught flies, but as though at rest, static participants in an ancient yet transformed ritual. Journalists quit writing, just watched. Nobody interviewed anybody. No one sought autographs and no women shrieked or fainted at the feet of heroes. McCaffree swiveled in silence, Winthrop silent. Umpires jerked thumbs or spread their hands, but no one complained. Good pitchers threw strikes, bad ones gave up hits to good hitters, while bad hitters went hitless. Boys watched grimly, older than old men, and old men hardly watched at all, just closed their eyes and nodded, nodded. Even Pappy Rooney, waterlogged in his own sweat, wrapped a towel around his bony old shoulders and sank back on the Haymaker bench, accepting, accepting, come what may. Sycamore Flynn and the Knickerbocker club-owners went to see Chancellor McCaffree about forfeiting the rest of the schedule. Nobody stood in their way now, but they couldn't seem to win. Just too much, Fenn. McCaffree understood, strange, yes, but what do we know about it all, Sycamore? Do your part, play the game, play it out. So they did and dropped the last nine games in a row. Contrarily, Barney Bancroft's Pioneers, as though released from some inexplicable burden, began to win. Barney ceased all subterfuge, called his plays open-handed, other teams knew perfectly well what was on—and still everything seemed to work. Nothing flashy: he just got men on base and brought them in, while his fielders and pitchers routinely retired the opposition.

The team with the most Stars and Aces, the Pastimers, won the pennant. The final three-game series found the second-place Haymakers, trailing by two games, in the Patsies' ballpark. Rooney, old trouper, stood up, tried gamely to get some life into his boys, but they'd been driven to play over their heads too long, they just collapsed, lost the first game and thus the pennant, so Pappy sank back again. Swanee Law finally did win another game, though, last one of the season, his twentieth, striking out his 303rd man, fifth best mark in UBA history—wonderful, but few cheered, not even when he got named Most Valuable Player. The Pioneers took three at the end from the Keystones to wind up in third, while the Knicks lost all theirs to sink to the cellar. Final Year LVI standings:

TEAM	WON	LOST	PCT	GB
Pastime Club	49	35	.583	–
Haymakers	46	38	.548	3
Pioneers	42	42	.500	7
Beaneaters	41	43	.488	8
Keystones	41	43	.488	8
Bridegrooms	40	44	.476	9
Excelsiors	39	45	.464	10
Knickerbockers	38	46	.452	11

So: into blue season. Time to bring all the records up to date, summarize the year's play, plan for the future. It was, in a sense, the static part of the game, this between-seasons activity, but it was activity all the same, and in some ways more intense than the ball games themselves, a concentrated meditative concern with history, development, and equilibria. Especially this one. He'd let things slide the last half of the season, had a lot of catching up to do. But more than that, it was simply a season that would demand a lot more thought than usual. Already, it seemed incredible to him that it had all happened.

He wanted some way to mark it, some special event, down there in the Association. Fenn was thinking, the old-timers, too, and the Council of Elders, but nothing yet. Of course, they'd already named both Damon Rutherford and Jock Casey to the Hall of Fame, joining the twenty-six other great all-time stars—including Damon's father and Jock's great-grandfather—but it didn't seem to be enough. He'd considered a UBA anthem, a monument, maybe a violent change in the playing rules, even a revolution, led by Patrick Monday perhaps, a revolt that would establish, ultimately, a rival league. He'd always wanted some kind of World Series, but on the other hand an entire new league would mean a terrific slowdown in the seasons. Going full time, it already took him two whole months to get a season played and logged, and if anything, he needed ways to speed it up. Another possibility was to imitate the majors and create a ten-team league, but for one thing it upset the record books (seasons would have to be six games longer), and for another it seemed somehow central to the game to maintain the balance provided by any power of two. To say a team finished in "first division" implied the possibility of further divisions, but a five-team division couldn't be further divided. Moreover, seven—the number of opponents each team now had—was central to baseball. Of course, nine, as the square of three, was also important: nine innings, nine players, three strikes each for three batters each inning, and so on, but even in the majors there were complaints about ten-team leagues, and back earlier in the century, when they'd tried to promote a nine-game World Series in place of the traditional best-out-of-seven, the idea had failed to catch on. Maybe it all went back to the days when games were decided, not by the best score in nine innings, but by the first team to score twenty-one runs . . . three times seven. Now there were seven fielders, three in the outfield and four in the infield, plus the isolate genius on the mound and the team playmaker and unifier behind the plate; seven pitches, three strikes and four balls; three basic activities—pitching, hitting, and fielding—performed around four bases (Hettie had invented her own magic version, stretching out as the field, left hand as first base . . .). In the UBA, each team played its seven opponents twelve times each, and though games lasted nine innings, they got turned on in the seventh with the ritual mid-inning stretch.

Well, he'd think of something, record Sandy's songs maybe, order a commemorative painting, he'd find a project, there was time, and meanwhile, ahead of him lay the winter player trades and contracts, the announcing of the new crop of Year LVII Rookies, balancing of the club financial ledgers, individual team elections and awards, plus this season the UBA-wide elections for Chancellor, reorganization of managerial and coaching staffs, death rolls, essays and obituaries and forecasts for the Book, as well as the traditional blue season basketball and bowling leagues, ice hockey, billiards, and auto racing, and in the spring, the UBA Golf Open, tennis, and the annual Olympiad. Maybe even another pinball tourney. Some of these sports were limited to active team players, but most were open to veterans as well. Helped bring them all together once a year. Big Bill McGonagil, for example, was a perennial contender on the golf links, though now in his fifties, and Willie O'Leary had long been the undisputed billiards king. Chin-Chin Chickering, who'd failed as a Beaneater shortstop, was making it big as a basketball center, while Brock Rutherford Jr. had taken up car racing. These other games were enjoyable, usually fast and full of action, played off in an hour or two, but ultimately simplistic, shallow, no competition for the baseball league. Relaxations only. Exercise, too, since he played out the bowling tourneys and billiard matches on real alleys and tables.

His immediate task, though, was the compilation of all season LVI statistics, and this he'd pretty largely accomplished by the time Benny Diskin brought up sandwiches and blue-season supplies about sundown, at least well enough to know that the Patsies' Bo McBean had won the batting title, that Damon Rutherford's ERA at the time of his death was far and away the best in the league, that his teammate Witness York had hit the most home runs and had the highest slugging average, and that Swanee Law led in games pitched, complete games, games won, shutouts, strikeouts, and had the second-best ERA. As usual, a number of the LVI Stars slipped below the line. The one that troubled Henry most was Pioneer catcher Royce Ingram, Damon's courageous battery mate and the man swinging when Casey got killed: he wound up with a .284, twenty-sixth among hitters and thus just out of the twenty-four man Star grouping for LVII. Of course, he could make a comeback next year; Henry hoped he would. But maybe it was worse than that. The instrument. Watching Damon, he missed Casey; watching Casey, Ingram . . . where would it end?

Before posting all the statistics in the permanent records, of course, he'd have to run a complete audit of all box scores and computations—couldn't risk mistakes, it was the one thing that frightened him—but he had enough now to pass out the MVP award to Law, the Rookie-of-the-Year posthumously to Damon Rutherford, and the Manager-of-the-Year prize to the Haymakers' Rag Rooney, his third time to win it, and to name the UBA All-Stars, the dream team of LVI . . .

First Base: Virgil (Virgin) Donovan, Pastime Club
Second Base: Kester Flint, Keystones
Shortstop: Bo McBean, Pastime Club
Third Base: Hatrack Hines, Pioneers
Left Field: Bartholomew Egan, Beaneaters
Center Field: Witness York, Pioneers
Right Field: Walt McCamish, Knickerbockers
Catcher: Bingham Hill, Haymakers
Pitcher: Swanee Law, Haymakers
Pitcher: Damon Rutherford, Pioneers Ⓚ
Manager: Raglan (Pappy) Rooney, Haymakers

When Benny Diskin brought up the sandwiches, along with a couple of cans of good coffee, a box of cigars, a few six-packs of beer, sour pickles and a carton of slaw, crackers, a thick slab of rich cheese, bacon and dry sausages, and a couple quarts of orange juice (Seabrooke Farms . . . Seabrooke Orange . . . Seabrooke Bacon . . . Stogie Seabrooke . . . hmmm, yes, Stogie Seabrooke, could be, catcher maybe), he wanted to know if Mr. Waugh was on vacation or something. Miss one day of work and old man Diskin began to worry about the rent. Henry gave Benny a fifty-cent tip to go out and buy him a bottle of brandy, and said nothing about getting fired. Summer, spring, or winter, blue-season was hot-stove-league weather for Henry, and so he always drank hot grogs. Yeah, I'm all washed up, boys, I got the axe, I got the aches. . .

Henry had been dragged out of a deep and peaceful sleep a little before noon by the telephone. He'd been dreaming, something to do with Fanny Lydell neé McCaffree, she'd been thanking him for something, he couldn't remember what, probably not important what, and he'd awakened to the ringing of bells. It wasn't Fanny, though, it was Lou Engel, calling on behalf of DZ&Z to say, in effect, he'd done all he could, nothing more to be done; hang up your cleats. "But what I, why I called, Henry, is, well, Mr. Zifferblatt here found these, uh, papers in your desk, with funny, you know, like names and things on them . . ."

"That's a horseracing game, Lou. You'll also find a couple dice there—"

"Unh-hunh. Well, we, uh, he found those, all right. But what he wants to know, why he asked me to call you, is what do you want him to do with them?"

Henry yawned. "Is he there beside you, Lou?"

"Yes."

"Well, tell him, if he wants to know where to put them, to look in the folder marked DERBY, year—or I mean page number forty-nine, top horse on the list."

"(He says if you want to know where to put them, Mr. Zifferblatt, to please look on page, uh, forty-nine in the folder marked DERBY, uh, yes, that one, page forty-nine, the top horse, or I mean, name—) Henry? What does it say? Why don't you just tell . . . ?"

"It says, Up Ziff's Ass."

On the other end a squeak. "(Mr. Zifferblatt, listen, never mind, I'll take care of—)"

"(WHAT THE HELL DOES THIS MEAN—!!)"

"*Now* see what you've done, Henry!" Click! and that was all, nothing more the rest of the day. Didn't know why it should've upset him so, that horse never won a race.

It was down in Jake's old barroom
Behind the Patsies' park;
Jake was asettin' 'em up as usual
And the night was agittin' dark.

At the bar stood old Verne Mackenzie
And his eyes was blood-shot red,
And he turned his face to the people,
These're the very words he said:

"I jist come from the boss's office,
I been up to see ole Number One;
He said: 'Verne, hang up your suit now,
Cause your playin' days is all done.'

"Yeah, I'm all washed up, boys,
I got the axe, I got the aches;
Now you'll find me when you want me
On the sack in the back of Jake's!"

Old Verne Mackenzie! Been some great shortstops since . . . Sycamore Flynn . . . Winslow Beaver . . . Jonathan Noon . . . and nothing wrong with young Bo McBean . . . but the greatest of them all was probably Verne. Hired and fired by young Kester Flint's great granddaddy Abe, himself a fine old gentleman, the appointed UBA Chancellor the first twelve years—

though back then the office was little more than that of league secretary, so he had time to be skipper of the Excelsiors as well. Though Abe Flint played no ball in the UBA, his son Phineas—the boys called him Skinny Ass—pitched for Dean Sullivan's champion Beaneaters, and his grandson Madison Flint played right field for a few years on the Bridegrooms. And now young Kester.

Maybe that was it, thought Henry, maybe *that* was the project for this blue season: a compact league history, a book about these first fifty-six years. Needn't be an official history, could even be a little controversial, the exposure of some pattern or other. And in fact, by God, that next verse of Sandy's "Verne Mackenzie" song might be just the perfect epigraph for it . . .

"Well, boys, I've played some ball now,
I could hit and I could run,
And some of the games we was losin'
But most of the games we won . . ."

Yes, some of the games we was losin', but most of the games we won—the more he thought about it, the more excited he became! Cover it all, the origins, the early stars, the making and breaking of records, the growth and transformation of the political structure, Dean Sullivan's ball-busting Beaneaters and the Keystones of Tim Shadwell's day, the Brock Rutherford Era, the fabulous Cels of Hellborn Melbourne Trench's heyday, the rise of Fenn McCaffree's Knicks, right up to the fantastic events of Year LVI, with all the Hall of Famers, and all the great personalities like Jaybird Wall and Verne MacKenzie and No-Hit Nealy, Long Lew Lydell and Sandy Shaw and Jake Bradley and Holly and Molly and Yip Yick Ping! It was all there in the volumes of the Book and in the records, but now it needed a new ordering, perspective, personal vision, the disclosure of pattern, because he'd discovered—who had discovered? Barney maybe—yes, Barney Bancroft had discovered that perfection wasn't a thing, a closed moment, a static fact, but *process*, yes, and the process was transformation, and so Casey had participated in the perfection, too, maybe more than anybody, for even Henry had been affected, and Barney was going to write it . . .

> "*Now, they say I cain't play no more, boys,*
> *They say I'm agittin' old;*
> *Ole Abe he showed me the door, boys,*
> *Sent Verne Mackenzie out in the cold!*
>
> "*So I hung up my ole jersey,*
> *Yeah, I hung up ole number seven,*
> *And I'll never play ball agin, boys,*
> *'Less they's a league up there in heaven!*
>
> "*Oh yeah, I'm all washed up, boys,*
> *I got the axe, I got the aches;*
> *Now you'll find me when you want me*
> *On the sack in the back of Jake's!*"

And what would Bancroft call it? *The Beginnings*, maybe. Or: *The UBA Story. Abe Flint's Legacy. The UBA in the Balance*. "Yes, that's it!"

"That's what, Mr. Waugh?"

"*The UBA in the Balance*—how does that sound to you, Benny?"

"Is it a riddle, Mr. Waugh? I'm not very good at riddles."

"Ha ha! Yes, that's what it is! A riddle! You hit it on the head!"

"Uh, well, they only had American brandy, I told them—"

"That's okay, Benny, we got nothing against Americans. They invented baseball, didn't they?"

"Well, I guess so, but the—"

"Here's an extra quarter, Benny. My best to your father!"

"Well, I went to see my woman,
I said, 'Baby, I'm feelin' blue!
The boss he turned me out, babe,
My playin' days is through!'

"My baby she started laughin',
She said, 'Verne, don' bother to call,
Cause I got me a brand-new man now,
He's young and he's still playin' ball!'

"Oh yeah, I'm all washed up, boys,
I got the axe, I got the aches . . ."

Not really, though. After Lou had called, Henry had phoned an employment agency where he was registered, told them he was semi-retired and wanted half-time work, starting after Christmas. They asked for an updating of his record, but told him there might be part-time work for an accountant there in the agency itself after the first of the year. And meanwhile, he had a drawerful of checks he'd never cashed. So old Ziff, ho, ho, ho, he sent to hell.

Well, I went to see my woman . . . hmmm, true, bunch of the boys probably be gathering at Jake's tonight, little Monday night blue-season politicking, oil the machinery, work up a new pitch or two, try to score. Lot of things to talk over, like who was going to take over the shell-shocked Knicks now that Sycamore Flynn has resigned, what to do about Mel Trench of the sunken Cels and Wally Wickersham, whose Grooms just can't seem to get going, who to run for Chancellor on the Guildsmen ticket against McCaffree and Maloney, and whether or not Patrick Monday would get up his new party this year, and what to call them if he did. Paragonists. Nonesuchers. Optimalists. Perfectionists. Yes, a good night, this new Monday, to play with all these problems, good night to drink a little, make out a little . . .

First, though, he decided to push through the death rolls. They often affected managerial and political situations, and it was pointless to worry about them until he knew for sure who was going to be around. It was a somber event, he never took it lightly. The shock of their deaths often dismayed him, though later he usually enjoyed the writing of their obituaries. He dreaded, in short, the death blow, yet it was just this rounding off in the Book of each career that gave beauty to all these lives. Even the forgotten ballplayers who never made it; doing research for their obits often led him deep into forgotten corners of the past, helped him rediscover some of the more unusual and poignant moments of UBA history, and reminded him always that there was no such thing as excellence without the foundation to measure it by. It was like baldpated old Jake Bradley always said: Yes, we needed him, too, even him.

His formula for the death rolls was based on a combination of insurance actuarial tables and league population: he tried not to let it drop below about a thousand living veterans. As to *how* they died, he made his own decisions while composing the obituary; if he was uncertain, he had another chart that provided him general descriptors, but usually he just *knew,* a certain definite feeling about it that would come on him suddenly while considering the ballplayer's past—Abe Flint's heart failure, Verne Mackenzie's liver, Holly Tibbett's tumor, Rupert Allen's suicide. His sign for death in the records was a Ⓚ

> "*Oh, when I die, jist bury me*
> *With my bat and a coupla balls,*
> *And jist tell 'em Verne struck out, boys,*
> *If anybody calls . . .*"

This year, the rolls brought few surprises, nor were many really great stars caught. Kester's grandfather Phineas Flint. Three of the other Elders with him, but with undistinguished careers. The politicians all survived. Ironically, the dice picked off young Jacinto Abril, the jockey. Violent death, no doubt, an accident . . . probably the reason they decided to close down the tracks for a while. On the whole list, only one really great shock, but it, all alone, was enough to make Henry gasp, sit back, ponder, let fall a tear or two: Jake Bradley, old Jake, second-sacker and barkeep, patron and paraclete, had died of a sudden heart attack!

> "*And when I'm down in my grave, boys,*
> *Drink a toast and sing me a song,*
> *And tell 'em you knew ole Verne Mackenzie*
> *When he was still young and strong!*
>
> "*Yeah, I'm all washed up, boys,*
> *I got the axe, I got the aches;*
> *Now you'll find me when you want me*
> *On the sack in the back of Jake's . . .*"

Henry pulled his door to, paused a moment under the hushed glow of the bulb on his landing, then drifted down the dark stairwell into the night street. Full moon outside. Maybe it was the moon that gave that peculiar floating luster to the bottom of the stairs. Old Jake Bradley! A real shock! That bald dome, the soft ironic manner, one of the finest! Oh, they all knew about that camera he'd let Fenn McCaffree install, he joked about it himself sometimes, they knew and didn't care because they loved the old bastard. And now he was gone.

Henry wandered through the moonlit Monday night streets thinking about Jake Bradley and wondering where he could go now for a drink, wondering where they'd hold the wake. At Jake's maybe, but not at Pete's. Or maybe they'd close it down. Too painful to go back in there and not see Jake. So where? He didn't know. Leave it to chance, leave it to Barney. "Come on, Barney, lead the way!" Yes: *Lead the way!* Of course! Suddenly it was all falling into place! *Barney Bancroft for Chancellor!* That was why he was writing the history, after all! Or maybe not why, but it was enough to do the trick. He'd lived through it all, hadn't he? Yes, the Guildsmen picked him up, he said no, but they persuaded him. The Man Who Couldn't Quit. The Old Philosopher. I'm not a politician, fellas. That's why you're *right*, Barney! And then, and then, the Pioneers would go hire Sycamore Flynn to take over for Barney, and the Knicks? Why, Brock Rutherford, of course! Wow! A perfect set-up! *The UBA in the Balance!* Ho ho! And so Barney's history of the Association: revealing the gradual evolution toward Guildsmen principles, and using the Rutherford-Casey event as the culminating moment, revolving toward the New Day, how the league had progressed from individualism and egocentrism—the Bogglers—through a gradual recognition (perhaps by the mere accretion of population) of the Other—the Legalists—to a moral and philosophic concern with the very nature of man and society: the Guildsmen. Of course, Pat Monday might want to carry that history another step, but never mind, for the moment he's no threat—and, in fact, think a moment, yes, he would probably swing his weight behind Bancroft in an effort to upset the McCaffree machine. The machine indeed! "What we want in this Association is participation—not in real time—but in *significant* time!"

A couple heads turned his way; he brought his arm down, ducked his head . . . better get in off the streets . . . light down there a couple blocks ahead: lead on, Barney! lead on! Yes, by God, old Fenn had been right about that wake for Damon—out of the ashes had risen the new leading light of the UBA. And brought to consummation at another wake.

The Circle Bar. Looked pretty much like Pete's on the outside, and from the inside, he heard country music. Give it a try. Push in . . .

> *"Well, boys, I've played some ball now,*
> *I could hit and I could run,*
> *And some of the games—"*

Inside, Henry pulled up short. He could hardly believe it! There he was, behind the bar, white-aproned, smiling moon face, paunch and all: *Hellborn Melbourne Trench!* Henry smiled back, though inside it was damn near a belly laugh, hooked up his hat and coat, asked for brandy, VSOP, the best. Yes, he must have given up that hopeless job of running the Cels to open a bar, carry on the great tradition of Jake Bradley, oh yes, and all the boys were gathering, coming through the door, *grand opening!* even the young ones now that the season was over and the training rules were down, Witness York and Ham Craft and Maggie Everts and Walt McCamish and Bo McBean, here they come! and Rag Rooney and Jaybird Wall and Cash Bailey with his champion Patsies, the whole goddamn whooping and hollering lot of them! and Chauncey O'Shea and Royce Ingram! Have to find a new manager for the Cels, who'd it be? Well, worry about that tomorrow, maybe easygoing old Mose Stanford, hey yeah, how about it, Mose? and old Mose, coming through the door, shrugged noncommittally and laughed to watch Jaybird go into his famous wind-up, pitching himself at the plate instead of the ball; and there was old Gus Maloney to catch him, holding up his derby and laughing around his big black cigar. "Yes, set 'em up! it's a goddamn holiday!" And Jake Bradley's old teammates, forgot about them! Burgess and Parsons and Bacigamupo! Darlin' Harlan Hansome and Philpott Loveen! and there's Willie O'Leary and Brock Rutherford and Sycamore Flynn and, goddamn it, even old Fenn McCaffree—hell, yes, Fenn! Come in and have one! Tune it up, Sandy! And yes, by God, there was a new song in the making, a Jake Bradley song, that "paraclete" idea had given it to him: "pair o' cleats"—and second sack, that sack in the back, hot damn! And the girls, too, that's right, let 'em in, fill 'em up, and if they hold out on us, boys, well, maybe old Willie O'Leary will drop by Mitch Porter's later on and see what sweet Molly's got up her skirts for the evening! It's the great American game! And *hey!* there's Tuck Wilson and Grammercy Locke and Tim Shadwell with his boy Thornton! and Toothbrush and Hard John and Swanee and Jumpin' Joe! *Here they come!*

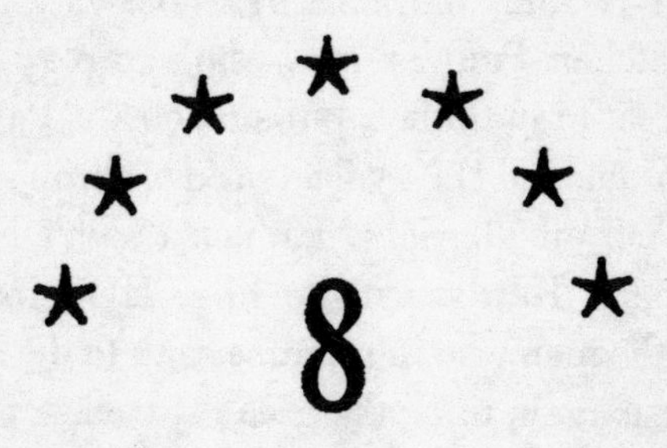

DAMONSDAY CLVII. Down in the Pioneer locker room, Knickerbocker rookie Hardy Ingram pulls on the old jersey with its bold antiquated "1." Was it really his? Probably not: too pat. Numerology. Lot of revealing work in that field lately. Made you wonder about a lot of things. Like the idea Damon was killed in Game 49: seven times seven. Third inning. Unbelievable. Or like that guy who's discovered that the whole damn structure from the inning organization up and double entry bookkeeping are virtually identical: just multiply it by twenty-one, the guy claims, and you've got it all. Grim idea. As Hardy tugs the shirt on over his head, there's like a—some said always a sudden chill—the others pause to watch: he gives them no sign. Fakes a yawn. Still, there *is* something strange—what is it? Fits too well. Coincidence. Or maybe they made it for him, new shirt, not the old one at all. In fact, the original must be in tatters by now.

When he arrived at the ball park a few minutes ago, Hardy was set upon by the usual runty mob of kids wanting autographs, but there was this one, standing at the fringe, just looking on. Peculiar, and it's still bugging him. What to make of it? Nothing, forget it. Trick probably. Get him upset. They all know the story from the catechism. Have a big laugh about it later. Next to him, the Universal Baseball Association's best rookie catcher, Paul Trench, who's to play Hardy's own great-great-great-grandfather, pulls on cleats. Paunch is good, but a Bridegroom, and Hardy isn't used to throwing to him. He hopes it'll come off all right. Paunch doesn't have much to say. Stage fright. Hardy grins at him: HOF Royce Ingram, the Avenger, the man who in remorse sank to the bottom of the UBA, then rose again to be the greatest backstop of them all, the Great Atonement Legend.

Sudden roar! Crowd. Big one. Ceremonies beginning. Take an hour or more, no hurry. Makes his throat catch just the same, though, and he grabs too fast for his pants. Take it easy, plenty of time. Still watching him, the bastards. Hardy Ingram isn't sure what might happen out there today. The annual rookie initiation ceremony, the Damonsday reenactment of the Parable of the Duel, is an Association secret. Lot of rumors, unnerving hearsay, but you can't be certain. Maybe it's like some claim and he won't come back. Doesn't make sense to him to knock off your best young talent every season, but he knows people aren't always rational. And if that's the way they want it, if that's how it's got to be, Hardy Ingram wants to take it like a man. Like *the* man himself. Poised. Knowing. Cool.

Really got them packed in up there. Not only a holiday and a good show, but in the middle of another centennial year as well—one hundred years since the assassination of HOF Barney Bancroft, the ninth UBA Chancellor, and the subsequent Monday Revolt. Weird times they had back then, all right. Still: ninth Chancellor, nine innings—all just so much bullshit, probably, like Cuss says. Centennial of everything these days. Enough to give a guy the creeps.

"How ya feeling?" Trench asks, standing. He tugs his belt one notch tighter under his belly, clops his cleats a couple times on the cement floor, picks up his mask and guard.

"Okay, I guess, Paunch." He uses the real name on purpose and grins to see Paunch blink.

"Good boy! Nothing to worry about. See you up on the field . . . Damon." He squeezes Hardy's arm, not looking at him, and leaves him. The rest watch this exchange, looking for—for what? some sign. Sign of weakness. Or sign that he knows . . . Nothing to worry about: hah! like hell! Hardy yanks on his knickers, feeling suddenly a little sore: why *him?* Because, goddamn it, you're the greatest, that's why. Rather be a second-rater like Squire? No. Well, then, shape up. Talks to himself like that, keeping his nerve up, hoping the others don't see the cold sweat of doubt starting to prickle his face.

Paul Trench is Hardy's age, but already looks and acts like an old man. A company man, a loyal Damonite, at home in the world, incurious and doltish. His old man was a Damonite, so is he. All there is to it. Well, it'd be nice to have it so simple. Attractive ideas, though, Hardy has to admit. Not easy to love the establishment, but on the other hand, if he'd been born back in the days of the Damonite origins, he'd have probably joined them. Return to the simplistic and pious view of Damon as Good and Jock as Evil. Seems silly now, but back then, the Caseyites having turned despotic and fractious, and the Association at the tag-end of two bleak decades of unalleviated mediocrity, it all must have made some sense. And something about Damon the man, legend or no, always excites Hardy. Genius. Yep, he'd have joined.

And the Damonites didn't lift an arm and still they got their way. Plain simple-minded faith in the ultimate power of justice and truth. Must have excited the hell out of them to see it happen like they said it would. Of course, once they got in, they grew a little muscle. Lot of different ways to get what you wanted, but only one to keep what you had.

Hardy hauls on socks, watching his teammates-for-a-day head out on the field to warm up, nodding back when they nod to him, reading their numbers . . . Stan Patterson . . . Grammercy Locke . . . Hatrack Hines. The strange resonance those names have! well, the childhood programing, the catechism, all the mythic residue hidden away in daily life. Still: hard not to feel it. Squire Flint shuffles by looking cast down—whose . . .? oh yes, Drew McDermott. Well, understandable. He has to relieve Halifax, suffer an humiliating shelling, then get his finger busted by Casey's line drive. Squire, like most failures, is in love with Casey—he's one of the new breed of radical Caseyites, heretical sect attempting to bring back the golden age of Patrick Monday, celebrate the mystery of Casey's uniqueness, his essential freedom, God active in man, and, as Cuss McCamish would say, all that shit. Hardy has noticed these guys have a way of using "must" pretty often. "Man *must* achieve authentic transcendence . . . Casey *must* be made relevant to our times . . . Man *must* have interiority . . . We *must* support human aspirations that cry out for fulfillment" . . . and who don't like it, bust his balls. Of course, Hardy has to admit, there's something exceptional and appealing about Gawky Jock the Mad Killer, too, something fascinating about the way he altered the entire course of UBA history. With one pitch. Hardy feels a tingling just behind his left ear.

So the Squire Flint types are saying that Damonism is

a perversion and a tyranny, while others say the original Damonites had the truth, but have been betrayed by opportunists; others—like Paul Trench and his dad—hold that power itself is proof they are still in the right, that the continuing strength of this story through time is evidence that it is somehow essentially true, while guys like Cuss McCamish think everybody concerned should just go diddle themselves and leave the league in peace. Amen to that, thinks Hardy, but feels burnt by a wave of guilt. How is it that a goddamn renegade like himself got Damon Rutherford's part to play today? How does Trench feel about that? Ironic? Or just a proper victim? Don't think about it, man. Just remember how you love the guy, that second son who pitched such great ball and died so young, and do him justice.

Book he's been reading lately. *The Doubter*. One of the flood of centennial Bancroft biographies out this year. Author tries to show that Barney Bancroft, not Rutherford or Casey or Hardy's own progenitor Royce Ingram, was actually the central figure, the real heart and point of the Parable of the Duel, as they call it now. Rutherford and Casey seem to be giants, this guy claims, but are really only subhuman masks, predesigned roles, while Bancroft is the only one wholly rounded and thus truly human participant in that incredible drama. Maybe the only *real* one. Skepticism, doubt, fear: yet the ability to act, to participate. Cute idea: old-fashioned humanism founded on abiding ignorance and despair, but who says man's condition is, eternally, dread and doubt? Funny how you can play that game so many ways. Other theories have Brock Rutherford, Sycamore Flynn, Fennimore McCaffree, Chauncey O'Shea, even Flynn's or McCaffree's daughters at the center. Can't even be sure about the simple *facts*. Some writers even argue that Rutherford and Casey never existed—nothing more than another of the ancient myths of the sun, symbolized as a victim slaughtered by the monster or force of darkness. History: in the end, you can never prove a thing.

Crowd noise over his head following a rhythmic pattern now. Speeches. Awards. Eulogies. Special ceremonies this year for the man who coached Damon Rutherford. HOF Barney Bancroft. The Old Philosopher. The Man Who Couldn't Quit. Real tear-jerker. Interesting guy, just the same. *UBA in the Balance* was the first book Hardy read, and he's never quite got over it. And Bancroft's assassination does bring that story full circle, when you think about it. But whether it makes it more or less human is hard to say. Who killed him? Doesn't really matter. They hanged Long Lew Lydell for it, but nobody really believed he did it. Part of the parable. Cuss McCamish's parody of the Long Lew and Fanny ballad in which Long Lew uses his fabulous dong as a life-saving crutch while on the rope—Fanny comes to tell him she's pregnant again: it goes soft and that's the end of Long Lew. Damonites like to claim it was Patrick Monday who killed Bancroft in a plain power grab. To be sure, given the collapse of the familiar patterns and the emotions aroused, it was easy for Monday and his Universalists to take over. On the other hand, Squire Flint is sure Barney killed himself. Remorse. But the point is, Bancroft's death was a kind of synthesis for the Duel, no matter who you think Rutherford and Casey really were or stood for, no matter who finally did the job. Must have been a poet who shot him. Sandy Shaw maybe. Good stuff for another song. Or maybe it just happened. Weirdly, independently, meaninglessly. Another accident in a chain of accidents: worse even than invention. Invention, even by a Monday or a Trench, implies a need and need implies purpose; accident implies nothing, nothing at all, and nothing is the one thing that scares Hardy Ingram.

"Well, as I live and breathe! *Hang down your heads, old pricks, and pee, it's the boy with the matchstick arm!*" A familiar voice: his friend Costen McCamish, dressed as Tuck Wilson.

With him is his drinking buddy Gringo Greene, who sings: "*The corpse it stinks most lov-huh-ly!*" Greene is in the togs of Goodman James. Soft jobs; they've both lucked out.

"I think you guys got your dates mixed up," Hardy says. "The Holly and Molly Show is next week." They're pretty drunk and for some reason that irritates him today.

"Say, tell us, glorious hero," says Cuss, "is it true what they say about the Virgin Daughter?"

"I don't know, what do they say?"

"Why, that:

Anyone could get in
To Harriet Flynn,
The problem was how to get out!
When she got you pinned,
Her daddy'd come in,
And give you one hell of a clout!"

Hardy has to grin at that one, but feels that tingle behind his ear again. "You drunken irreverent bastards! How you malign our common mother!"

"*On the sack in the back of Jake's!*" sings Gringo. Then, in a hush, leaning forward: "Hey, I just got the word, men, this game is fixed!"

"*That*, my boy," declaims Cuss McCamish, "is the immortal parable's very message!"

"What?" asks Hardy. "That the game is fixed, or that Gringo gets the word?"

"The only thing I'm getting outa this," grumbles Gringo, "is a pain in the ass."

"Which is more than you deserve," says Cuss.

"Deserve!" croaks Gringo. "I deserve love, truth, beauty, meaning, and eternal life . . . but I'll settle for a fuckin' drink."

They start to move away, but first Costen turns back to say: "Now, you know the rules, Hardy: no intentional wild pitches thrown at the Chancellor, no soiling of the immortal skivvies at the moment of truth, leave all your unconsumed liquid assets to your old buddy Cuss, and remember: you've got first crack at the Kill—"

"Get outa here, you sonsabitches!" hollers Hardy, "before I bust a few immortal skulls myself!" He looks for a ball to throw but before he can find one, they've staggered out in a drunken gallop, whooping and snorting as they go.

His roommate Skeeter Parson, dressed for the role of rookie Toby Ramsey, wanders over. He and Skeeter get along fine, play hard, accept everything with a grain of salt, josh each other out of the dumps, and when in doubt, go chasing tail together. Skeeter is wearing his usual one-sided grin, but doesn't look his old happy-go-lucky self. Hardy bends over his laces. Looking at his right hand, he thinks suddenly: by God, I've got something there today, all right . . . something different. He flexes his fingers.

"I don't see why we can't reenact 'Long Lew and Fanny' instead of this old doggerel," Skeeter complains. Hardy straightens up, half smiling. The grin on Skeeter's face fades. Something peculiar crosses his expression, like awe, something Hardy hasn't seen before. "Hardy . . . is that you?"

"Sure!" laughs Hardy, taken aback. He notices now that he and Skeeter are alone down here. "What's the matter?"

"I don't know." Skeeter's color comes back, makings of a grin again, but he keeps eyeing Hardy in a funny way. "For a minute there . . ."

"You thought I was Fanny McCaffree herself."

Skeeter laughs, but that funny look doesn't leave his face. "Do me a favor, roomie."

"Name it."

"When that pitch comes today, step back."

"You kidding?"

"No, Hardy, I'm dead serious." The grin is gone and Skeeter's gaze is fixed on him. But can he trust even Skeeter? Isn't this just another trick, another prearranged ploy to see if he'll break? Cuss hinting he should deck Casey when he pitches to him in the top of the third, Skeeter tempting him with cowardice. Won't know for sure until the initiation is over. "Seeing you there just now, I don't know, I got the idea suddenly that maybe this whole goddamn Association has got some kind of screw loose, Hardy."

"You just finding that out?"

"No, wait, Hardy, I'm not joking. Maybe . . . maybe, Hardy, they're really gonna kill you out there today!"

Hardy feels a cold chill rattle through him, tingling that patch behind his ear, pulverizing his organs and unhitching his joints, but outwardly he laughs: "Bullshit, Skeeter. The old-timers just build it up this way to give the rookies a little scare each year. They'd have to be crazy to—" He's sorry the minute he's said it.

"Exactly!" Skeeter cries. "Crazy! Why have we been assuming all along they weren't? *Listen!*"

Above them, the crowd growls spasmodically. Do sound a

little mad at that. Like a big blind beast. "Well, if that's what they want," he says, troubled, and tucking a glove in his armpit, clops out of the locker room.

Skeeter trails, sighing. He's still trying to tell Hardy something, but the autograph hunters in the passageway are making so much noise he can't hear him. Mostly kids, sprouting girls, a few women who can always be found outside locker rooms. Hardy grins, pauses to sign a few scorecards, and Skeeter does, too. Going by the rules, they sign the names they are playing under today. Hardy notices that Skeeter is leaving the "e" out of "Ramsey." Rebellious streak. Get him in trouble someday. Lot of these cards will end up in the Chancellor's office.

They push forward, through the young bodies, crowd roars egging them on. Time soon. Have to warm up. Sun slicing through open bleachers on to the ramp ahead. Brilliant day. Always like that on Damonsday. Or so they say. Signing a baseball, he notices it already has a lot of autographs. He looks closer. They're all Damon Rutherfords! He swallows, looks up uneasily: Yes, by God, *that same kid!* Who the hell are you, he wants to ask, but something holds him back. He adds his version of the signature—not all that different from the others, he notices—and hands the ball back. A girl, grabbing at his fly, distracts him—by the time he's got her hand out of there, the kid has disappeared.

"Come on, let's get up there!" he snaps at Skeeter Parsons —but where is Skeeter? There, way up ahead, alone on the ramp, looking back, oddly aloof. Hardy plunges ahead, but they're all over him now. Excited, all right, he's never seen anything like it. "Damon!" they're screaming, and "Damon!" and "*Damon!*" Excites him, too, damn it. Their hands and mouths are all over him. He realizes he is walking on some of them. Looks down, but they swarm so thickly over him, all he can see is an occasional thigh or face down there. They groan under his cleats and praise his name. He struggles: "Come on! For God's sake, let me go!" Suddenly he is in sunlight and breaking free. He staggers forward, propelled by his own thrust, blinded by the sun, dragging the more desperate with him—and a tremendous stunning roar brings him up short! As one, the fans in the stadium stand and cheer, stand and cry the magic name: "RUTHERFORD! RUTHERFORD! RUTHERFORD!" Appalled, in pain, terrified, he wrenches one kid off his shoulder, kicks free of another, pries loose the fingers of the girl who hangs on between his legs, her poor face cleat-battered, pulls up his shorts and his knickers, and marches, suffering more than he'd ever guessed possible, to the bull pen. "RUTHERFORD! RUTHERFORD!"

Well now, a sight for whore eyes! Those immortal hairy cheeks ablush in the blazing sun, immortal ankles in a bind of antiquarian knickerbockers, the whole immortal creation pirouetting gracelessly bullpenward, and the whore of whores, Dame Society, in all her enmassed immortal fervor, fixes her immortal eyes thereupon, missing not one mote and mentally putting the measure to the royal shillelagh—well, a whit bulkier than last year's, though not so far reaching perhaps, nothing to compare with the Hall of Famer of two years past, to be sure, but 'twill do for a bit of a turn, dearie, 'twill do—and lets fly from the black and cavernous depths of her immortal bosom a lusty approbation: "RUTHERFORD! RUTHERFORD!"

Costen the Rotund Transient McCamish, not to be confused with that lord of old whose musty Pioneer woolies he wears now, nor even with that grand paterfamilias Walter R. F. McCamish (and who was his preterient lodger today? Warwick was it? Or Raspberry Schultz?), only he, Cuss the contemned and contemning, side by side with Gringo Greene, the heavy-lidded atheist, he Cuss remarks this strange scene: the Association of the Stars. "Gringo, I swear by the holy cock of Saint Brock the Great, we've been born in a wondrous world, borne to a wondrous pass!"

"God bless our mothers," is Gringo's yawning reply.

"We have no mothers, Gringo. The ripening of their wombs is nothing more than a ceremonious parable. We are mere ideas, hatched whole and hapless, here to enact old rituals of resistance and rot. And for whom, I ask, for whom? For that old whore?"

Gringo Greene in affectionate accord turns and blows kisses to the old girl, the mass assembled, now crying wet-lipped for Casey (and who is it to be? is it Galen Flynn, as they have rumored? proper response to the immortal lust for sentiment and pattern, and yet . . .), and "The one true thing!" cries he.

"I can't believe it, Gringo. If all this fuss is just a rash in the old girl's crotch, then pray, where'd she get the rash?" Cuss McCamish, negator even of negations, surrenders to the paradox, surrender facilitated by his conviction that paradox, impossibility, confusion, and emptiness are the natural abode of a mind at rest; and proposes: "Let us hie us to the immortal pen and commend ourselves to yon heroes!"

"So be it fenn mccaffree!" vows Gringo, already in his cups it would seem, and off they go there, the thin and the stout of it, the good man Goodman and fat Tuck, reluctant participants in a classic plot, too wise to fable a future fortune, too distressed ever to invent their childhoods, left with nothing but the spiky imprint of their cleats upon the turf and the passage from envelope to maddening envelope of inscrutable space. Behind them, electronified voices recount the miracles that graced the ruptured but still radiant reign of the lofty Barney Bancroft HOF: well, there have been worse. As a point of fact, Gringo is himself celebrating this greenhorn season the centennial of the founding of his own inglorious line, his patriarch Copper Greene having been the most fabulous fly-by-night in Association history: up in LVII to whale out a record .411 and out of the league a year later with a .138.

"Greetings, personages of large consequence!" hails he of little consequence, Costen McCamish. In company out here with Hardy Ingram *cum* Damon Rutherford are his diminutive sidekick Skeeter Parsons, the party proselyte and jackstraw Paul Trench, the star-crossed iconoclast dire Squire Flint—and who is that slackbritches in the raiment of the greatest Witness of them all? Why, Raspberry Schultz it is, the gentle folklorist and gamesplayer. Hmmm. So in grandpop's knickers it's to be Wicked Willie Warwick, after all: may he reflect due honor on the happy clan, shy of immortals though it be.

"Where's the bar?" asks Gringo Greene, his emblematic salute.

"Ah, it's Cuss and Gringo!" complains the raspberry-complected Witness York with a turn of his knobby head. "As if things aren't already bad enough!"

"Pull the switch on that thing, man!" Gringo hollers up at the sun. "I can't even find my drink!" And clutches blindly before him, not so blindly punching Squire Flint in the chest. No love there, and feckless Flint flicks the hand away.

"Look up, good man, cast your eye on the Ineffable Name," intones Cuss, "and give praise!"

Gringo stares gapemouthed upward. "Oh yeah!"

"Do you see it?"

"Yeah!"

"What does it say?"

"100 Watt."

"Imagine!" cries Cuss into their laughter. "I always thought it said, 'Sandy lives!' "

"So it's Tuck Wilson, is it?" observes Raspberry Schultz, having orbited to the rear to read the magic number.

"Might have known McCamish would wrangle a deal for himself like that," snipes Squire Flint with a squint of ire. True, of course.

"In the giant's very gear," Cuss says. "Lucky Tuck!"

"Not all that much of a giant," notes Skeeter Parsons. "You appear to be coming out at the seams."

"Yes, Tuckered Son of Will was a bit low on the bone," confesses corpulent Costen, and they admire the parting threads. Hardy Ingram, proud scion of the avenging giant of the bloody past, and Paunch Trench, humble Damonite, do not join them, intent upon their pre-game task. Between pitches, Cuss sees, Hardy flexes his fist, staring curiously at it, probably thinking he's got something special there today, poor fool.

"You mean, *long* on the bone," cracks good man Greene. "I notice the crotch is holding."

The beast roars, startling them all. Casey has entered the Knickerbocker bull pen. Can't see him.

"If we could only get to whoever's playing Casey," Squire Flint says, half to himself, staring toward that distant figure.

"Awake! Awake!" cries Costen McCamish across the verdant pastures. "Put on strength, o arm of the league! Awake, as in days of old, the generations of long ago! Was it not thou that didst cut Rutherford in pieces, that didst deck the daemon? Was it not—"

"*Cut it out!*" cries Squire Flint.

"That is going a little too far," says Raspberry Schultz soberly. They all glance guiltily over toward Ingram and Trench, who, undisturbed, are still pitching, pitching, pitching. "I don't believe in just making fun of things you don't understand."

"What's this?" demands Skeeter Parsons. "You been converted, Razz?"

"No," says the Witness, blushing Raspberry, "but, well, legend, I mean the pattern of it, the long history, it seems somehow, you know, a folk truth, a radical truth, all these passed-down mythical—"

"Ahh, your radical mother's mythical cunt!" sniffs Gringo Greene. "It's time we junked the whole beastly business, baby, and moved on."

"I'm afraid, Gringo, I must agree with our distinguished folklorist and foremost witness to the ontological revelations of the patterns of history," intercedes (with a respectful nod to Schultz) Professor Costen Migod McCamish, Doctor of Nostology and Research Specialist in the Etiology of Homo Ludens, "and have come to the conclusion that God exists and he is a nut."

Skeeter Parsons *cum* Tubby-ass Ram's-Eye laughs: "Why, that's funny, I was just thinking . . . !"

"I think you better shut up," snaps friar Squire over his shoulder, still facing out toward the Knick bull pen where Casey works.

"Say, you're pretty lucky yourself," quoth Cuss to Squire's numbered back. "I see you drew McDermott."

Flint spins around full wroth. "You trying to be funny, you bastard?" Now what did he say that . . . ? Well, of course, Flint wanted to be Casey himself.

"Who do you think Casey is today?" asks Skeetoby.

"Galen Flynn, I hear," offers the occult Schultz, man who has turned, so Costen has heard, to the folklore of game theory, and plays himself some device with dice.

"Flynn!" snorts Flint, whose line in this league is the longest of them all, indeed to the first of the vicars. "That damn toady!"

"Easy, easy!" cautions Raspberry Schultz, nodding with squinted eyes toward Paul Trench, son of the establishment, now receiving Hardy-Damon's warm-up pitches. "Even the eyes have spies!"

But fiery Squire McFlint in a temper is no easy man to hush. "A bunch of *idiots,* that's what we got running this league! Nobody understands Casey anymore! Nobody understands *history!*" Paunch, asquat, uniformed as Royce Ingram, mighty arm of divine retribution, is faceless behind his mask.

"Anyway," proffers the conciliatory Parson Ramsey, "maybe it isn't Flynn."

"Of course, it isn't," Cuss-Tuck McWilson informs them.

"No?" asks Witberry Yultz. "Then who do you think that . . . ?"

"Why," quoth this hero who shall *walk* today from home to home to the inevitable satisfaction of all parties under the sun, "that it is Jock Casey himself!"

"Ho ho!" cheers Skeetoby Ramparts. "I might have guessed!"

"But how . . . ?" asks the witless Jerkberry.

"You're crazy," grumps Drusquire McWormy, lover of the Casey dead, but not alive.

"Crazy? Well, yes, I am," Cusstuck confesses nobly. "Else how account for my stuffing body and bunghole into this museum piece of a rag bag?" He flexes a leg to rip a stitch and spring a general laughter. "But as for Casey, what do we know?"

"Aw, let's find a bar, for God's sake!" butts the good Gringo impatiently in.

"That no man ever lived a life like his," responds Squire Flint, the humorless one.

"First, we know that—"

"Thirst is first!" gripes Gringo Greene. But as Cuss McCamish knows full well, it is all bravado; the first sack will be tupped many times over by the sober Pioneer cleats of Goodman James today.

"He thirsts for the True Church," wry Raspberry smiles.

"And what of your fans, Gringo?" asks Skeeter Parsons.

"Mother can smother in her own vat of fat," Gringo grumbles.

"A dogmatist," Cuss McCamish complains, and all nod, pitying. "Now, as for Casey, the first thing we know is that he was still pitching long after Damonsday the First."

"Everybody knows that," is Squire's reposte. "They've just squeezed the two deaths into one ceremony in order to—"

"But if *this* is a falsehood, dear comrades, where is truth? We know who buzzarded about the immortal remains of our friend Hardy here—or I mean, Damon—know when and where he was immortally interred, even know the music performed at his immortal obsequies, but of Casey what can we say? That Hardy's own glorious ancestor knocked Jock on the block and fixed his clock? A mere fairy tale, adorned with the morbid imaginations of a century of sentimental artisans!" His efforts to draw in Hardy Ingram avail him not. Hardy Ingram he is no more. "We don't even know if his corpus delicti was scraped off the rubber, or if it just sank into the premises! As the great historian U. R. Obseen has informed us:

Said Long Lew to Fanny
Whilst inspecting her cranny:
'Why! someone inside I have found!'
Said Fanny to Lew:
'Dear, don't you know who?
It's the Man Who Sleeps there in the Mound!' "

"You're sick, McCamish!" is the reward the noble historian reaps from the furious Flint, though elsewhere he fares better.

"So I say it is he, in the flesh of the bone and the bone of all flesh, the Man in the Mound, Jock the Mad Killer Casey, come back this day once yearly to victimize us all, we of the green hinderparts and the wives and daughters of honest men!"

"Casey died to prove his freedom!" Squire Flint blurts out. "And ours! And all we do—"

"Well, a great man, Casey, but not the greatest."

"Who was the greatest, Cuss?" asks the grinning Skeeter.

"Why old Pappy Rooney, of course."

"Rooney! What did he do?"

"Lived to the age of a hundred and forty-three and, so they say, could get it up to the very end!"

"To the very end of what?" asks the Green Gringo.

"That's stupid!" Drew McSquire snaps.

"Stupid? I should say not! In fact, may we all, my friends, meet such a reasonable demise!"

"Death is never reasonable," argues Squire the great denier, "even for an old fool at one hundred and forty-three."

"Take it easy on Squire," laughs Skeeter. "He's writing a book on Jock Casey."

"So I've heard," says he whose very seams split with a loathing of giants. "It's *The Man Who Stood Alone*, isn't it?"

"That's right," says Squire grimly.

"If Squire writes it, then I shall bring out my long-awaited biography of Long Lew Lydell!"

Raspberry Schultz laughs and claps. "Wonderful! What are you going to call it, Cuss?"

"*The Man Who Stood on his Bone!*" Full-bellied laughter at last, which he gathers in, then adds:

> "*Said Fanny to the spectre*
> *As soon as he'd decked her:*
> *'Why, sir! you're positively pneumatic!*
> *Unlike my old feller,*
> *You tickle the cellar*
> *Without making a mess in the attic!'* "

But no rewards this time, for it's Dame Society herself who responds, a terrible roar dredged up from the very gut of the beast, a horrendous witless bellowing, that sucks up all their scrotums, and makes them catch their breath. Skeeter Parsons checks his timepiece: "It's time," he says. Trench and Ingram depart, under a cascade of cheers. But yes! It is really they! See how they go! Two still-young heroes of the golden past: miraculous transformation! And soon even he, Costen McCamish, will shrink instinctively to Tuck Wilson, step over the crushed skull and blinded eyes of that one who, in spite of all, must be loved, and walk the magic bases while the whore weeps. No cheers for him. Only survival.

Paul Trench, at the grim edge, too wise to step back and too frightened to leap, walks miserably toward the diamond beside Hardy Ingram, wanting to speak of it, his gloom, and why, but not knowing where to begin. Paul is a plain-spoken man, and his despair is too complex for plain speech. Though none would ever guess it, the thunder of the crowd only makes it worse. He is afraid. Not only of what he must do. But of everything.

Beyond each game, he sees another, and yet another, in endless and hopeless succession. He hits a ground ball to third, is thrown out. Or he beats the throw. What difference, in the terror of eternity, does it make? He stares at the sky, beyond which is more sky, overwhelming in its enormity. He, Paul Trench, is utterly absorbed in it, entirely disappears, is Paul Trench no longer, is nothing at all: so why does he even walk up there? Why does he swing? Why does he run? Why does he suffer when out and rejoice when safe? Why is it better to win than to lose? Each day: the dread. And when, after being distracted by the excitement of a game, he returns at night to the dread, it is worse than ever, compounded with shame and regret. He wants to quit—but what does he mean, "quit"? The game? Life? Could you separate them?

High in the stands, enjoying the rewards of mere longevity, sit the twelve Elders, his grandfather among them. In the government's official box, beside the Chancellor himself, sits his father. Though he knows they watch him, he doesn't look their way, afraid his own doubts will betray him. It began with them, after all. Discovering their fallibility, he encountered the pathos of all life, then reasoned that the Age of Glory was perhaps no different than this, his own inglorious times.

At first, he thought of it as tragic, saw himself as a kind of Damon Rutherford: young, brilliant . . . dead. He became suspicious when he realized the idea gave him a certain grim pleasure. He became interested in Jock Casey then, felt the terror and excitement of the Great Confrontation, asserted himself and learned to hate—but discovered that, even here, there was something he was enjoying that seemed wrong, a creature of false pride. It was Barney Bancroft who led him to the final emptiness; at every point in the man's life, he found himself asking: but why go on? Bancroft *went* on, but gave no reasons. And wasn't that, finally, a kind of cowardice?

The green grass at the edge of the infield feels spongy to their cleats. They walk in silence, beneath the loud blessing of the exalted and exultant populace, onto the diamond itself. A sacred duty, his father said. But "sacred," what is that? The Whore-Mother, Costen calls the people: Is it they, is it she who defines it for them? Is it in her name that he must kill today? Or is it for the record books that we go on, exposing our destinies? "Exposing our destinies"—that book Raspberry gave him, called *Equilibrium Through Intransigence*. It was Raspberry Schultz one day who told him: "I don't know if there's really a record-keeper up there or not, Paunch. But even if there weren't, I think we'd have to play the game as though there were." Would we? Is that reason enough? Continuance for its own inscrutable sake?

He noticed back there in the bull pen how they all avoided him, how they talked about him, wrong about everything. They think he's a Damonite. He isn't. He has read all he can find on the Association's history, and he knows now he is nothing. He has relived the origins and growths of the Bogglers, the Legalists, the Guildsmen, has examined their aspirations and how they tried to realize them, has suffered the pain and shock of Bancroft's murder, has watched the rescue of the Association by Patrick Monday's Universalists—later called the Caseyites—and their efforts, honest enough, to bring order to the chaos, has cringed under their ultimate tyranny and joined with the first courageous Damonites in their small and secret meetings, then ascended with them, pious and forever amazed, through the long slow years, to power—and has discovered, in the end, his own estrangement from them all. If anything, he is simply a willing accomplice to all heresies, but ultimately a partisan of none—like fat Costen, a negator, without any hope of rediscovering affirmation. Not that Cuss is any help to him. Cuss mocks the regime and everything else, but his mockery encapsulates him, cuts him off from any sense of wonder or mystery, makes life nothing more than getting by with the least pain possible, and somehow, to Paul Trench, such a life seems less than human.

Casey, in his writings, has spoken of a "rising above the rules," an abandonment of all conceptualizations, including scorekeepers, umpires, Gods in any dress, in the heat of total mystic immersion in that essence that includes God and him equally. Of course, some say he never wrote it, it's all apocryphal, inventions of Monday and his Universalists, distorted by redactions without number, but no matter, the idea itself remains. What it leads to, though, is inaction, a terrible passivity: Casey on the mound, shaking Flynn off, waiting—but who is playing Casey today? And will he wait? Trench, alias Ingram the Avenger, squatting dutifully behind the plate to receive the last of Hardy Ingram's warm-up pitches, feels a tingle in his hands, a power there he neither wants nor asked for.

He'd like to trade places with Hardy. Against the rules, of course; Hardy couldn't do it, can't play your own progenitor. No, even better, he'd like to trade with Galen Flynn or whoever it is that's playing Casey. What would he do? He'd burn them in, that's what he'd do, try to strike Ingram out. Or: why not an intentional pass? Or bean him. How about that? Is Flynn-Casey thinking about that? Going for number two? Namely, him? Royce Ingram tries to kindle up an anger, but Paul Trench can't bring it off. I'll strike out.

The idea excites him. A rising above. Yes, why not? He feels better than he's felt for months! Of course, so simple! What will they do to him after? Is he martyrizing himself? It doesn't matter: death is a relative idea, truth absolute! Yes, it was Squire who said that. He understands it now. Or did Squire put it the other way around? Stop and think. But he is too upset to think. He forgets now which is relative and which is absolute. If either. It is all falling apart on him. And either way it's coming. Yes, now, today, here in the blackening sun, on the burning green grass, and the eyes, and the crumbling—they shout. He sweats. Damon's pitches sting his hands. Can't hang on to them. All like a bad dream. And die. They're all going to die. And nothing he can do about it. Foolish things pass through his head. Rooney reaching the age of 143. The mystery of Casey's burial. The Brock Rutherford Era—

"*Play ball!*" the umpire cries, and he feels a terrific grabbing in the chest.

That dead boy. And the wake. Sandy's songs. The sack in the back of Jake's—cordoned off with a rope now and overseen by a museum guard, just like his ancestor Mel's Circle Bar, so they won't tear it up and carry off the pieces as souvenirs. They! Pieces! He laughs.

He flings the ball to second; then, impulsively, he walks out there, to the mound, not because it's a rule of the game, but because he feels drawn. The ball goes from Ramsey to Wilder to Hines. Hatrack comes in halfway from third, tosses the ball to Paul. He hands it to Damon, standing tall and lean, head tilted slightly to the right, face expressionless but eyes alert.

Paul tries to speak, but he can find no words. It's terrible, he says; or might have said. It's all there is.

And then suddenly Damon sees, *must* see, because astonishingly he says: "Hey, wait, buddy! you *love* this game, don't you?"

"Sure, but..."

Damon grins. Lights up the whole goddamn world. "Then don't be afraid, Royce," he says.

And the black clouds break up, and dew springs again to the green grass, and the stands hang on, and his own oppressed heart leaps alive to give it one last try.

And he doesn't know any more whether he's a Damonite or a Caseyite or something else again, a New Heretic or an unregenerate Golden Ager, doesn't even know if he's Paul Trench or Royce Ingram or Pappy Rooney or Long Lew Lydell, it's all irrelevant, it doesn't even matter that he's going to die, all that counts is that he is *here* and here's The Man and here's the boys and there's the crowd, the sun, the noise.

"It's not a trial," says Damon, glove tucked in his armpit, hands working the new ball. Behind him, he knows, Scat Batkin, the batter, is moving toward the plate. "It's not even a lesson. It's just what it is." Damon holds the baseball up between them. It is hard and white and alive in the sun.

He laughs. It's beautiful, that ball. He punches Damon lightly in the ribs with his mitt. "Hang loose," he says, and pulling down his mask, trots back behind home plate.